AUTHOR	CLASS
KERSH, G.	F

TITLE

THEY DIE WITH THEIR BOOTS CLEAN

THEY DIE WITH
THEIR BOOTS CLEAN

THEY DIE WITH THEIR BOOTS CLEAN

GERALD KERSH

HEINEMANN : LONDON

FIRST PUBLISHED DECEMBER 1941
REISSUED 1967

PRINTED AND BOUND IN GREAT BRITAIN BY
BOOKPRINT LIMITED, CRAWLEY SUSSEX

DEDICATION

From Guardsman Gerald Kersh, No. 2663141,
Coldstream Guards, to

Sergeant Bill (Spider) Kelly; Trained Soldier Phillips;
Sergeant Ding-Dong Bell of the Musketry Class;
Lance-Sergeant Muddy Waters; Corporal (Blondie)
Fletcher; Corporal (Starting Price) Perry; Sergeant-
Major (The Commander) Knott; and my very good
friends the Guardsmen Jack Shaw, Tommy Swales,
Charlie Rose, Grouser Doughney, Les Essex, Spencer
(now Lance-Corporal), Rudd (the golfer), Puttock (The
Blond Beast), Frank Buttery, Carter of Lancashire, Harry
Allen (the Genius of County Durham), Middlecote (of
Gloucestershire), old puffy-faced Edwards, Alfie Abdale
(the Worksop Nightingale) the Good Boy from Godalm-
ing, Ginger Dennett, and Gant, the Blackpool window-
cleaner. Also Saunders, the timber-feller of Berkhamp-
stead and James. We had some good times in Caterham.
. . . Who forgets, for example, Ossie Osborne-Joyce
(afterwards Scribe at Caterham), Geordie Wood, Geordie
Benson, Alan Simpson (I always called him Wilson), and
all the rest—my best of pals?

Again to my friends in the Training Battalion—to
Corporal Warr (who still has a book of mine), to Sergeant
Allen (now an officer), and Lance-Sergeants Hitch
Hitchens, "Captain" Kidd, good old "Dagwood" Travis
(and why they called him Dagwood, God only knows),
Kilham (and kill 'em he did), Darkie Matthews (whom no
man dared face), Company-Quartermaster-Sergeant

Pickergill, Company Sergeant-Major Arthur George (Iron) Duke, R.S.M. (Charlie) Yardley; the good old Drum Major; Drill Sergeants Pinder, Reason, and Nippy Kirk; Albert Aunger, M.M.; Leadham, that ace of Sarnts; Corporals or Lance-Corporals Ling, Bell, Bateman, Piggy Hinsley, Wacky Jones . . . but this is getting to be a Directory, an Army List.

This book is about my friends of the Coldstream Guards; my pals of what they call "the other ranks".

I got to know and love them. I think that they represent all that is finest in army life. They will permit me to call them my friends? I was happy to live with them, and could never wish for better men to have on my side in a battle. I regard them as representative of the Guards—which is what is best in the British Army: best, because it is so completely in accordance with the British spirit as a whole. They are my friends. The honour is mine. I am proud to know them. When I go back, Sergeant Travis will chase me for this, fearing that I have been currying favour. He chased me before, on Defaulters, anyway. What is a chasing? These are good fellows. They are the backbone of things. Therefore, to them, this book, unworthy as it is, is dedicated.

GERALD KERSH,

Pirbright,
1941.

PROLOGUE

"A MAN gets knifed. A throat gets slit. A bomb goes off. The Wogs are out for blood!"

As Sergeant Nelson talks his right eye blinks in the smoke of his cigarette. Pensively pursing his lips, he takes his left eye out, polishes it against the bosom of his battle-blouse, and puts it back again. "Is it in straight, Dusty?"

Sergeant Smith says: "A bit bolo."

Sergeant Nelson blinks hard. The glass eye stares rather angrily through the smoke. "You've got to close the left, or disengaged eye, when you fire," he says. "What's an eye?"

We wait, very quiet. We want to hear about the Wogs, the Arabs. Evening is coming. The moon is already out—a pale, thin little moon, no bigger than an eyebrow.

"Ah," says Sergeant Smith. "We used to see a bit of fighting in peace-time."

"Definitely, Dusty," says Sergeant Nelson, and his story goes on:

The Wogs was around us. The desert was alive with Wogs. You couldn't see 'em. You couldn't hear 'em. But you knew they was there. They can hide, those Wogs can, behind a grain o' sand. Ain't that a fact, Dusty? They wears robes the same colour as the desert. They digs themselves little bits of cover. Puzzle, find 'em. You *know* they're there, but they're invisible. And the Wog can wait. He can wait hours. . . . Then *bomp!*—and *wheeee!*—he's letting loose atcha. He ain't a bad shot at three hundred yards.

What was I saying? The Wogs was around us, quiet as mice, but all you could see was lousy sand. We come to a road block. We takes it down and marches on. Now mind you there's nothing stirring—nothing in sight, only the lousy great sun and the lousy old desert. I say we marches on. Quarter of a mile on, round a bend, we comes to another barricade. Walk on, and walk into a jolly old death-trap. We about-turns and goes back. We definitely does.

Now mind you, nobody's seen anything. We rounds the bend and Sergeant Tuck says "Blimey". There lies both scouts with knife-holes in their backs and their rifles and ammo gone. And the block we just took down, so help me Gord, it's up agen. Definitely up.

The officer says: "Well, it looks as if we've got to fight it out here." He talked like his mouth was full o' hot potatoes, but he wasn't a bad sort—I've heard that fellow swear something terrible, blinding and bloodying like a bargee, just like you and me. Didn't 'e, Dusty?

Then all of a sudden, poppity-pop! Old Charlie, my pore old china, pore old Charlie, he says *Gug!*—just like that, didn't he, Dusty?—*Gug!* and goes down plonkety-plonk on the road. Definitely plonkety-plonk.

And we see sort of . . . kind of bits of desert getting up and charging us. So help me Gord they seemed to be right atop of us. And somebody yells: "The Wogs! The Wogs!"—and we're firing for our lousy old lives, biff!—bosh!—bang!—with the Wogs going down like coconuts. Where one fell, ten seemed to spring up. Didn't they Dusty? Yelling. It sounded like "Lulu! Lulu!" Remember that, Dusty? That's their God—Lulu. . . . Allah? All right, Allah: but it sounded like Lulu to me, Dusty; definitely Lulu. Definitely.

Well. You rooks can grouse and grumble about discipline, but in a time like that you want it. You horrible little men. You over there—you funny creature, you—stop picking your horrible little nose and pay attention to me when I'm talking to you. Whaddaya mean, you *are?* In my day, if I'd answered back to a sergeant I'd of been run into the moosh so fast me feet wouldn't have touched the ground. Why, you miserable twillip!

Discipline. We was outnumbered about twenty-five to one. I was shivering in my shoes. I was dead scairt. Wasn't I, Dusty? We didn't stand the chance of an ice-cream cornet in hell. Definitely not the chance of a penny cornet. But we had to hold out to the last man, if only as a matter of principle. Our mob never say die. Definitely never. Do it, Dusty?

That was just about twelve, noon, when the fun started. Quarter past, was it? I would of sworn it was just on the hour. Well. The Wogs tried to rush us. But in a time like that, without stopping to think, mind you, you remember the stuff we knock into your soft little heads when we train you here. Don't you, Dusty?

We fired like on a range. The good old Lewis was going thumpity-thump, and the Wogs was going down. At last they got back under cover to snipe. And snipe they did—they snipe all right. And we gave it 'em back. But they had the advantage of cover. Poor old Muddy—you knew Muddy Waters, Dusty? The bloke what threatened the Sarnt-Major? Yeh, back in '28—poor old Muddy gets one, bip, right in the forehead. The joke of it was, it didn't kill him: didn't touch the brain; he never had no brains: he's in Palestine, now, still keeping the Wogs in order.

The day wore on. Didn't it, Dusty? Definitely it wore on. And about a third of our fellows was out. But we held 'em. Discipline. Morale. *Es pritty corpse*, to put it in Froggie lingo. And at last, towards sunset, we could see that the lousy old Wog was going to make one big, determined rush and scoff us that way. And the devil of it was, we was pretty near out of ammo. We was, wasn't we, Dusty? Are you listening to me, you, Dopey, over there? Give him a poke in the eye, somebody—he's going to sleep.

Near out of ammo. Okay doke. So now it's going to come down to good old cold steel. We see the Wogs gathering. They fluffed our ammo was out. They gathered in the open, luluing like mad—hundreds of 'em. We was absolutely certain we'd never get away alive. Remember, I shook 'ands with you, Dusty? Funny, wonnit? Then the Wogs charged. We stood firm. We was going to die in proper order, by crummit we was. You don't get yourself took prisoner by no Wog, not if you use your loaf you don't. The Wog's a torturer. Well, over they comes, and we gets ready to snuff it.

And then, all of a sudden, what do we hear? That lovely old scalded cat of a lousy old bagpipe! *Mee-yow . . . mee-yow . . . mee-yow . . .*! And I says: "By God Almighty—the Jocks!" And the Jocks it was, screaming like madmen. Firing? Nothing! The pig-stickers was out. It was knives, me boys, bayonets! They came pouring over the ridge, they did, and they tore into them Wogs from the rear like lions—and we comes out, we does, yelling red white and blue murder—*Yaaaah! Yaaaah!*—and what we leave of them Wogs is scarcely worth the trouble of picking up. Eh, Dusty? It was a whatsiname, definitely a whatsiname. A triumph. A triumph for training and discipline. Without it we'd of been wiped out in the first half hour.

And training and discipline is what you're going to get here. See? And if you don't like it you can definitely lump it. Because you're going to beat the pith out of old Herr von Fritz. You're going to batter the tar out of Old Adolf. You're going to kick old pigface Gooring from hell to breakfast. Ain't they, Dusty? Definitely from hell to breakfast. Don't let me hear no lousy old alarm and despondency about tanks. I'll spit in the eye of the next man who mentions tanks. England's an island, see? And while we hold this lousy old island, old Hitler's blocked. See? And we can make all the tanks we're going to need, given time. And if we hold out, we've *got* time. Get it? And with trained men we hold out. Men are more important than tanks. You can bust a tank. You can't bust a proper man. And I'm going to make proper men of you—you horrible creatures, you. You'll give old Hitler a coating in Africa, and Greece, and hell and all. You will! Won't they, Dusty?

Who said "What about Musso?" Musso? I don't count Musso! I could take on Musso and the whole Wop army single-handed, five at a time, couldn't I, Dusty? . . . All right then, three at a time. Remember the time I laid out three Wogs with a spare Bren barrel? Swords, they had— swords and knives. They was the mob that mutilated poor old Charlie. Ah, it was fun being in the army in peace-time. Definitely, Dusty.

Now, you mummy's darlings, get a rift on them boots. Definitely shine 'em, my little curly-headed lambs, for in our mob, war or no war, you die with clean boots on.

PART ONE

THE RAW MATERIALS

IT WAS a big, dim, grim, high, wide, unhandsome room, smelling unpleasantly of too much cleanliness. Discipline has an odour of its own—a smell of scrubbing-soap and floor-polish mixed with just a little too much fresh air. You sniff it in prisons, workhouses, and other places where men abandon hope: the smell of organised scouring; the smell to end smells.

Men were talking; not loud. A beardless boy with a pink face and a queer mop of hair like a copper-wire pot-scourer had been smoking a cigarette. He was holding the butt of it between finger and thumb, looking anxiously from side to side. A crisis was approaching: soon, he wouldn't be able to hold it; but how could he dare to throw it down and put his foot on it? A large plump man with a deep, round voice said: "Chuck it out t' winder, lad." The wire-haired boy said: "Ah, but say there's a rule agin it . . ." He pinched out the glow, rolled the remaining crumbs of tobacco into a little pill which he poised in his hand like some undisposable, incriminating mass. At last he put it into the huge cold stove, slammed the door, and walked hastily to the other side of the room.

"Scared, lad?" asked the plump man, and the wire-haired boy replied: "What, *scared?* Who, *me?* Me *scared?* Not me."

"Homesick, like?"

The wire-haired boy scowled. "No."

6

Two men were trying to play billiards with a sawn-down cue and three odd balls on a table not much bigger than a tea-tray. The boy watched them. One of the players, a long, saturnine man, addressed the spot-ball with elaborate care, and miscued. I heard the woody scrape, and saw the ball roll slowly away. The saturnine man swore briefly and bitterly, handing the cue to the other player, who took it, held it, stared blankly at it, and then said: "Ah dinna wanna play na more."

"No more do I. Let's turn it up."

"Play draughts?"

"No."

Somebody else asked the company in general what was going to happen to them now.

A glum blond man who had been turning over the pages of a bound volume of *Punch*, 1893–1894, said: "We get another medical examination. First of all we get our hair cut off. Then, if we're okay, we get injected."

"Injected what with?" asked the wire-haired boy.

"Germs."

"Oh, blimey."

"Germs," said the glum man. "Your arm swells up like a thigh. You throb like a damn great aeroplane. Your head aches fit to bust. A scab comes. Then it drops off. Then there's a scar."

"What's that done for?"

"Because it's healthy."

"And what happens then?"

"A trained sweat is put in charge of you. You go and draw your kit."

"Do we get rifles right away."

"Yes. Then you're put in a hut."

"What kind of a hut?"

"A *hut.* Then you're squadded. Then . . ."

"Ah?"

"God help you," said the glum man.

"What d'you mean, God help you?"

"What I say. God help you. You're here. You're in the Guards. It's like being in jail, only there's one difference."

"What's that?"

"In jail you sometimes get a bit of time to yourself."

"Oh, blimey. Do they give you hell?"

"Hell," said the glum man, "hell. If they gave you hell, it wouldn't be so bad. Hell is Paradise to what they give you here."

"Can you go out?"

"After a few weeks they let you out maybe once, for an evening, every eight or ten days."

"And where can you go?"

"Nowhere."

"What's the food like?"

"Horrible."

"What are the officers like?"

"Terrible."

"What beds do you get?"

"Planks."

"What are the sergeants like?" asked the wire-haired boy.

"Son," said the glum man, "did you ever see a picture called *Beau Geste?*"

"Um."

"Remember the sergeant that put them dead men on the wall, and sent them blokes that was dying of thirst out into the desert without a drink o' water?"

"Oh, ah!"

"He chased 'em in the sun till they fell down dead, didn't 'e?"

"Ah!"

"Would you say he was tough, just a bit?"

"Not half he wasn't tough!"

"Well," said the glum man. "He was a Godfrey Winn compared to the sergeants here."

"Oh, blimey," said the wire-haired boy.

There is a silence; then a little outbreak of uneasy laughter.

"Join the Army to see the world," says the glum man. "Join the Guards and scrub it."

We look about us.

Each of us sees twenty or thirty other recruits, raw and inconsolable as new-born babies. The man with the volume of *Punch* is riffling the leaves, blackened at the edges by the fidgeting of countless uneasy thumbs.

This is one of those awful gaps of silence. You know such moments. Talk limps to the edge of a chasm and falls in. Ten thousand pounds couldn't buy a spontaneous word. Men become suddenly engrossed in silly trivialities. A big Nottingham man sits scrutinising a razor-blade wrapper with the intentness of a merchant poring over a rare vase.

The purr of the pages is the only sound we can hear . . . *prrrut* . . . *prrrut* . . . *prrrut*. . . .

The weather has got into us, also. The day has blown hot and cold, wet and dry, light and dark; and now, settling into a uniform dirty whiteness, threatens rain. The sky sags like a wet sheet.

From the asphalt below comes a *ka-rup*, *ka-rup* of disciplined iron heels, and a great, strained voice shouts:

"Get a hold of the step! Get a hold of it! *Eff*—ite! *Eff*—ite! Eff. . . . Eff. . . . *Eff*. . . . EFF. . . . *EFF!*" It is a squad of Grenadiers being marched to their baths. In this place no man walks. A recruit represents two feet on a brown caterpillar: his paces are measured; his movements are predestined; his day is divided into equal squares. "Eff. . . . Eff!" The voice and the footsteps fade . . . walking *en masse;* a community-singing of boots. . . .

From an unknown distance, a flat, sore-sounding bugle blows a melancholy call of unknown significance. From different distances other bugles pick it up. The notes blend. They combine in a strange, sad discord . . . a rich weeping of vibrant brass. Then, right under the window, a little grim boy puts a bugle to his lips, puffs his cheeks, and blows. The red, yellow, and blue tassels on his coppery bugle hardly stir. A gathered flush empties out of his neck and face, into the mouthpiece, round the coil, and out in a great trembling note. He sounds the call again. Two scared swallows flutter from the roof. Simultaneously, a flat loud-mouthed bell in the clock-tower clangs an hour; and sliding down a slanting wind comes a rattling volley of raindrops.

Somebody sighs. The man with *Punch* throws down the volume and yawns.

The bugle is our masters' voice . . . and the swallows will go where the sun goes, and we shall be here under the treacherous English rain, kicking the soil into mud for our feet to slip in.

But all England is here.

We men in this Reception Station are unreserved, inessential.

Individually, we are necessary only to the tiny nooks and crannies of England into which life, like a wind carrying seed, has dropped us. We have our roots, of course, like all men. Pluck us up, and an empty space is left. But not for long. Without us things do not change. Only the appearance of things changes. Life moves differently, but still goes steadily on.

We lived our peace-time lives; worked, enjoyed things a little, suffered a little; built what we could, struggling, more often than not, for just enough bread and rest to give us strength to struggle with; made homes and supported them, turning sweat into milk for the babies. We were part of the mass of the British.

We are here. The things we lived for are behind us. All the personal importance of our own lives has been washed down in the gulf of the national emergency. Other hands were there to take up the tools we laid down. The machines still drone. The fires still roar. The potatoes still grow, and will be plucked when their time is ripe. Our work is behind us, still being done.

And we wait here, to be made into soldiers.

There is scarcely a man among us who did not volunteer. How does this happen?

We come out of the period between 1904 and 1922— that wild waste of years, strewn with the rubble of smashed régimes. The oldest of us is thirty-six, Shorrock of Rockbottom. The youngest is Bray, eighteen, of London. Those of us who are not old enough to remember the war-weariness of the century in its 'teens, are children of the reaction of the nineteen-twenties—when "No More War" was the war-cry; and the League of Nations seemed more solid than the pipe-of-peace-dream that it was; and the younger generation—our own generation—was sworn

to eternal non-belligerence in the face of the futility of war.
We haven't forgotten that. If only our own propagandists
took a little of the blood and thunder that the peace
propagandists so effectively used to move us!

From page after laid-out page, the horrors of war
gibbered at us . . . stripped men, dead in attitudes of
horrible abandon . . . people (were they men or women?)
spoiled like fruit, indescribably torn up . . . shattered
walls that had enclosed homes, homes like ours, homes of
men, men like us . . . cathedrals shattered; the loving
work of generations of craftsmen demolished like condemned slum tenements . . . children starving; nothing
left of them but bloated bellies and staring eyes . . .
trenches full of dead heroes rotting to high heaven . . .
long files of men with bandaged eyes, hand-on-shoulder
like convicts, blind with gas . . . civilians cursing God
and dying in the muck-heaps of blasted towns. . .

Oh yes. We saw all the pictures and heard all the
gruesome stories, which we know were true. We were the
rich culture-grounds of the peace propaganda that said:
*If war was like this then, what will it be like next time, with all
the sharpened wits of the death-chemists working on new poison
gas and explosives, and the greatest engineers of all time devoting
themselves to aeroplanes that can come down screaming like bats
out of hell?*

When we heard that first siren on the Sunday of the
Declaration of War, things like damp spiders ran up and
down our backs. We expected the worst.

And then came a flow of something hot and strong. We
went out and begged to be allowed to fight Jerry. We
insisted on our right to do so, and to hell with the age-
groups. Men of sixty, who had seen the things at the
pictures of which we had lost our breakfasts, and who had

spent twenty post-war and pre-war years saying: "Never again," declared on oath that they were forty and beseeched the authorities to give them rifles. There was a rush and a heave. Because it wouldn't take us all at once, we cursed the War Office from hell to breakfast.

Men like Shorrock, who had argued the futility of all war in his grocery shop in Rockbottom (cotton and coal; pop., 21,369; near Blackburn; finest town on earth), did a *volte-face* like the pirouette of a ballet-dancer. (I say nothing of his mulish insistence that Britain, being an island, had no concern in the affairs of Europe; nor of the imbecile satisfaction he seemed to suck out of the statement that there had always been an England and always would be. That Shorrock, in his fossil-ivory tower!) He left the business to his wife, clapped on his durable bowler hat, and, arguing about nothing for fifteen minutes with an old sweat in the Recruiting Station, passed A1. and got his fifteen stone of maddening self-assertion into the Coldstream Guards.

It is what they call "Being there when the bugle blows." He sits by the window on a little collapsible iron bed, filling a pipe with Sidebotham's Unscented Cut Plug which, in the tone of a man who stands by some ultimate and glorious truth, he declares to be the finest tobacco on earth. Let his neighbour, Whitaker of the West Riding, swear that Sidebotham's is manure and there is nothing in the universe to touch Cooper's Fragrant Twist at one-and-five an ounce. Shorrock stands firm. Put Sidebotham's label on old bootlaces, and Shorrock will smoke them and die in defence of them.

He is a big man. Assume that three of his fifteen stone are so much fat, food for worms. They will get that off him here, it is grimly hinted.

Meanwhile it fills his waistcoat, the good waistcoat of his everyday suit, which still has a year of wear in it. (The best suit—five pounds; no guineas; worth fifteen; made by Joe Hindle of Rockbottom, greatest tailor in Great Britain, one-time cutter to Jim Leach, finest tailor in the world, also of Rockbottom—hangs full of moth balls, ready for his homecoming. He will be back in one year. Germany will capitulate next spring. Who says so? He says so. Why? Because.)

All right. He will admit he has a few ounces of weight to lose. The Shorrockses eat well. You could not get Jack Shorrocks' Agatha's potato-pie for ten shillings a portion at the Savoy Hotel, London—no, nor even at the Rockbottom Commercial Hotel. And he will say that, though careful with the brass, he begrudges nothing when it comes to food.

He knows what it is to go without. He doesn't mind admitting that he worked in the Mill. He saw Boom and Slump; knew Cotton as King and as Beggar. A man must not be ashamed of anything in the way of honest work. When circumstances demanded it, he got a job labouring, and happy to get it. The whole point is, the children ate, had shoes, and never had a day's illness. That's little enough to brag about, but at the same time it's something, he reckons. Well, gentlemen, he got together a pound here and a pound there, by going without everything except potatoes and sleep. He likes his grub but can go without it. He took a little shop, starting with a few packets of stuff on tick. Now he owes no man a farthing. It is a good business. It took him five years to make it what it is. He had a vast scheme for a mail-order business, a fair and square one on new lines, which, in another five years, might make Shorrock as big as Sainsbury. He hasn't the slightest doubt that Agatha, though the finest lass in the world, will ruin everything. Well . . . happen she will, happen she won't. He'll still have his own two hands——

—that is to say, given reasonable luck. He reckons that very few men lose *both* hands. . . .

He sits, pink and stubborn, like a skinned bulldog. His expression does not change. He has got his left-hand dog-teeth into the hole they have bitten through the stem of his pipe: pincers could not wrest it from his mouth before he chose to lay it down. Somebody asks him why he volunteered so soon. A year or two might pass before the thirty-sixes are called; and in that time a lot might happen. . . .

"If we've to fight," says Shorrock, "let's get it over and done wi'. Let's get on wi' it. I look at it lak this: it takes months to train a man. Ah. A year, eh? Ah. I reckon that year between now and t' call-up o' t' thirty-sixes as eighteen months. Ah. Any'ow I don't like foreigners gettin' cheeky. So let's get on wi' it, and quick, too."

His little blue eyes glitter as he talks, and he spits rather than puffs the smoke of his pipe. You agree with Shorrock or you quarrel with him. He is a man of unyielding spirit. He loves England for one smoky dent in her wind-blasted northern moors—the unlovely valley of Rock-bottom which reeks to the rainy sky.

The wars of all the world never moved a hair of his scanty eyebrows. He never gave a damn for all the Japs in China. He wanted only to be left alone.

In this he gets his way, in the end.

There were other Shorrockses, just like this one. They were the dawn-men of Britain. There is little doubt that they looked much the same; had the same stubborn, rosy, primeval English face; the same stalwart carriage; and talked something like the same language. If Shorrocks on the bed wants to "talk broad", or lapse into Lancashire dialect, up pops the old Angle. He never yielded a thing—not even a phrase—to foreign influence!

The ancient Shorrocks went about his business in the same way and the same place when there was a bit of a Roman villa standing where the Jubilee Memorial Tower stands to-day. The Romans had come and gone. Shorrocks ploughed his land, and rose at dawn, and lay down at dark, and owed no man a farthing; kept a cautious eye on what came in and what went out, and cared not a rap for the heaving world. Yorkshire was a foreign land. Leicester was a traveller's story. London was a legend. Soldiers were a pain; they ate and drank but grew no barley for bread and beer. Shorrock was unimpressible. He wanted nothing. He had Rockbottom. He had a world.

And when they said that the wild men were coming from the north—giants with winged helmets, swordsmen in long boats—Shorrock snorted and sniffed and called the panting newsmonger a Silly Fewel, and told him to be damned.

But when he smelt the smoke of something burning, and heard that the long boats were up the Ribble, Shorrocks put down his scythe and put on a steel cap—not unlike his best black bowler—and got down a buckler and honed up an axe, and told Gurth to look after the swine, and kissed his wife, and went out to do battle with the raiders. He fought like the pig-headed yeoman that he was, and is. In due course he came back; or didn't come back. But he got what he gave himself for.

Rockbottom remained with the Shorrockses.

Snatch the cubs from under the she-wolf. Filch the kittens from the wildcat. Then try to take something that Shorrocks lays claim to—his wife, his child, his living, his prejudices; or England.

What is this strange stuff that runs in English veins? God knows, who shakes the cocktail of human blood. The English mixture is smooth and dangerous, always well iced, yet full of an insidious fire. Many elements go to make it. The English lay no claim to racial purity.

Racial purity! If blood were pure, man would still have no chin and walk on all fours. Even if there were un-adulterated primeval blood, who would boast of it? A liquor might as well boast of being crude from the still. Rotgut might as reasonably vaunt its mad harshness over the gentle strength of a tempered liqueur.

The predominant English flavour is potent but bland, like good old blended whisky. You blend a whisky by balancing proportions of many different crude whiskies of various ages and qualities, until you happen upon some-thing individual and of its kind perfect. In a blend, you mix the rough with the smooth, and so achieve a happy medium; power and sweetness.

Blood is like that, especially English blood, which of all the blood in the world is the most widely and subtly mixed.

Sometimes some ingredient predominates. Thurstan, for instance, although he has the national flavour, is a little too fiery. He is knockout drops, taken in im-moderate quantities; best left alone. Shorrocks has the heavy, strong, fundamental stuff predominant in him—the Blend would be lost without it, but on its own it can become a shade monotonous.

Dale is one representative sample of the balanced whole—the decent Dale, who sits next to Shorrocks on the bed.

Dale is the Man In The Street if ever I saw one.

Abiding by all written and unwritten laws, right or wrong; adhering to all established beliefs, wise or foolish; patient as an ox, unopinionated as a spring lamb; moderate of appetite, diffident of manner—he looks at you with the clear, anxiously trusting eye of a child who has once or twice been unjustly punished. He is: he has: he is the English Man In The Street.

Dale is a Londoner. He was born in the black heart of that monstrous jungle of soot-eroded brick round Battle Bridge. Now, he has a home in Ilford, which, to him, is deep countryside; practically agricultural. He is a good, steady boy, married to his female counterpart who loves him and whom he loves. Their home is their own. They were saving up for a baby as for a piano when the War broke out. When they had so much put away, then they were going to have a family—for Dale loves to pay his way, and feels easy in his mind only as long as no man calls him debtor. He was happy on his wedding day; but even happier, in a deep and strange kind of way, when he posted the last instalment on the furniture.

Once he was an office boy. Now he is a fairly highly-placed clerk in the offices of a firm that has sold wine since 1755. Dale is proud of this date. If you take him to a pub, he will ask for a small glass of Sheraton Port, which is the produce of his employer. Not that he likes port very much: he is simply loyal in all matters, and feels that in supporting the Company he is also doing right by himself. If he worked for a brewer, then he would drink beer;

though never more than a little of it, since any expenditure beyond his budget would take milk out of the bottle of his unborn son—or, as his wife insists, daughter. He knows his job and does exactly what is required of him. He can tell you that a hogshead of Claret holds forty-six gallons, while a hogshead of Hock holds thirty, and one of Brandy fifty-seven. Don't ask him why: it doesn't concern him. Dale will accept all the discrepancies of life without a murmur.

His face seems familiar to you. You feel you've seen it before. So you have. Where? Everywhere. Agencies pick that face for the type of Mister Everyman. The streets are full of it. At Cup Finals myriads of it make a great pink bank in the rain. It has straight, ordinary features; eyes neither grey nor blue; complexion neither fresh nor pale; hair neither light nor dark . . . everything about him is *ish*—greyish, bluish, brownish; in size tallish; in dress darkish—the whole noticeably unconspicuous and unmistakably English.

The coming night will be the first he will ever have spent away from his wife. He has started to write a letter, already, but having written the words: *Dear Mavis, I have arrived safely*, chews his pencil disconsolately, not knowing what more to say; or rather, having so many things he knows he wants to say, that he does not know where or how to begin. He won't sleep a wink. At home he couldn't shut an eye unless he was lying on the outside of the bed and could hear his watch ticking. Dale is a man of habit. His habits are chains which he has forged about himself in the thirty years of his peaceful and uneventful life.

Then why is he here, now, when others of his age-group still await the call-up?

Ask Time. Ask History. A lamb to lead, a ram to oppose: such is Dale. He heard the trumpet and smelt the smoke. Somewhere in Dale's veins something craned up crowing like a fighting-cock. He screwed the cap on his fountain-pen and asked what they would kindly let him volunteer for. Vacancies in the Guards. Guards? Since Dunkirk, good God yes, alas! Dale is here for examination by the Guards M.O. (You need two A.I.s to get in here . . . but these townsmen, under their serge and shirtings, have good strong hearts and straight bones.)

He is thinking: *To-morrow's Saturday. Mavis will spend her first week-end without me, in six years.* He is depressed to the verge of tears.

There was another occasion, when another Dale spoiled his good wife's week-end. Sunday was his only day off, too. He was a George Dale, exactly like this one. He ruined the family Sunday on June 18th, 1815, when he put in a bit of overtime from ten in the morning to five in the afternoon. He, also, worked in a counting house. But that Sabbath he put paid to the account of a Dictator called Napoleon, and the day of reckoning goes down in history as Waterloo.

Greyish-white as the paper on which Dale is trying to write; threatening as the sky; sullen as a thundercloud, Thurstan sits behind him, rolling a cigarette and staring at the floor.

He has the habit of staring at a thing as if he hated it. His eyes are holes full of shadows, in which dim, menacing things wait, slightly stirring. There is a rumour that he has been in jail. Who knows? Or perhaps his pallor is natural to him; some men are born pale. It may be that Thurstan has done time: lots of people have. If he did, it was for some outburst of violence, rather than petty larceny or sneak-thievery, for there is a savage recklessness in every line and curve of the man.

His lean hand with its bitten nails holds the tobacco against the paper. Blue veins like whipcord writhe over and around tendons that jump and snap taut-like wires in a musical instrument. That would be a bad hand to have on your windpipe. The knuckles are dented and scarred. From one angle the hand looks like pincers: from another it resembles an old mallet. Thurstan is not a big man: he just touches the minimum five-foot-nine-and-a-half. And he is fleshless. His cheeks are sunken: he has had bad times. He can't possibly weigh more than nine stone. Yet there is about him an air of appalling force; a nervous power that could drive him through an iron plate. Was he a boxer? He won't talk. His nose is smashed to the four points of the compass . . . but boxers don't have such knuckles. You do not often see scars such as Thurstan has on his face. It is not that they are very terrible scars: simply that they are queer. High up on his right cheekbone there is a rough oval of white indentations. Toothmarks! Where he comes from, men fight with fangs and claws and hoofs. His forehead is marked with two depressions, circular in outline, equal in depth and size. You may make scars like that by hitting soft wood with a carpenter's hammer—and that is what somebody did to Thurstan, only there is nothing soft about his ferocious little skull. You would hate to receive such blows. You would hate, still more, to be the man who dealt them, if Thurstan lay under your hammer.

Life has beaten him like iron on an anvil.

He comes from the region of Durham City. That is, he lived there before he came here. His origins lie a little further north. His is the wild blood of the Border. He was a collier, once. He knows what it is, to lie in the hot darkness pecking tons of hard coal out of the seam. He doesn't have to tell you this: he wears the miner's trade-mark—blue freckles of buried coal in his face. He talks a dialect difficult to comprehend. Since the moment of his arrival, three hours ago, he has spoken only three words. A harmless old man, a Scripture Reader, called, and asked the recruits to gather in a far corner of the room. Thurstan said: "Ah no gang," meaning, "I will not go." He is a dangerous man, a rebel, inflammable as fire-damp, touchy as a half-broken pit-pony and equally willing to kick or bite—obstinate, morose, savage as a caracal, quick as a lynx, courageous as a wild pig and twice as hard to stop. He has a wife, somewhere in the stormy north, whom he has forgotten like a parcel in a bus. There will be trouble with Thurstan. We can smell it, like something smouldering.

There always was trouble with Thurstan. Hadrian built a wall to keep him out, but he came right in and thumbed his busted nose at the iron might of Rome. He was always something of a rebel and a raider. A Thurstan drew a wicked bow alongside Robin Hood in the black age of the Robber Barons. He is unblended fire-water; a patch of unmixed hot stuff, here because he wants a fight. He comes to war as his grandfathers went to feud. He can't live without the thrill of the pounding heart and the slamming fist. He itches for the mad moment of the bayonet-charge. When this moment comes, "controlled charge" will not include Thurstan. He will swell. He will yell. He will rush forward in front of everybody else, a live projectile, a horror, a bloodthirsty nightmare; the kind of fight-mad killer that panics an army. Whichever way he turns out, he'll be dangerous. Thurstan would butt against a bull, gore against a boar, trade bites with a leopard, impervious to pain or fear.

Disciplined, that force of his will be overwhelming. Discipline to him will be the brass shell round the packed explosive. But to discipline Thurstan, you must make him like you. God help the sergeant that has to break in Thurstan. But God pity the Nazi that comes up against Thurstan let loose. He is the old, old wildfire of ancient Britain.

In this room also sits John Hodge, a giant, reading a small black book which, under his huge thumb, looks no bigger than a playing card. His left arm hangs over the bedrail. It has hung like that for fifteen minutes, during which time he has pored, motionless, over the same page. His great square-blocked head droops, pressing his massive chin into folds against his chest. Hodge sits astride the bed, dwarfing everything; still as a man carved out of one mighty chunk of ruddy brown rock. You look twice at his back before you notice the rise and fall which indicates that he breathes.

Suddenly he moves. He closes the book. A grave suspicion has been whispered, that this book is a Bible: this is not the kind of accusation one shouts round the place, for fear of slander; but it has been whispered. It has black, shiny covers. Perhaps he promised his mother that he would read a page or two every day; in which case, of course, one may say that there are extenuating circumstances. Hodge raises his arms and yawns. Chest rises, belly flattens, things like ropes run taut under the bronzed skin of his throat. The Cockney called Barker says: "Blimey, it'd take a hell of a drop to 'ang that geezer."

John Hodge is muscled like a Percheron stallion: his hands are hard and shiny like hoofs. A horse of a man; a work-horse; patient, powerful, docile, and simple.

This is the story of John Hodge:

He was born to a farm-labourer in Gloucestershire twenty-seven years ago. Fourteen years later he went to work on a farm. Week in, week out, for six hundred and seventy-six weeks, he worked stolidly. Then War came. John Hodge told the first lie of his life. He said he was a casual labourer, fearing that farming men might be reserved. The gentlemen gave him a railway warrant and four-and-six. He gave the four-and-six to his mother, who said nothing much, but privately wept. And he came here in a train.

Complete history of the main events of twenty-seven years in the life of a giant.

His father did the same in 1914. Back and back, generation upon generation, the seventeen-stone Hodge men, mild and unshakeable as the hills, went to the wars. There is something in their blood that makes them do it. You can slap a Hodge in the face without necessarily stirring him to fight; and in the event of an inescapable private quarrel he will go into action apologetically, uncomfortably. Ordinary insults arouse in him only a sad surprise. What does anybody want with him, Hodge who wants to hurt nobody? You could harness him to a plough, like a gelding; or to a millstone like Samson in Gaza. He asks only a little food and a bed, first for his mother and then for himself. He belongs to the earth; can tell you, intuitively, the productive potentiality of a field by the feel of a handful of its dirt; knows stock, and all the permutations and combinations of time and rain.

He wants nothing. He has got it. He is happy.

Yet he is here, a little worried about the subterfuge. Do you see?—he *wasn't* a casual labourer, so now he's a liar. He reckons that it was not a very bad lie . . . not like lying to avoid something, or to get something. Still, a lie *is* a lie. . . .

Once upon a time another of the Hodge men, also tearing himself up by the roots on a point of conscience, similarly told a lie. He was walking with a limp. Somebody asked him why, and he said he had a bad leg. Well, he didn't have a bad leg: far from it; he had a very good leg. But he couldn't very well say he had a sword hidden in his breeches because he was going to join a band of good Protestants further west in a species of uprising under a certain Duke of Monmouth. God approved: the Law didn't. God, thought the ancient Hodge, would overlook the lie.

The Monmouth affair turned out badly. Monmouth ran; that pretty, gutless gentleman. It was a nasty business. The good peasants went down like wheat under hail, calling upon Heaven for gunpowder. *Powder, for Christ's sake, powder!* It must have been one of the most piteous cries ever heard on a battlefield. The King's troops poured over, and the good Hodge, laying about him like a stag at bay, died singing a Puritan hymn, leaving an orphan son.

It was bad, for Hodge to leave an orphan son; but it would have been worse if he hadn't—for here is John Hodge! May I be with him at the last ditch!

In one of our fitful bursts of talk we had discussed the retreat from Dunkirk.

The Cockney, Bob Barker said: "But it was a bit o' luck the sea was smooth, anyway."

Hodge, opening astonished blue eyes, said: "Why,

don't 'ee see? The Lord God stretched out his hand over that water. He said: 'Now you hold still, and let my children come away.'"

To that, Bob Barker said nothing. He knows when to laugh and when not to laugh. He is sardonic as a general rule, and believes in nothing much. If he laughs at Hodge, it will be in his sleeve. In his odd way he draws his own kind of power from his faculty for laughter. D'Annunzio told a story about a man like Barker in the last war.

I forget his actual words. The poet was looking over a little soggy black hell of shot-harrowed mud between front-line trenches. A handful of British soldiers held a trench. They were wounded, and tired almost to death. You must imagine the scene . . . the unutterable melancholy of autumnal Flanders, and the rain, and the cold, and the hopelessness, and the heartsickness, and the ache of throbbing wounds and empty bellies, and the helplessness of exhausted ammunition. . . . Suddenly one of the soldiers shouted: "Are we downhearted?"

A pause.

Then, from a pit of mud out in No Man's Land, animated by its very last flicker of life a thing like a scarecrow out of a slaughterhouse leapt up, and screamed:

"*Nao!*" And died.

That could have been Barker.

He is a long, gaunt man of twenty-eight or so, with the kind of face one associates with adenoids. He hasn't got adenoids, but looks as if he ought to have. His eyes are prominent, under thick, arched eyebrows as mobile as caterpillars which almost meet at the beginning of his beaky nose. His upper lip is long and outstanding. His mouth is always half-open, so that his chin, which at its firmest is far from prominent, seems to slip away down to his big, wobbling Adam's-apple. He has a bass voice. When he swallows his throat expands and contracts in the tight compass of the white rayon scarf he wears knotted round it. The ends of this scarf are tucked into a flash waistcoat. Barker dresses for show. It is for Barker that unknown heroines in mass-production tailors' shops sew on fantastic superabundancies of buttons, and fix incredible pleats in extraordinary coats. If anything new appears in the way of purple suitings or velvet collars, Barker will be the first to wear them. He knows, and carefully specifies, the circumference of his trouser-legs—no less than twenty-four inches, though the heavens fall. He crams his big feet into torpedo-shaped shoes . . . unless the salesman tells him that America is wearing square toes, in which case Barker will wear square toes too.

For work, he wears his flash suits gone to seed. Barker shoves a barrow: fruit. He is the one permanent type of the Londoner—the indomitable, the virile, the astute, the nervy, the brave and cocky Cockney of the markets, who speaks a language, and has a background of colour and misery. His phraseology is debased. He uses slang. To Barker, a row is a Bull-an'-a-Cow; a suit is a Whistle, or Whistle-an'-Flute; a kid is a Gord-Forbid; a car is a Jam, or Jam-Jar; talk is Rabbit, or Rabbit-an'-Pork; beer is Pig's Ear . . . and so on, up and down the language. He has a secret code; for sometimes Barker and his brothers have to hold their own against organised, English-speaking society: they can exchange conversation in slang and hint, spoken fast, and incomprehensible as Hungarian to the man or woman of polite pretentions. Barker has his own financial jargon. If the Stock Exchange can speak mysteriously of "Clo-to-clo" and "At the mark," Barker can refer to "Forty tosheroons" or "Six o' Clods."

He loves a rhyme, has as keen an ear for euphony as James Agate, and speaks in irony and satire. "*Who made that hole?*" asks the Rookie, at the shell-hole; and the Old Sweat replies:—"*Mice.*" This is a Barker joke, pure and simple. If it is pouring with rain, he will say, not "Isn't it a terrible day?" but "Ain't it lovely?" As a free trader, he will starve rather than take a steady job. He has got to be his own master . . . even if he, as master, drives himself out at four in the morning and pushes himself round the streets with the barrow until midnight, when there is a chance of selling a bit of fruit at an advanced price to the girls and the drunks. He will short-change the prosperous without pity . . . or recklessly give stock away to the children of the poor. His father, a costermonger of the old school, was an Old Contemptible, who spent about a third of his Army life in the Glasshouse, but got a D.C.M. for some crazy impossibility with a bayonet against a machine-gun. That same old man Barker, having, in his cups, bored ten thousand listeners with ten thousand bitter curses on the Army and all concerned with it for the last quarter of a century, now makes everybody's life a misery with his savage denunciations of the corrupt authorities who, just because he has only one arm, turned him down in 1939. He says he hopes Hitler wins. If he hears anybody else say that you have to admit that Jerry hasn't done too badly, he has to be held down while he brandishes his solitary fist and yells that Jerry doesn't stand a chance and asks everybody to wait till he gets hold of Goering.

Bob Barker is much the same, only he is young and humorous. If he goes out under heavy fire and saves somebody's life, he will say he did it because the man had some cigarettes. When he is decorated, he will curl his lip at his medal and call it a bit of tin . . . and secretly polish it for hours.

He says he volunteered out of spite, because of the shortage of bananas.

He admires above all things the quality of toughness. I don't mean toughness in the current sense of the term—not the toughness one associates with naughty little hats, tight lips, scowls, criminality, and offensive manners. I mean the quality of resistance: the quality that makes man survive. Galileo would have been a Tough Guy to Barker because he couldn't find it in himself to deny that the earth revolved round the sun. He would regard as tough the gangster who never squealed: also, Scott at the Antarctic or Sir Richard Grenville sailing into the guns of the armada of fifty-three, or Tom Sayers fighting with bare knuckles against Heenan, or Van Tromp hoisting at his masthead the broom with which he was going to sweep England off the seas, or Blake battering Van Tromp; or Ney fighting Wellington, or Wellington fighting Ney. Barker loves cold courage—in effect, the triumph of the soul over the nerves.

Thus, it is safe to prophesy a friendship between Bob Barker the Cockney and Harry Bullock of Bedfordshire.

Barker flips Bullock a Woodbine. Bullock gives Barker a light. He is a dark man, with a dour expression, a knotted forehead, a sombre glow in his eyes, and a swollen upper lip. Bullock is a bruiser. He is one of those boxers of whom nobody ever heard. His greatest fight was against one Nippy Oliver. Nobody ever heard of Nippy Oliver, either. Neither of those two fighters will ever get more

than a five-pound note for an evening's mauling. Yet
Bullock thinks he could beat Farr. Maybe he could. If he
couldn't, Bullock would never know it. He has no idea of
the meaning of defeat. If he lost his hands he would fight
on with the stumps of his wrists, and feel that the advantage was somehow with him. He augmented what he
earned in a boot factory by fighting in booths: shattering
battles, murderous combats in which the ring ran red;
for a few shillings a time. It began when the kid wanted a
fairy-cycle for her birthday. He has never been knocked
out. Something in Bullock holds on to consciousness and
makes him always fight. He is big enough and heavy
enough to fight anything on legs; gloomy, good-natured,
taking all things seriously.

One of his front teeth is missing. This imparts something oddly wicked to his smile . . . to say nothing of the
formidable look of his swollen lip, bridgeless nose, and left
ear which resembles half a walnut.

Barker says: "Scrapper?"

"Yum."

"Fourteen stone?"

"Thirteen-ten."

"Ever meet Pinky Stallybrass?"

"Nump."

" 'E couldn't 'arf go."

"Yum?"

"A souf-paw boxer. But stone me, wot a left!"

"Um . . ."

" 'Oo you met?"

"Nippy Oliver."

"Zat so?"

A Trained Soldier, with a pale, patient face fixed in an
expression of permanent disgust says:

"Well, my chickerdees, come and get yer hair cut."

There is a dreadful finality about this. Condemned men in American jails feel the same cold thrill that we feel, when their head is shaved to facilitate the passing of the shock that kills them.

"Hair-cut. Then medical inspection. Then good night," says the glum man, rising and flipping away his cigarette-end.

We go out. The wire-haired boy is as pale as ashes.

The rain holds off. The wind has stopped. The world is holding its breath. There is an awful silence in the Barracks. I have a dreadful feeling that the world has paused in its spinning. Looking up, I see something that makes me jump. Sixteen barrage-balloons stand still in the air. They look like bombs which have been falling but have stopped dead with the wind, the world, and time. In a moment there will be a sickening jerk. . . . Everything will move again. . . . Bugles will bray, the bombs will fall, and as life moves, so it will cease to move in one last red whirl of disintegration.

There is a dream-like quality about this place, at this time.

First day at the Depot! It is too new to be real. We look round at the bare plane of concrete, as a new-born baby, being smacked into life, looks down at the counterpane. We don't see it, but it gets into our minds. We'll never quite remember, and never quite forget, what it looks like.

"If they spoil my quiff," says Barker, fluffing up his forelock, "blimey if I don't run away to sea."

We straggle into the barber's shop.

Later we were to hear dark, emphatic tales of barrack barbers; old soldiers' stories, punctuated with fearful oaths and paragraphed with pregnant pauses, of atrocities committed with 4-0 Clippers on unsuspecting skulls. Ah, the good Old Soldier! He will make a history of oppression and a drama of unutterable crime out of every grain of sand in the midday cabbage.

Months later I was to hear Sergeant Tug's tale of early sufferings in the barber's chair.

Tug, with burning eyes, talking of that barber as an Armenian might talk of Turks; thrusting forward his flat-nosed, stubborn-jawed, dour, hard face, morosely smiling, and saying:

"You're issued with a comb. Get it? A comb. And a brush. D'you foller me? A brush. What are you issued with a brush and a comb for? Answer me that? What for, I ask? I'll tell you what for. To comb and brush your hair. Do you see that? To comb and brush your hair. Now listen to me. Some blokes round this camp are vague, if you get what I mean, vague about hair-cutting regulations. Right. Some say your hair mustn't be more than two inches long on top. Be that as it may. I say, *you got to be left with sufficient hair to brush and comb*. King's Regulations, by God! And to crop a man's head is to defy the King. To defy the King and country! Do you foller me? It's like saying Pooey to King George the Sixth. It's like putting your thumb to your nose and wiggling all your fingers at Winston Churchill and the whole British Government, to go and take all the hair off of a man's head.

"So. I was proud of my headervair. Laugh. But I had a headervair any woman might have been proud of. Oh, *I* know it's a lot of bull. But I was a youngster. And I tell you, I was proud of that headervair. And I says to the barber: 'Leave it on top,' and he says to me: 'God blimey, where d'you think you are? In a bleeding orchestra? Fond of music, are you? A pansy, ha?' And I says to the barber: 'I'm not fond of music—cut out the insults.' And he says to me: 'Bend your 'ead forward and cut out the back answers.' And I says to him: 'Cut off that top bit that waves and so help me I won't stand for it,' and he says: 'Oh, then lie down to it, Paderooski.' And I waits. And I feels them clippers going up my neck, and so help me God Almighty in Heaven, I feels them clippers going right up to the top of my head. And I jumps out of that chair and I runs out of the barber's shop, and I goes on parade with me hair uncut, and a sort of bald strip running from me neck to the top of me skull. And the officer says: 'What the devil do you think that is?' And I says: 'Sir, permission to speak, sir. Am I here to be shaved like a convict, sir?' And the officer says 'No.' And I says: 'Sir, permission to speak, sir, the barber wanted to shave my head, sir.' And the officer says: 'Oh,' and as true as I sit here that barber got fourteen days. Ah. Fourteen steady days. They run him into the moosh, they did, and they took him on Orders, and they give him fourteen solid days C.B. Yeah, it was jankers for that lousy rotten barber, for flying in the face of the King's Regulations. My headervair. I don't mind telling you, it just about broke my heart, what they done to my headervair.

"That's a fact. I was a good boy till then. But after that, I didn't care for nothing or nobody, I didn't! I been made up three times and busted three times, and when I was a Corporal they bust me for something I never done, ah, they did that! But Detention, Spud-Hole,

Jankers, Reps, Royal Warrant, and everything else—
nothing 'urt me so much as what they done to my lovely
headervair.

"Murderers! Murderers! That's what them barbers
are, murderers! Jerry kills your body. But the barber, he
murders your soul. Look at me now. Bald. Me mother
cried when she saw me last. She cried, I tell you, she
broke down and she cried like a child, and I don't mind
telling you that I broke down and cried with her, too. . . .
I was ashamed of myself, but I couldn't help it. I sobbed
as if my heart was breaking, I did. And my old dad, a
lump came into his throat; he couldn't touch supper. I
can show you a photo of myself with a headervair that'll
make you look up a bit . . . just like a mop. Call me a
liar if you like. I say a mop. Everybody used to talk
about my headervair. Girls used to say: 'Tug, I envy you
only one thing; your headervair.' I got a picture of
myself took in Ramsgit in 1910, when I was seven. Curls
down to me shoulders. The Army ruined all that. I
forgave 'em everything, but I'll never forgive 'em
that."

And Sergeant Tug, who led a bayonet-charge on the
road to Boulogne, or thereabout, and carried six men's
equipment twenty-six miles, and looks upon the awful
discipline of the peace-time Brigade of Guards as "cushy,"
and has seventeen years of service behind him, and is as
impregnable as a tank, fingers his scalp, from which the
hair just naturally receded, and sighs, and scowls at the
memory of the barber.

Somebody says: "Sarnt Tug—you got shot in France,
didn't you? What's it feel like?"

He replies: "What's that? Feel like? Oh . . . sort
of hot and cold. Golden, it was . . . spun gold, my

mum used to call it, and I'm not telling you a word
of a lie. Spun gold. That's life for you."

"Where d'you get hit, Sarnt Tug?"

"Machine-gun burst: thigh and backside: two in the
face, teeth splintered to hell. Blimey, I was proud of that
headervair . . ."

Recruits have been pouring in. The Corporal in the
barber's shop is harassed. Recruits are dreary cattle to
shear . . . terrified, dumb, stupid, paralysed with
novelty.

The floor is sprinkled with clippings, red, yellow, black,
brown, and, above all, plain English mouse. The grim
soldier is playing barbers: there are two cut-glass bottles
on the shelf in front of the chair.

We cram ourselves into the room. The Corporal says:
"Well, siddown, siddown, siddown, siddown, siddown
. . . don't block up the gangway."

The wire-haired boy is first to take the chair. There
isn't a mirror: we can't see his face; but a look of terrified
expectancy spreads, somehow, to his neck. No doubt a
neck looks like that when Monsieur Paris has his hand on
the string of the guillotine. There is a *tickety-tickety-
tickety-tickety* of clippers. It is like husking a coconut. Out
of a mass of fibre emerges something pale, oval, top-
knotted, and seamed. "Next," says the Corporal.
"What?" says the wire-haired boy. "Fancy a nice
shampoo?" says the Corporal. The boy who used to have
wire hair says: "I don't mind."

"Any particular kind of shampoo?"

"I don't know. I don't mind."

"Ashes of Roses?"

"If you like."

"Or would you rather have violets?"

"Well, I think I'd rather have violets."

"Oh. And a friction? Or a nice massage?"

"Never mind about that. Just a shampoo."

"Just a shampoo?"

"Yes, please."

"Well go and put your head under the bloody tap. *Next!*"

The boy rises unsteadily, feels his head with an incredulous hand, blinks, looks at his palm as if he expects to find blood upon it. "Where d'you come from?" the Corporal asks him.

"Widnes."

"Then," says the Corporal, "you ought to be ashamed of yourself. *Next.*" He cuts a man's hair in about forty-five seconds.

"It ain't 'umane," says Barker. "You ought to give us gas wiv 'air cuts like these."

"*Next.*"

Hodge's naked head emerges, still massive. Thurstan, shorn of a dense dark growth, looks blacker and paler and even more dangerous.

"I've seen your face before," says the Corporal to the glum man. "What's your monicker?"

"Alison."

"You been here before, ain't that so?"

"That's right."

"And now you're back, eh?"

"Worse luck."

"You pore thing."

One by one we pass under the clippers. He shears us like sheep. One man lurks near the door, half in and half out of the shop, as if he contemplates flight. He is very young and slender, dark and sunburnt yet lacking the look of one who lives in the open air. *Town* is written on his forehead, so to speak; the streets are his destiny. You can't help feeling that he got his tan in a city park: like inordinate skill at billiards, it seems to indicate a mis-spent youth. This is John Johnson of Birmingham; of Brummagem, gentlemen, the breeding-ground of the Fly Boys from time immemorial.

He has talked too little and too much during his few hours in the Depot. He wants everything tough—in the silly sense of the term. When Bates, that garrulous and amiable brewer's drayman from Leicester, said: "Well, Oi 'ope they'll fill moi teeth," it was John Johnson who snapped, in his aggressive burr: "Oi want 'em to take all moine out. Oi can't be bothered with teeth." He has a lank, saturnine face; eyebrows which collide in a black plume in the middle of his low forehead; little green eyes, and a sloping chin. He keeps his mouth compressed; sports a green coat, green flannel trousers, green suède shoes, green fancy sports-shirt with pompoms; a tricky cigarette-case which won't open and a cunning lighter which won't light—to say nothing of a novel watch on a doggy leather lanyard, which like Johnson, looks smart but doesn't work. When simple Bates said he earned a good, steady three pound two-and-six a week, Johnson said: "Oi drew twelve." He carries a box of fat cigarettes, and a paper packet of little black cigarlets, which, he maintains, are too strong for ordinary men. . . . The tobacconist warns you that you smoke those cigarlets at your own risk: if you pass out cold in a sweat of nicotine poisoning, don't come and ask for your money back. Nothing is too powerful for John Johnson of Brummagem.

Barker, to whom fly boys, both of Brummagem and

The Smoke, are an open book, smiled at this, and said: " 'E chews nails and spits rust. 'E shaves wiv a blow-lamp." Barker knows fly boys as Professor Huxley knows flics . . . what they eat and drink, where they breed, if and when they sleep, how many eyes they have, and where they go in the winter time. But Bates permitted himself to be impressed, and said: "Are they noice?"

Bates, displaying his blond head, with anxiety in his big, bony Anglo-Saxon face; wide-eyed, wide-mouthed, wide-cheeked and friendly, says: "Do Oi look funny? Do Oi?"

Johnson replies, with patronage: "All right. You're in the Army now, yer know," and comes away from the door. He has lank black hair, heavily creamed, extraordinarily long, carefully arranged with a parting one inch to the left of the centre. I believe he would sooner part with his right arm than lose that gallant mane. But he swaggers forward, now, and says:

"Cut it off, Corp-rerl. You can't cut it too short for me. Oi can't be bothered with it." *Tickety-tickety-tickety*, chatter the clippers.

"One o' the Brylcreem Boys, eh?" says the Corporal, with a little smile of enjoyment: he looks forward to heads of hair like this; they give a zest to his life; he talks of them in the Mess. *Tickety-tickety.* . . . Johnson is scalped. A raiding party of Iroquois couldn't have done a much completer job on him.

"That looks noice," says Bates.

"Honest?" asks Johnson.

"It makes yow look toof."

"Tough, eh?" says Johnson, and represses a smile of gratification. "Don't talk soppy. You wait a minute and I'll give you one o' my cigarlets."

Bates has said exactly the right thing, for the first—and perhaps the last—time in his life. He beams, that simple soul; his face cracks into a smile like a split pumpkin. He has given pleasure: he is delighted beyond words. He lights one of the little black cigarlets. It isn't anywhere near the stuff he rolls, for strength and irritant quality. Bates sucks in a cloud of smoke and blows it out.

"They're noice and moild," he says.

Johnson's lips tighten again.

Clipped to the bone we walk back and wait for the Medical Officer to send for us.

A dentist looks at our teeth. An old sergeant, who appears to be nailed to an invisible backboard, shuffles eye-testing cards. There are some unscrupulous recruits who, having bad eyes, try and learn the rows of letters by heart, and so slink into the Guards. They have several cards, which they change from test to test. A big Exeter man named Septimus Plimsoll, seventh son of a seventh son, but far from psychic, is cast out as astigmatic.

"But my hair! They've cut my hair! They can't turn me down now . . . they've cut my hair!" he says.

"Cutcha hair, son?" says the old Sergeant, looking at him.

"Yes."

"Well, I'll tell you what. You go straight to Corporal Philips at the barber's shop—tell him Sergeant Robson sentcha—don't forget to mention my name—and he'll give you your hair back agen. Next!"

We take off all our clothes except our trousers. Bodies emerge, pallid as maggots. You see, now, the herculean thews of Hodge; his biceps like grape-fruit, his pectorals like breast-plates; Thurstan, all tendon and gristle, with a back that writhes with muscle like a handful of worms; lanky Barker; the Widnes boy, still padded with puppy-fat; the inconspicuous pale Dale; suety Shorrock; Johnson, thin but fast-looking, with long flat muscles and not enough chest; Bullock, dark and knotty; Bates, starch-fed, starch-white, but built for power; Alison, the glum old soldier, with *Death Rather Than Dishonour* tattooed on his left arm and *I Love Millie* on his bosom . . . out-door workers with brown forearms and necks which make their torsos look like cotton vests . . . sedentary men, run to skin and bone . . . miners, with great backs and arms . . . a timber-feller, with wrestler's shoulders grafted on to the body of a clerk . . . a steel-worker, like a mummified Carnera . . . men who push things and have loins like Samson . . . men who pull things, and have deltoids like half-moons and hams for forearms. . . .

Barker says: "Hallo, Tarzan: if I 'ad me barrer ahtside I'd go an' get yer a banana."

The man he calls Tarzan smiles a slow, white smile. He is a tall, strong Cornishman called Penrowe; Barker's nickname will stick to him, for he has a hairy chest. Barker, looking at him for the first time, said: "Look—a Five." A Five is a Five-to-Two, or Jew. Penrowe has something vaguely Semitic about him—a swarthy skin, white teeth, glittering eyes of a hard hot brown, and a big hooked nose. Yet he, and his father, and his father's father, lived in the West of England all their lives, and no Penrowe ever was anything but a good Englishman. A Penrowe was among the first of the Englishmen who looked through a warm dawn and saw the New World loom on the western horizon. Sir Francis—they called him Franky—Drake knew the Penrowes. A Penrowe went out with Grenville off Flores, in 1591. A Penrowe terrified his fellow villagers by smoking one of the first pipes of Elizabethan Cut Plug; and a Penrowe got a Spanish ball in his head when the Great Fleet Invincible, the hundred and twenty-nine ships of the Armada, sailed against the eighty ships of England. Eighty ships, and Admiral the North-West Wind. "God blew and they were scattered." But Penrowe helped, the black Cornishman; moody, calculating, proud, quarrelsome, hard man of the sea.

The sea is in his blood, and has been since the beginning of history. The sea washes its sons inland sometimes: our Penrowe comes from some messy hole in the ground where they get china-clay. He has two brothers in the Merchant Service, at present engaged in the stout old Cornish sport of harassing the modern equivalent of the Dons on the high seas.

But what dark stranger left that complexion and that profile in England? Who left the name of Marazion in the West? The very first of all the sea-rovers, the Phœnicians; dark, Hebraic-looking gentlemen, out to do business, as usual. They called at Britain to barter trade-goods for tin, before the Romans came, before the Three Wise Men cut their first teeth. The remote, forgotten grandmother of Penrowe saw the coloured sails of their great galleys, and saw them land—very dark, very suave, very well dressed, and smelling of perfume, with dress-lengths of exclusive materials and all kinds of household goods. They had come out of the Great Sea, over as rough a piece of water as anybody could wish to struggle against, right over the rim of the world, just to trade . . . the eternal, wandering Semites with their eyes that itched for new prospects. They were the first mariners. They came and went in Britain, always on friendly terms. The time came when

Ancient Briton women brought forth dark, curly-headed boys and girls in the far West of this country. And then, no doubt, there slunk into the blood a restlessness and a yearning . . . a craving for the unknown seas.

And here is Penrowe, English as Land's End but dark as high Barbary, with his hairy torso and high square shoulders, holding up his trousers and waiting for the M.O. to listen to the strange strong blood pumping through his powerful heart. . . .

Penrowe, swarthy Phœnician; Hodge, Bates, straight clear Saxon, fair as corn; Thurstan, black Gael. These are three rough, stinging, formidable elements in the Blend of Blood. What a devil of an island this is—this mixing-bowl of all that is most fierce and enduring in man, stirred by war in its beginnings and matured in its iron-bound cask of tradition in the rat-infested cellar of the centuries! Ancient Briton. . . . Ancient Roman—look at Allan of Cumberland, an English yeoman from the Pennine Chain, the Backbone of England—with the high-bridged nose and fine-drawn face of one of the Roman gentlemen who lived here, and laid the Great Wall, and Watling Street, and Uxbridge Road so long ago. The Romans were in Britain for four hundred and sixty-six years: they left blood, too! The red-headed monsters of Arthurian legend, the Saxons, came after them; and then the Norsemen cracked through. Johansen and Holm have been Yorkshiremen for centuries; yet there are no two between Heligoland and Hammerfest whom you could more easily visualise in a longboat under a ragged sail on a grey sea. And the Normans came, with a dash of Baltic madness and a dash of Gallic finesse; and we hated their guts, but assimilated all they had. Angle, Jute, Pict, Scot

—it all soaked in. And you see it here, blended into a type, yet distinguishable in its separate elements . . . fermenting into Thurstan, mellowing into Dale—blood of the stolid Shorrock, blood of the light John Johnson—blood of the cold English, the mad English—rough as Usquebaugh, smooth as Mead—strong red liquor!

Most of us are stolid and reserved, shy of strangers and of the sound of our own voices.

But there is a dark fire under the crust, and a hard current under the ice of the poker-faced Englishman. The expressionless Englishman, mouse-whiskered and talking at the ends of his teeth and greeting his best-beloved friend with a curt "Hallo," demanding mutton chops and strong tea of the luxurious restaurateur of the *Hermitage*, yet drinking like a Russian, duelling like a Hungarian, gambling like a Chinaman, or swearing like a Croat if the occasion demanded it, was always a little mad and curiously colourful to the amazed peoples of the Continent when he went on tour.

Heavy and immobile, or high-strung and variable blond; enigmatic black; mercurial red; or primary blond, red, and black ground into the prevalent common nondescript brown—in these men there is a strange way-ward will. Dash of ferocious Britain, spot of aromatic Asia, jigger of crazy Celt, splash of gentle and murderous Saxon, tinge of iron Roman, shot of haughty Norman, drip of fierce Norse—the elements, even when they are blended to neutrality, give birth to something queerly individual. You can imagine the baffled astonishment of Napoleon, when Wellington, in Spain, imported some hounds and rode after local foxes in the blue coat of the Salisbury Hunt . . . grown men, tough soldiers, but serious gentlemen, *mon vieux*, dozens of them, all riding belly-to-earth after a species of vermin, blowing shrill notes out of a little brass trumpet! And these same gents, with the dead-faced shopkeepers who followed them and took it all for granted, were the rock against which the Irresistible broke itself.

Fou! . . . Wahnsinnig! . . . Loco!—quite crazy, demented, nuts—mad Englishman! Methodical in his eccentricity; cool to man and openly affectionate only to dogs and horses; stirred to applause or catcalls by nothing in the world but the struggles of twenty-two men with a ball; seemingly more engrossed in the defence of three stumps and a pair of bails against a five-and-a-half-ounce ball, than in the defence of an Empire against barbarism; prone to forget everything in his eagerness to ascertain that one horse can run faster than eight others; regulating all combat by rules as of sport; unassuming as a mole and arrogant as a lion; an islander of islanders, regarding his salty wet rock as a universe, and the universe as too foreign for serious consideration; looking upon himself, in a strange land, as the one Briton in a world of gibbering aliens; blindly despising and blindly tolerating all outlandish things; incredibly blundering into chaos and fantastically blundering out of it; conspicuously inconspicuous; insanely cheerful; bland as a fat man in an asylum who thinks he's the Buddha; and maddeningly calm . . . always bewilderingly calm.

Calm. What looks calmer than a flywheel at top speed? What is calmer than the heart of a whirlwind?

Men like this sailed on the *Birkenhead*. It is a simple story. They had a pride of birth far deeper than any sentiment born of false reasoning or well-hammered propaganda. The *Birkenhead* struck a submerged reef.

Think of the thing as a scene in a film: the night, the stars, the heaving, shining sea. Then the crash, long and grinding. Furniture goes mad: immovable things fall and movables fly. Women scream. You catch a glimpse of men's faces in the vague half-dark: black gaps of shouting mouths, pale teeth. Then the list of the gutted ship and the swinging out of the boats. There is barely enough space in the lifeboats for the women and children, and the *Birkenhead* is sinking damnably fast.

There are some hundreds of English soldiers abroad.

These were soldiers like any other English soldiers. The same kind of men went down at Hastings and at Pass-chendaele—inveterate grousers, individuals who would sometimes skive if they got the opportunity, and frequently chanced their arms in the matter of boots and buttons. They saw off the women and children. Clouds came over. Night had put on the Black Cap.

These condemned men were formed up on deck. I do not doubt that even then, and there, there was a bucko sergeant who yelled "Order yer arms when you got yer dressing!"—or words to that effect—"Dress forward number three in the centre rank! God damn it, any soldier'd be ashamed to stand in a rank like a dog's leg! Stand still!"

They stood still. The sea rose. The ship sank. The soldiers stood to attention on deck until the water closed over them—Tom, Dick and Harry, saying forever good-bye to beer and skittles, tea and wads, the dawn they'd never see again, wives and children, love and life. They drowned by inches in the cold, empty ocean, because it was expected of them that, there being no chance of getting away, they die like Englishmen.

That's an old story, like the death of Nelson. We—it is

typical of us—hide our admiration in our hearts, and giggle at "Kiss me, Hardy," and "England expects . . ."

But Nelson knew exactly what to say on his last memorable naval occasion. Emotional as a ballerina, but calm as the Angel of Death in crisis; sick as a dog at the heave of a ship, yet dragged out onto the ocean by the ancient sea-wolf that tugged inside him; Norfolk Puritan salted with old Scandinavian—there was plenty of the pale fire-water in his mixture; and something sweet, too, for he could be gentle as a woman. He was a very gentle Englishman; a very English gentleman.

But you can imagine the French admiral making a song and dance about glory, honour, death, the France, liberty, the Emperor, Marengo, Austerlitz, the illustrious memory of Monsieur Chose, and so to the peroration. Nelson merely said, in effect: "Being Englishmen, fight to the death."

That was the duty England expected of them. And there is no doubt at all that in every ship in the English fleet, sailors, treated much worse than dogs and scarred as much by punitive flogging as by battle, growled that England expected a hell of a lot. . . . England expected a bloody sight too much . . . and England could go and do something impossible to itself . . . and they were browned off, and to hell with England. Whereupon they fought furiously and won the day.

The Englishman, that inveterate gambler, has loved the feel of long odds against him, since the dawn of his history. You can't breed out what is in the old blood. And here, there is plenty left of the blood that got splashed about when Caractacus threw his handful against Rome—the Caractacus who said to Cæsar, as we might say to Hitler: "You fight to make men your slaves: we fight to stay free men." There is plenty of the spirit that came out best in affairs like Agincourt, where 9,000 knights and bowmen engaged an army of 27,000, and killed a man apiece and sent the rest flying. History is veined like an inflamed eyeball with our Thin Red Lines!

Crazy Englishman! Incomprehensible Englishman, who would die rather than admit his satisfaction in finding himself outnumbered and out-equipped, perched on a rock with all the weight of a swollen Dark Age in front of him, and three thousand miles of terrible sea behind him . . . who sourly smokes the wayward butt of a Wild Woodbine and gathers his strength for the most terrific struggle in the red calendar of homicide which is the History of Mankind.

PART TWO

THE FOUNDRY

THE calendar says early August, but the sky says late
September. The world is stuffy, like an unventilated
room, and the clouds crawl slowly like melting grease
under the dim sun. The brick and asphalt Depot has
strange acoustic properties. It rings and echoes like a sore
head. We shamble across to the Receiving Station. At
this point we are neither flesh, fowl, nor good red herring.
Clipped heads protrude from civilian collars; a bristly
residue of our first haircut still clings in the folds of our
ears. Yet we are in the Army. We are in the Guards,
rather, which represents a fate somewhat worse.

We have had our first Army bath, in sinks under showers
in cubicles which to some of us seemed strangely familiar.
It was Barker who said: "Where's the clurk to write out
the tickets?" Those cubicles were very much like the ones
they have in pawnshops.

We were a little shy. Thurstan, strangely enough, went
to extraordinary lengths to prevent anyone watching him
as he washed. Even Barker stood like the girl in "September Morn"; while Dale seemed to suffer with a
primeval embarrassment, and the Wire-Haired Boy from
Widnes crouched under the shower like shamed Adam in
the rain. He couldn't adjust the temperature of the water
and struggled with the lever of the tap, while his body
became red, white and blue. Hodge just turned cold
water on himself, and stood with an expression of dumb

48

suffering, soaping himself conscientiously from head to foot. Johnson of Birmingham dashed madly in, protesting too much that he was not afraid, and repeating again and again that he bathed almost every day and liked it. Bullock the bruiser, inured to nakedness in little athletic dressing-rooms, looked at us with sombre astonishment. Alison, the old soldier, went through the process of washing as one who carries out a fine but hackneyed ritual: he bathed as some men recite the Lord's Prayer— as if he felt that it was doing him some incalculable good, but was best got over quickly. . . . "Our Far chart nevn, Harold bethy Name"—he was bathed and dried in no time at all, and out, gloomily smoking, in the dim humid daylight.

So we went for inoculation. Bates asked: "What do they do to yow?"

"Stab you in the arm," said the Old Soldier.

"Is it noice?"

"Horrible."

"What 'appens?"

"Your arm swells up. Sometimes you get a temperature. Some men have to go sick with it."

"And what 'appens when yow go sick?"

"You soon wish you hadn't."

"And 'ow do yow go sick?"

"You get a form filled up."

"And say yow're sick and don't go sick?"

"You get into trouble."

Bates became sad and thoughtful. At last he said: "Do yow get shot for deserting?"

"Not unless it's in the face of the enemy."

"Are we in the face of the enemy now?"

"It's hard to say."

"If they don't shoot yow, what do they do to yow?"

"Send you to the Glass House."

"Is that noice?"

"I've done twenty-eight days there," says Alison, and pauses, struggling between two strong desires. Like all old soldiers, he wants to terrify the recruit. Like all men who have been In Detention, he wants to laugh it off. He says: "You heard of Devil's Island?"

"Where there's crocodoiles and sharks?"

"Well, Devil's Island is like the Y.M.C.A. compared to Aldershot."

"Whoy did yow go there?"

"For nothing."

"Oh bloimey!"

The time will come when, to us, an inoculation will be just another Jab—when we will even hope for a serious one, which will mean forty-eight hours off duty, "Attend C, Bed Down." But now, everything connected with the Army is strange and slightly terrible. We file past the M.O. As we wait, we hear the thud of a heavy fall. A big buck Jock who would laugh at a bayonet has fainted at the prick of the needle. He is revived, and left to his shame: the world will end before that moment of weakness is forgotten. In years to come, on remote bivouacs in the hearts of awful deserts, or in the mud of questionable positions under earth-shaking barrages, there will be somebody who will say: "Remember Jock?" And somebody else will reply: "Got the D.C.M. Captured a tank with a jack-knife. Won the heavyweight title in such-and-such a year. Nearly got a V.C. for taking on seven Jerry tommy-gunners with a Bren-gun cleaning-rod, and licking 'em. Carried an anti-tank rifle sixty miles. Toughest guy I ever knew. They once mounted a three-inch mortar on his back and fired seventy bombs off him while he held it." And then the first speaker will say: "Yet—funny thing—first time that feller got a Jab, he went out like a light. It only goes to show." "You're right, son: it only goes to show . . ."

We emerge from the Receiving Station. Bates, by the power of suggestion, has a paralysis of the arm. Johnson maintains that it doesn't hurt; that no Jab can hurt him.

At this point there rises the banshee-howl of a siren. Something in the upper air goes poppity-pop. We stand and gaze at a flattish grey nothingness, until an old sergeant, medal-ribboned to the condition known as "fruit salad", roars "Genna shelter! Gorn, you silly great things, you, genna *Shelter!*" We take cover, and sit still, looking at one another. Can it be that the Excitement is starting? An old sweat, decorated with a round badge bearing the words "Trained Soldier," says:

"Another 'Red'. *There's a Jerry in the sky.* Bah. I'll tell you the honest truth: I'm losing patience with this 'Itler. This is on the up-and-up: I'm gettin' browned off with this 'Itler. I'll tell you straight: sometimes I begin to get sort of annoyed with this so-called 'Itler. Oo do 'e think 'e is, *any*way, this '*It*ler? Shell I give you my honest opinion? Right from the shoulder—politics aside— every man is entitled to 'is own opinion, and I'm entitled to mine, and I tell you, between you and me and the lamp-post, it's my candid view that 'e's beginning to get a swollen 'ead, this 'ere 'Itler. *Adolf.* I'll *Adolf* 'im. 'Im and 'is 'Mine Camp'. Adolf! If I come acrost 'im I'll say 'And oo are you?' and if 'e says 'I'm Adolf 'Itler,' I shall say: 'Never 'eard of yer.' And then if 'e cuts up rough— *bif!—boff!*——"

The Trained Soldier shadow-boxes. Shorrock says to him:

"Been here long, lad?"

"What did you say?"

"Been here long, lad?"

"Lad? *Lad?* LAD? Now look. You're a Recruit, and as such you're ignorant. I pity your ignorance, Rookie, and so I shan't be 'ard on you. You're as ignorant as gorblimey, otherwise you wouldn't dare to call me 'Lad', any more than you'd call Lieutenant-Colonel the Earl of Romney 'Old Cock'. Do you realise who I am? *I am a Trained Soldier!* It's all right: don't be frightened. You didn't know. Well, you'll know in future. You always, always, mind you, *always* address a Trained Soldier as 'Trained Soldier', and stand smartly to attention when you talk to 'im. In the Brigade of Guards, you address me as Trained Soldier; a Lance or Full Corporal as 'Corporal', a Lance-Sarnt or Full Sarnt as 'Sarnt', and everybody else as 'Sir', and you stand smartly to attention. Nor are you, strictly speaking, supposed to speak unless spoken to. A guardsman is a Man. A recruit is not a man yet. A recruit is a child. Bear that in mind."

Somebody asks him, with full title, how long he has been in the Guards. He replies:

"Seven years, four months, eleven days. And let me tell you, you get it cushy 'ere now. You ought to of joined the peace-time Guards for real soldiering. Ah, those were the days, son. Those were the good old days. You couldn't call your soul your own. Why, when I come 'ere as a recruit, like you, they pretty near broke my 'eart. Three suits o' scarlet, S.D., and everything. White webbing, mind you, and it 'ad to be perfect. Perfect? More than perfect. If it was only perfect, you went in the

book. We used to blanco our webbing day and night.
Then, if there was so much as a sponge-mark on it, our
Trained Soldier would chuck it plonk into the coal-box.
As for brasses, well, all I can say is, gorblimey. The
slightest speck, and you was run into the cooler faster than
your legs could carry you. As for chasings on the square,
we used to faint in 'eaps. I remember when I was on a
Buck Guard . . ."

"Buck?"

"Buckingham Palace. Buck is the Palace. Jimmy is
St. James. I lowered my butt less than a quarter of an
inch. I got seven days. Blimey. Some of you will be in
my squad, I suppose. I tell you 'ere and now: do as
you're told, and you'll be all right. Nobody'll worry
you, just so long as you make your minds up to do just
what you're told. You've got to get yourself into the Army
way of doing things. You've got nothing to worry about.
All the worrying is done for you. Get that. All you do
is, obey. If you've got a loaf to use, you'll be given a
chance to use it later on. Meanwhile, you got no responsibility, except in obeying an order exactly as it's give you.
My name is Brand, Trained Soldier Brand. Bear that in
mind. . . . Ah-ah, there goes 'All Clear'. Now get
outside. You rooks are going to 'ave to draw your kit."

There is a general feeling that all we need to do is,
get a gun and a uniform, and there we are. But when we
get to the Quartermaster's Store, we find ourselves in a
kind of forest of equipment. There are sacred groves of
boots, avenues of battle-dress, hanging gardens of slippers,
a foliage of vests, undergrowths of socks. We hear the
Quartermaster blasting a wicked man.

"So. Your slippers are too small. What size do you

take? Eight. And what size are those slippers? It *says*
eight? Then they *are* eights. And they're too small. Then
why the hell didn't you take nines? Obviously, you take
nines. You tried them on before taking them, didn't you?
What do you mean, you suppose so? Stand to attention!
You did try them on. You know you did. And weren't
they too small for you then? What d'you mean, you don't
know? Did they *feel* small? Oh. *Oh.* A bit tight, eh? They
felt a bit tight, did they? And so you took them away, and
now you bring them back, do you? Could you do that in
civvy street? Could you do that in a shop? After you've
worn them for three days? Who's going to wear them after
you? No consideration for yourself or anybody else. Where
there's no sense there's no feeling. Just because you're in
the Army, you think you can take all kinds of dirty rotten
liberties. All right. I've got my eye on you. Stand still!.
Give him a pair of nines. . . . Now, do they fit? Are you
sure they fit?"

"Yessir."

"Are you positive they fit?"

"Yessir."

"They fit, then?"

"Yessir."

"You won't come back and say they don't fit, the day
after to-morrow?"

"No sir."

"Then go away."

"Please, sir . . ."

"What is it now?"

"They're too loose."

"Oh God, give me patience! Oh, Good God in Heaven
Almighty, give me strength! Oh God blind O'Reilly
suffering Christ in Heaven above so help me! You . . .

you . . . Take him away. Take him away before I tear him to pieces! . . . What's all this? Recruits? *More* recruits? The Guards used to be exclusive, and look at it now! If my poor father were alive to see it he'd turn in his grave. Lead 'em in."

The men who work in the Store have an eye for size. They can look at you and issue, without wasting a word, equipment that more or less fits you. Each man gets a blue kitbag. Then comes a cataract of clothing.

Boots, ankle, pairs, two; a pair of braces; socks, knitted, pairs, three; slippers, pairs, one; shorts, gym, pairs, one; vests, gym, two; caps, F.S., one, and a hard cap with a cheesecutter peak that covers the eyes and makes you hold your head up; two pairs of underpants; one stocking hat; holdalls, one; housewives containing needles, thread, thimble, and spare buttons—one; knives, one; forks, one; spoons, one; shirts, three; suit of canvas, consisting of blouses, denim, one, and trousers, denim, pairs, one; battle-dress . . . blouses, serge, two, and trousers, serge, pairs, two, or one suit of Best and another for Second Best; a greatcoat. The kitbag bulges. Trained Soldier Brand sweats and strains like a man with a thirty-mule team. Do we think we're done yet, he asks. Oho. Let us not think so for a moment. If we want his candid opinion, we haven't begun yet. There is Web Equipment yet to be drawn. We draw it . . . a large valise, a small pack, two ammunition pouches, bayonet frog, a tangle of strange strips with brass D's and dim buckles, a thing to contain a water-bottle, and a water-bottle for it to contain. Is this all? Ha. This, says Trained Soldier Brand, is far from all. This is by no means all. There is still a ground-sheet to come; and an anti-gas cape; and a respirator, and a respirator-case, and a strap to hang it on; and another kind of anti-gas cape, rubberised and obsolete, but useful for training purposes; and a badge; and mess-tins, and a canvas bag to keep mess-tins in; and a steel helmet complete with chinstrap and lining; and a clothes brush, and a button-stick, and a button-brush, and a shaving-brush, and two boot-brushes, and a toothbrush, and a nailbrush, and a safety-razor complete with blades, one, unusable except by downy creatures not more than six months on the wrong side of puberty. Then, of course, every man must have a rifle, a Short Lee Enfield, together with a bayonet.

There is a stupendous clicking of pressed triggers, and an uproar of "You're dead", until the Trained Soldier says, very sourly:

"Say there was bullets up the spouts of them rifles. Say there was live rounds. There couldn't be, but just *say*. Well, you'd all be dead. It is strictly forbidden to point your rifle in the hut. I'm decent. I'm good-hearted. I'm one o' the best, I am. But I can be a lousy, rotten swine if I want to. And I'll put any of you inside that I ketch pointing rifles or assing about with bayonets—fencing, and throwing 'em, and chopping up wood or anything. So don't you go and do it. School-kids. Who goes fencing about with dangerous bayonets in huts? Soppy little girls do that, not Guardsmen. Now look. You're in Lance-Sergeant Nelson's Squad, Z Company, Coldstream Guards, Guards' Depot, Caterham. Got it? And I'm your Trained Soldier, Trained Soldier Brand. Got it? Well, get it if you ain't got it. This is your hut . . ."

We look. A great, scoured box; two stoves; ninety planks on sixty trestles, making thirty little wooden beds; a coal tub, two galvanised iron buckets, three brooms, a long scrubber, a mop, two scrubbing-brushes.

" . . . This is your hut. From now on, this is going to be your home. And it will be kept as such—so clean you could eat fried eggs off the flour, just like you do at home. God help the dirty man in the Brigade of Guards. God help the man who goes around in tripe! Personally," says Trained Soldier Brand, in a burst of friendly confidence, "I never used to use a nail-brush myself, for the simple reason that I used to bite my nails down to the quick. But then I lost all my teeth. And look at my nails now. Look how clean. I want to see every man's nails like them. I'm proud of my finger-nails, now.

"Everybody pick himself a bed. Keep it. You're responsible for the tidiness of your bed-area, and everything connected with it. There is only one right way of doing a thing, and that is the Army way. I am here to show you what to do. Come round me in a circle, and I'll have a chat with you. I want to get to know you."

He looks us over. He says: "It takes all sorts to make a world . . . and *then* what have you got? What's your name?"

"Shorrock, Trained Soldier."

"What was your job in Civvy Street?"

"I was a grocer. I've got my own business."

"What's your religion? Not that I care a damn."

"Congregationalist."

"Well, every man is entitled to his own whatsiname. I'm a bit of a Mohammedan, myself. But I goes down as C. of E. There's services for C. of E-ers and Roman Candles. Any other fancy religions—Baptists, Jews, Congregationalists, Methodists, Seventh Day Adventists, Peculiar Methodists (whatever they may be), Mormons, and what not, get along as best they can. If anybody's got any religious arguments to make, he can go and have it out with the Company Commander. I 'ad a Buddhist in my squad, once. A white man, mind you, but a Buddhist. Gord bless you, *we* didn't mind.

"While I'm talking, by the way, you can take off them civvy clothes, and put on proper ones. You're expected to wear your underpants. In the first place, they're issued for you to wear. In the second place, it's un'ealthy not to. When cold weather comes you'll be issued with long winter ones, and woolly vests, and gloves. Roll up your civvies. They're to be sent 'ome; it's illegal to keep 'em now. You're in the Army. And look. I've got 'ere a cap-badge. It's the eight-pointed star, the Coldstreamers' star. Look at it. I've 'ad it seven years, and somebody 'ad it seven years before me. See? It's been polished and polished until the pattern's almost all wore off. Can you read what's on it? *Honi Soit Qui Mal Y Pense*. Evil be to 'e that evil thinks. Our motter. Got it? Well, a soldier prizes a cap-star that's wore down like this one. Now I'll tell you what I'll do. You're a decent-looking lot o' fellers. The man that gets the best shine on one of his pairs o' boots by the end o' next week gets this star. I tell you, you could offer a quid for a star like that and not be able to buy it, but I'll give it to the best-shone pair o' daisy-roots end o' next week.

"I'm warning you, they're 'ot on shining in this mob; and rightly so. We got a tradition to keep up. Anybody who remembers the last war'll tell you how the Guards went into action like a parade. Not only have we got to fight better, and 'ave better discipline: we got to *look* better. We're the 'Ouse'old Brigade, and the oldest foot-regiment in the British Army. I tell you, Jerry thinks twice when 'e sees us coming: we been getting ourselves a good name for thousands and thousands of years, ever since 1650, when Colonel Monk formed the Coldstream Guards.

"Other mobs aren't so fussy about cleaning, and I'll admit that when you're tired it can be a bit of a business, getting all spick-and-span. But it's worth it. You can tell a Guardsman anywhere for his smartness, especially a Coldstreamer. It can be overdone, this spit-and-polish, in wartime. But the principle of the thing is good. Like an old woman who's always spring-cleaning . . . it's uncomfortable, but the idea is all right. . . . Now what's your name, son? Thurstan? And where did you come from? Durham, eh? You been a miner, ain't you?"

"So what?" says Thurstan.

Trained Soldier Brand looks at him and says: "So what? So this: lemme give you a word o' warning. I know your type. You're tough, you are, or you think you are. Well, don't get tough with the Army, because the Army's tougher. See? And you'll get hurt. See? You're a miner. Well, you wouldn't 'ave a kicking-match with a pit-pony, would you? Well, don't try and beat the Army. Better men than you have tried to do it, and failed. You can be as tough as you like with 'Itler: you'll toe the line 'ere, for the sake o' discipline.

"How shall I put it? You ain't expected to be angels, but Gord 'elp you if you're not, kind o' thing. I'm warnin' you, Thurstan, if you got any idea of playing up in this Depot, don't do it. We're 'ot on discipline. Discipline makes the Army. The Guards hold their line and don't break: it's discipline that does it, and discipline means when every man has got confidence in his N.C.O., his Officer, and his pal. If you know just what everybody else in your mob is going to do, things are easy for you.

c

That's discipline, and take it from me, it's essential. I've seen some of it working out East, and so has your Squad Instructor, Sergeant Nelson.

"Sarnt Nelson. A word of warning about him. He's the decentest Sarnt you could wish to have. He never goes about punishing fellers. He never chases you more than you can stand. He won't bully you and chivvy you till you don't know where you are. He's never too tired to explain something to you. He'll stand by you through thick and thin in the event of trouble. Nelson is 'uman and a good bloke. But Gord 'elp you if you take liberties with Sarnt Nelson! Just that: treat 'im decent and 'e's a pal. Take liberties and 'e's a terror. You'll find that out, Thurstan, if you want to start something.

"You? Hodge? You're a big feller, Hodge, and they like big fellers in the Guards. What do you weigh? You don't know? Well, all I can say is, Blimey. Somebody told me you'd been seen reading the Bible. You'd be surprised how things get around 'ere. Remember that, all of you, and be careful what you say. Some'ow or other, news gets about in this Depot quicker than a tea-party. Well, there's nothing against reading the Bible. I've never read it myself, but far be it from me. That is what I say—far be it from me. Why, we've 'ad blokes here reading poitry before now, and one of 'em used to wiite it. I'm glad to see you, Hodge.

"And you. What's your name? Bullock? Scrapper? Good. You won't get a chance to box 'ere: you'll be too busy otherwise engaged. We've 'ad a few decent scrappers 'ere in peace time. Danahar. Jack Doyle. We used to 'ave some lovely fights in peace time, but I'm afraid there's none o' that at present. There's a war on. Religion? C. of E. I've got to put down a religion because of Church Parades. The Roman Candles go to Communion. The C. of E-ers go to a service.

"Now I'll tell you roughly what you do. You get up at five forty-five, when the second Reveille sounds. Then you wash and shave with great care, because they're 'ot on washing and shaving 'ere. Then you make your bed up. You make it up nice and neat—I'll show you 'ow—because they're 'ot on making beds up neat in this place. Then on top of your blankets you lay out your 'oldall, containing your knife, fork, spoon, buttonstick, razor, and shaving-brush, all polished till you can see your face in 'em, and your mess-tins, also polished, laid end to end, like this . . . with the canvas bag neatly folded in the middle . . . so.

"Got that?

"Now your lockers must be kept neat and tidy, because they're 'ot on lockers 'ere, In the top shelf, your battle-dress, neatly folded—they're 'ot on neat folding—and your stiff cap neatly placed on top. You will polish your chin-strap till it looks like patent leather, and get the buttons up till they sparkle, because if there's one thing they're 'ot on in the Guards, it's buttons. Got it?. Good. On the lower shelf you place your brushes, all properly numbered, sandpapered, and laid in proper order. You mustn't keep any personal property in your locker, because they're 'ot on that, too. When you make your bed down at night, you'll lay your battle-dress down to crease: I'll show you 'ow, because they're dead 'ot on creases in this Depot. Your boots go up there on top. Got it? And you'll 'ave to work on them boots. They're full o' grease: you've got to work it out, with energy, spit, and polish. Spit is the best thing for boots. A little polish: a lot of spit; that's the rule. And your greatcoat must be hung on the left-'and peg, with the buttons polished till they blind you; because they're 'ot on that, I can tell you. Kit-bag on the right 'and side, neatly tied up.

"You've got to salute an officer whenever you see one. You 'll be taught 'ow by Sarnt Nelson. That's *is* job, poor feller. You'll be 'ere for eight or nine weeks. It used to be four months, and will be again shortly, but at present recruits are kept eight weeks or so before going on to the Training Battalion. You'll 'ave Inspections, every so-often, to see 'ow you're shaping with things like drill. You won't be allowed out o' the gates for at least three weeks, and thereafter, once a week if you're lucky. That's so as you won't disgrace the Guards by lounging about the streets with a packet o' wine-gums in one 'and and a bag o' chips in the other. In three weeks or so you'll *begin*, you'll just about *begin* to appear to look like sort of soldiers. It'll take a long time before you get the unmistakeable Guardsman's Walk—straight as a poker, but supple as rubber; quick, regular, and easy. You watch Sarnt Nelson: 'e's a typical Guardsman. See? You're civilians, and walk as such, which is incorrectly. We've got to break you of the 'abits of a lifetime. You'll be sore at first. That's all right: it's good for you.

"You'll get your first leave in about thirteen weeks time, maybe. You can never be sure. Maybe thirteen weeks. For that time, consider yourself right away from Civvy Street. The funny thing is, you'll feel uncomfortable when you get back to your own beds . . . and all the girls 'll fall for you. Everybody falls for the Coldstream Guards. You know the poem?

"Why should England tremble when the Guards go 'ome on leave?
It's only for a short while, so why should England grieve?

"Very well, then. You'll get a lot of Physical Training 'ere. They're dead 'ot on P.T. in this Depot. You'll get a lot of drill, too, and weapon-training. The Guards always make a name for themselves with bayonets. You ask Jerry. When the Coldstream Guards take up a front-line position, Jerry knows that sooner or later it'll come to cold steel. And 'e's scared. It pokes the wind up 'im.

"Well, you ast for it. You volunteered. It'll be something to brag about afterwards, mind you. Not everybody's fit for the Guards, even in wartime.

"Reveille, 5.45. Lights Out, 9.30. You'll be on training till about four. Then, from four till seven, you're on Shining Parade—you get your kit worked up and in proper order, and sit on your ground-sheets going hard at the jolly old spit-and-polish, until seven pip emma. Then you're free to go and buy yourselves a beer or a tea at the Naffy. Got it? Or you can read books or write letters, or talk to each other. During Shining Parade, no talking or smoking is allowed, nor no singing, 'umming, or whistling. Dinner is twelve-thirty. Tea is at five. Break-fast, seven. You can buy pies and stuff in the Naffy if you can eat 'em. You'll be hungry enough, mind you; but Naffy pies . . .

"You mustn't form a trade union. You mustn't get girls into trouble. You mustn't go about with your hands in your pockets. You mustn't be immoral. You mustn't smoke out o' doors while an Alert is on. You mustn't smoke in shelters. You mustn't desert. You mustn't go absent. You mustn't be late for anything. You mustn't gamble. You mustn't get anybody else, for money or moneysworth, to do any jobs for you. You mustn't have financial dealings with Trained Soldiers or N.C.O.'s. You mustn't address me, or any other superior rank, with a fag in your mouth. You mustn't get drunk. You mustn't use foul language or tell filthy stories or possess filthy pictures. You mustn't associate with bad women. You mustn't steal, bear false witness against your neighbour. You mustn't do anything not in the Army Act. I've never read the Army Act, but, put it like this—to all intents and purposes it's safest not to do anything, much, unless you're specifically ordered to do it by a Trained Soldier, N.C.O., or Officer. You will always be clean, kind, courteous, and what not. If you see an old geezer getting on a bus, give him a shove to help him along. If you see an old girl standing up in a public convenience, you will give her your seat. Conveyance: I always get them two words mixed up.

"But I am 'ere to show you the ropes. It's not my duty to lecture you.

"Everybody will buy a tin of black boot polish, a tin of dark tan, a duster, a slab of Blanco Khaki Renovator, a tin of Bluebell Metal Polish, and a twopenny-halfpenny brush. With the possession of these here articles, your troubles begin, and so do mine; for your webbing must be spotless, your brasses must damn well flash like a gigolo's eyes. . . . Is there an educated man 'ere?"

A dark, quiet individual whom we call Old Silence, says: "I've been to school."

"Well, tell me. Is it *Gigolo*, or *Jigolo*?"

"Pronounced *Jigolo*."

"I thought as much. I was having an argument. Someone said *Gigolo*. Then someone else said *Jigolo*, and I agreed. Where are you from?"

"London, Trained Soldier."

"What business?"

"Unemployed."

"Do you mean you've got money of your own, or that you just couldn't get a job?"

"Both, Trained Soldier."

" 'Ow old are you?"

"Thirty-four, Trained Soldier."

"Well, son, we'll soon find you plenty jobs round 'ere . . . And your name?"

"John Johnson," says the Brummagem Fly Boy sullenly.

"Not so much of the 'John Johnson,' you. Address me as Trained Soldier! Don't tell me where you come from: I know. You're a Brummy Boy. I can tell by your accent. Well, don't get fly here, son. It won't pay you. And you?"

"Bates, Trained Soldier. Oi come from Leicester. Oi was a brewer's drayman. Oi'm Church of Englernd, Trained Soldier."

"Married?"

"One proper woife, Trained Soldier, but she left me. She took all the furniture. Oi got an unmarried woife, now, and she's noice, Trained Soldier. Would yow loike to see a pic-tcher, Trained Soldier?"

"In a minute. And what's your name?"

"Abbs, Trained Soldier. I got a brother in the Cold-stream Guards. Did you ever meet him, Trained Soldier? Abbs, from Walsall. Jimmy Abbs. I'm Alfred Abbs. Thirty-five. I got six kids, all girls. My wife's uncle just died of a growth in 'is throat—big as a babby's head. I——"

"—Every morning," says Trained Soldier Brand, "the hut will be swept and tidied, and everything will be put in its right place. Every Saturday, it will be scrubbed from top to bottom, and your bed-boards and trestles will also be scrubbed till they are as white as snow, because I don't mind telling you, they're 'ot on that. Also, you better take care to scrub your 'oldalls till they're like *driven* snow. They're 'ot on 'oldalls, too. Got it? One other thing: don't keep things under your mattresses in the day-time. More men get put in the book for that than anything else. And for God's sake see your rifles are clean. A dirty rifle is a serious offence. Oh well . . ." He yawns. "Muck in," he says, with conviction, "that's the great rule of 'appiness. Muck in. Muck in. That's what the Bible says: muck in. Do unto others as you would 'ave others do unto you. In other words, *muck in*. Got it? What 'ave you got to do, Bates?"

"Not leave nothing under your mattress, Trained Soldier!"

"Oh Gord lumme, I want my mummy and the puddens she used to make!" cries Trained Soldier Brand. "Why should England tremble, eh? Did you hear me say 'Muck in'?"

"I thought——"

"You thought. Wot with did you think? You ain't 'ere to think. You're not in Civvy Street now. Why, if everybody went around thinking, we wouldn't 'ave no army. Muck in. What did I say?"

Bates thinks deeply, and says: "Mook in, Trained Soldier."

"There now. You got it right that time, didn't you? You can do it if you try, can't you? That's the style. Go on like that and you'll be a Brigadier before you know where you are."

"Will oi really, Trained Soldier?"

There comes into the hut a man in shirt-sleeves and a

soft S.D. cap. You can tell, by his walk, that he is no ordinary man. He swings his legs out from the hip, and his iron heels cut little arcs in the floorboards. He is long and lean, sun-dried, wind-cured, boucanned, smoked, and sand-blasted. His face is brown as a kipper, and as expressionless. One of his eyes is fixed in a dreadful stare: it is of glass. The other blinks. There is nothing left of him but bone and sinew and vitals: years of service have sweated away all that was superfluous or decorative. He has an air of demoniac energy: a wild swagger, a steady, genial ferocity. Out of his neatly rolled sleeves hang arms as dark and gnarled as old Salami sausages. He has fists like mallets of black stinkwood; an aluminium ring; and a silly little blue bird tattooed on his left wrist. Quite effortlessly, he shouts, in a voice that makes us jump:

"I am Sergeant Nelson! (Ain't I, Trained Soldier Brand?) I am Sergeant Nelson! I've got one eye, but both me arms! I died at Trafalgar but they dug me up again, and when I'm mad I'm a one-man wave o' destruction! I'm poison! I'm terrible! I kill seven rookies before breakfast! I can spit fifty yards through the eye of a needle! D'you see that dead tree over there? They'll tell you it was struck by lightnin'. Don't believe 'em. I killed it! I slapped it down! You're my new squad! I'm your Squad Instructor! Silence! Nobody say a word! You do as I say or you suffer. You suffer 'orrible tortures! Now, when I say *Hi-de-Hi Squad!* you shout *Ho-de-Ho!*— and shout it loud! Now: *Hi-de-Hi Squad!*"

We roar: "*Ho-de-Ho!*"

"Right. Whenever I shout Hi-de-Hi, let me hear you reply pretty damn quick, or I'll chase you all round and round that square till the huts look like hen-houses. *Hi-de-Hi!*"

"*Ho-de-Ho!*"

"Good. Now we're introduced. I'm here to make Guardsmen out o' you. Are you going to help me? Well, answer, you unsociable lot of squirts!"

"Yes, Sergeant!"

"Good. You'd better. Soldiers get buried in a blanket. I'll make Guardsmen out of you if you have to pass out of here in blankets. If you turn out flops, as soldiers, I'm responsible. *I'm* the one that drops something on account of you. And I'd murder me best friend if he got me into trouble. I'd murder me great-grandmother. I'd cut her heart out and throw it on the floor and jump on it—wouldn't I, Brand? Now on Monday you'll be Squadded, and you start with me on the Square. I've got to drill you. I've got to hammer four months of drill into you in eight weeks. It's impossible. But I shall do it. You'll see. But you've got to play ball with me. You've got to give me all you've got, with a good heart." Sergeant Nelson becomes quieter, and very serious.

"Ask anybody in this Depot about me. They'll tell you: I hardly ever punish anybody. I never, never bully my men. But you've got to work with me. There seems to be a war on. Isn't there, Brand? So you've got to take things seriously. If there's anything you want to know, don't be afraid to ask me. If there's anything you don't grasp the first time, ask me again, ask me a hundred times: I'll tell you. If there's anything you want demonstrated, I'll demonstrate it. I'm the best demonstrator on earth, aren't I, Brand? Definitely, I am. If you're in trouble over anything except money, come to me, and if necessary I'll march you into the Company Commander, or the Commandant himself. I'll stand by you. But don't try any funny stuff. If anybody tries to treat me rough . . . By God! Call me Pig, and I'm Pig all through. Definitely Pig all through. Okay. Which is it going to be? Are you going to work with me?"

A chorus: "Yes, Sergeant."

He roars again. "Okey-dokey, my little fluffy-'eaded chicks! *Hi-de-Hi!*"

"*Ho-de-Ho!*"

"Good. Now look. Recruits are babies. In one second, Cookhouse is going to blow. By rights I ought to march you about everywhere, definitely everywhere. But I'm going to let you go on your own, just to show you I trust you. You won't get lost? Or make mugs of yourselves in any way?"

"No, Sergeant."

Come to the cookhouse door, *boys*, cries the bugle.

"Knives, forks, and spoons, and scram, then!"

We rush to the door.

"Halt!"

We stop, paralysed by that shattering voice.

"*Hi-de-Hi*, Squad!"

"*Ho-de-Ho*, Sergeant!"

We go to Dinner.

That afternoon we get our first Fatigue. There isn't much for us to do until we are squadded. Hanging around, putting twice-ordered bits of kit again in order, looking around, exchanging speculative horrors, we wait, killing time by inches. One or two of us—Hodge, Dale, and Thurstan foremost, as it happens—start on our boots. The surface of these Ammunition Boots is what the shop-keepers call "Scotch Grain": that is to say, it is all bumpy. This has to be smoothed out by the chemical action of spit and the mechanical action of polish. We have been warned that, at first, the more we polish the less there will be to show for our efforts. "Think of the Foorer," says Trained Soldier Brand, "think of Gobbles, think of Gooring . . . and spit." But the Ammos, or boots, would absorb the digestive juices of a shark. John Johnson watches us. Soon, he says: "You got no oidea, that's what it is, no oidea." And he picks up a boot and a tin of polish, and, baring his sunburnt arms, begins to polish away with a mad enthusiasm. All the misdirected energy of a little, misspent life, is being concentrated on a toe-cap. He polishes as if some strange fate has condemned him to it . . . which, indeed, it has. "Oi'll get that cap-badge," he says, "oi betcher a million pounds." A Bedfordshire lad who used to work in a Nottinghamshire boot factory talks of buffing leather. He takes out of a battered fibre case a tooth-brush; compares it with the Army issue, and finally strokes his boots with it. Everybody else follows suit. As any gentleman's gentleman will tell you, it helps if you beat the surface of a leather boot flat with a bone . . . but you've got to put your weight behind it. Alison, the glum old soldier, says that if you smear the surface of the boots thickly with polish and then set light to it, you get the grease out quicker. Trained Soldier Brand, hearing this, says: "That is a serious offence," and adds:

"Say you burn your boots. What happens? Boots are made of what? Well . . . what, Bates?"

"Oi don't know, Trained Soldier."

"Leather and stitches. Burn the leather, and you burn the stitches. Burn the stitches, and what happens? Well, Bates?"

"It's a serious offence, Trained Soldier."

"They bust. And if the stitches of your boots bust, what happens, Bates?"

"Oi don't know, Trained Soldier."

"One day your boots come apart. And remember—a soldier marches on his feet. On his . . . what, Bates?"

"On his feet, Trained Soldier."

"Good. You'll be a lieutenant-colonel inside of a fortnight."

"Will Oi——"

"So. Don't burn your boots. If you're without boots, you're what, Bates?"

"Uh?"

"Say you've got no boots, what happens?"

"Oi don't know, Trained Soldier."

"You're bare-foot."

"Oi knew that, but——"

"Then why didn't you say so? You can't march, and the war is as good as lost. So no burning. Leather," says Brand, "comes from abroad. It takes sailors. Sailors die so that you wear boots. Get it? Them boots are covered in the blood of sailors."

Bates says: "Trained Soldier, Oi thought that was grease."

"God give me strength," says Brand.

We polish away. Later, a sergeant with a book under his arm comes into the hut and shouts: "Stand to your beds and listen! Is there anybody here who's good at painting and decorating?"

Two men stand up.

"Anybody play football . . . I don't mean just kicking a ball around: I mean, anybody who can play it well."

"One man rises and says: "I played for Underwood Wednesday."

"And are there any market gardeners, or other men who know all about turfing and whatnot?"

Two more men rise.

"Excellent. Excellent. Lastly, is there anybody here of education up to matriculation standard?"

Old Silence stands up.

"That's fine." The sergeant with the book licks a pencil and says: "Names. . . . You will all report to the Green Lanes Cookhouse for spud-peeling."

("And let that be a lesson for you," says Brand, grinning: "In the Army, you never volunteer for anything except certain death.")

Those of us who have risen go out. A cookhouse sergeant says: "Do you mind eating spuds a little bit wizened?"

"No."

"Then bloodywell peel them."

The men left behind congratulate themselves, until a serious-looking Corporal, asking for men who know jig and tool making, the use of the typewriter, the elements of the banjulele and singing, salesmanship, care of livestock, bandaging, fire-fighting, bartending, building, haircutting, carpentering, ladies' hairdressing, platen-minding, type-setting, fancy lettering, high jumping, and box-making, drags in most of the others for floor-washing, and, tiring of the joke, asks, all humour apart, for one intelligent man. Johnson leaps us. "You read books, I bet," says the Corporal. "Ah," says Johnson. "Then go and swab out the library," says the Corporal In Waiting, and goes out, while Johnson swears that in this life there is no justice.

That Sunday is quiet. Recruits in the Naffy tell dark tales of discipline. Men three weeks squadded, already assuming the portentous air of old sweats, ask themselves rhetorically why they did not join something else. The Glorious Fusiliers, says one, do no drill; the Dagenham Foresters, says another, have dulled brasses for active service, and rightly so. Old Silence, pursuing the vexed question of spit-and-polish in the Brigade of Guards, asks the Trained Soldier about it.

Brand laughs. "You'll work your boots and brasses up," he says, "whether you like it or not. So you may as well do it with a good 'eart. When you get round to fighting, I dessay you'll be told to let your brasses go dull and grease your second-best boots. Meanwhile, you'll shine. Why, you might ask. Because the Guards have got a tradition of smart turnout, that's why. I admit you work harder in the Guards than elsewhere. Well, that's the price you pay for the privilege of being in the 'Ouse-'old Brigade. Don't worry—you'll learn as much of tactics and field-training and fighting as anybody in the Army; only you'll be made to get the 'abit of smartness in your appearance. Why? Because we're the Guards. We're the Lilywhites, the Coalies, the Coldstreamers. It's got to be kept up. At Dunkirk, our mob were still pick-outable on account of some of them still shining up their daisy-roots and working in a quick shave, even on the retreat. It's crazy, I know. But personally, I like it. And so do you. Or if you won't, you will. And if you don't, you'd better. Gorblimey, we've 'ad fellers 'ere like Wild Men o' Borneo, and turned 'em out neat as a new pin in a few weeks. Carriage! Smartness! That's the *real* uniform of the Guards. Because all battle-dress looks alike. And yet you could pick a Coldstreamer out of a thousand others. It may be a bit tough. Well, blimey, you've got to suffer to be beautiful. . . . Ain't you, you de-licious little peach-blossom?" he says, to Thurstan.

Before Thurstan can unload the insults which rise and

fill his mouth, a bugle sounds, a siren moans, and Brand says:

"Jerry in the sky. Get in the trench."

The Guards' Depot exploits air-raids, and makes prompt action a part of Guards' training. We run to cover, and it is then that Sergeant Nelson, who, for eight weeks, will never let us out of his sight, tells us about the Wogs, "light of ear, bloody of hand," the Arabs; and tells tall stories in short sentences, of discipline and training in the Guards. "And if I make your blood run cold—don't worry, because I'll warm it for you when I get you on the Square to-morrow. Definitely."

The Square is vast and flat; black-grey asphalt tickled by mysterious eddies of pale-brown dust. We have to pass a half-finished building to get to it. Bricklayers pause and look at us with some pity. One old man, splitting a speckled pink brick with one flick of a trowel, says: "Now you're for it, my boys." He is a little old man, incongruously got up in soiled blue serge, with a stiff collar and a bright strip of medal-ribbons. "Ah well, I was at Mons." To this, Barker, who is hiding his nervousness under a great froth of funny talk, says: "No wonder they retreated. Are you sure you don't mean Water-bloody-loo?"

"Laugh, my cock-oh," says the old man, "you'll never see what I saw!"

Sergeant Nelson is there, waiting for us. "Sheep!" he says, in such a voice that the distant echoes answer *Eep*. "Sheep for the slaughter. *Hi-de-Hi!*"

"*Ho-de-Ho!*"

"Now listen to me. I'm going to teach you some elementary drill movements. You don't have to be a

Bachelor of Science to do 'em. Millions have done 'em before. Millions will do 'em again. You don't need a matriculation certificate to do it. Just be confident. Don't be nervous. Keep calm, and do exactly as I tell you. *And work!* By God! Work with me and I'm as mild as your mummy's milk. But work against me and I'll kill ya! Look at me. I'm poison! I'm a rattlesnake! I kill more men than Diphtheria! Now for the time you're here, you'll shout the time of your movements out as you move.

"For example. Look at me. I'm standing properly at attention. See? Heels together, feet at an angle of forty-five degrees, fingers curled up, head perfectly still, eyes straight to the front, chin in, back like a ruler, and thumbs in line with the seams of the trousers. (That's what the seams of your trousers are for.) Now. I'm standing to attention. I get the order Left Turn. *Le-heft* ... *Tyeeern!* The heel of my left foot becomes a pivot. I push with the toe of my right foot, and turn left. That's *One.* I count a pause—*Two, Three*—then raise my right knee smartly and bring my right foot down in the correct position at an angle of forty-five degrees with a smash that cracks the asphalt—*One! One ... two ... three. ...* *One!* Get it? You'll only shout out the time while you're here. By that time, the correct pause will become instinctive. Now, you. What's 'Instinctive'? What's it mean?"

He has picked on Bates. Bates grins. Then he says: "Loike a dog, Sergeant."

"What d'you mean, like a dog?"

"Well, a dog's instinctive, Sergeant."

"Oh, so a dog's instinctive, is it? I'll dog you, you stuffed dummy, you. I'll instinctive you, you sloppy great Date, you! You horrible thing! The correct movement—

for the benefit of any brainless lout that doesn't know the meaning of the English language—will come to you without your having to think about it, and so will the correct time. Anybody here done any navvying? . . . Several of you. Well, do you have to think how to get hold of a pick or a shovel? No. That's instinctive. Definitely. Well, your arms will come to you like that. So will the proper use of your feet. Now listen," says Sergeant Nelson, dropping his voice to an ordinary, conversational tone. "Some of you guys may be sensitive. I dunno. Well, don't *worry* if I shout at you a bit and call you names. It's essential. It's impossible to get along without it. I've got to get you fairly proficient in eight or nine weeks. Always be sure that I won't dish you out more than you can take, and I won't punish any man unless he asks for it. Take everything in good part, and you'll be all right." He bellows: "Now, then! Come here. Lemme arrange you, like flowers in a garden . . . oh, you pretty-pretty bunch o' soppy-stalked shy pansy-wansies. God definitely blimey, blimey with thunderbolts, blimey with lightning! You, you rasher of wind!" He drags Old Silence into place. "Atcha, you great roasted ox." He pushes Hodge into position. "C'mon, you parrot-faced son of a son, Barker, or whatever your name is. . . . You, you gorbellied Geordie . . . yes, you, Shorrock. There's enough of you there to start a sausage-factory. . . . And you, Dopey . . . where are you from? Widnes? Get in there. . . . Cor damme and lumme! Why should England tremble, eh? *You*'ve been in the Army before, eh? I can see you have. Well, you come up here. Now look. You're in your positions. You'll always keep in those positions while you're here. Get it? When told to fall in, you will fall in in those same positions, one arm's length apart. Have you got it? Are you sure?"

To our left, thirty men, followed by a shrieking Sergeant brandishing a pace-stick, execute a left wheel which, to us, represents the ultimate perfection of military footwork.

"Gord milk the coconuts and stone me over the hurdles," groans Sergeant Nelson, "look at 'em. Three weeks squadded, and when it comes to a left wheel some of 'em right wheel, some of 'em about turn, some of 'em turn handsprings, some of 'em pick their noses, and some stand still. Definitely horrible. Now you're going to show 'em what you can do. To me, you look not too bad a squad. You might shape. Now look. Over there is a squad that came last week. I want you to do me a personal favour. I want you to beat them Things hollow. Your credit is my credit. I won't let you down. Will you let me down?"

"No, Sergeant!"

"I'm sure you won't. I like the look of you, you terrible-looking objects as you are. Now. You'll be on this side of the Square punctual to time. That is to say, ten minutes too early, always. You will be clean and tidy, smart and attentive. Now, I want you to try and stand to attention like this. . . . No, no, head straight, eyes straight to your front, arms straight to your sides, backs straight. . . . Now, when I say *Stand at Ease*, raise your left knee, so, and bring your left foot down with a *stamp*, your heels twelve inches apart; and simultaneously, shoot your hands to your rear . . . like this . . . your thumbs crossed, fingers straight, right hand over the left. Now don't worry if you can't do it properly first time. I don't expect you to. We've all got to learn. Now . . . *Stand* at Hoooe*ase!*" He looks at us. "Keep still. In the Army, right or wrong—keep still!" He walks round us, pushing up a chin here, tapping down a head there, straightening fingers, adjusting heels.

With the possible exception of a man in love, no man in the world is so desperately eager to please as the new recruit in the Army. He has his back to the yardstick of regimental tradition. For the duration of his time, his value will depend upon nothing but his proficiency as a soldier. The muscles of a rookie doing his first Stand at Ease are as taut as those of a man clinging for his life to a breaking branch.

"It'll come easy in time. *Squa*haad . . . Shun!" roars Sergeant Nelson. "Speed. Speed is the word. Smooth speed. Definitely smooth speed. And let me see one of you not keeping his head up. I'll make him wish he'd died ten years before he was born. I'll have him running round this square like Mister Nurmi the Flying Finn. I'll hare him up and chase him down so that his plates of meat don't touch the ground once in five hundred yards. Stone me definitely blind! *Stand*at Hooo*ease!* Now, when I says *Stand Easy*, stay where you are but let all your muscles relax. Stand . . . easy! And when I say *Squad*, tense up again, stand properly at ease. *Squad*. As you were! *Squad!* Just tense yourselves back to the At Ease. All right, stand easy and rest for a minute."

"Please, Sergeant, a dog *is* instinctive," says Bates.

"Shullup! Are you out of your mind? Whaddaya mean, a dog? Who asked anything about dogs? Insubordination, eh? Insolence, eh? Shullup! . . ." Sergeant Nelson looks to Heaven and says: "All these years have I lived, and it seems like a thousand years; and never, definitely never, have I heard such a load of Sweet Fanny Adams as this horrible man comes out with. Gord forgive him. He's mental. . . . Now, about saluting. They're pretty hot on saluting in the Brigade of Guards. I don't care what they do in the Boy Scouts or the Church Lads' Brigade or the W.A.A.C.S. or the A.T.S., or the Salvation Army. Here, saluting being a matter of discipline and proper courtesy and respect, they are hot on it, and rightly so. Thus, whenever you see an officer approaching you, you will salute . . . head up, chin in, shoulders back, hand in line with the forearm, thumb pressed close against the edge of the hand, fingers all close together; the whole to come up like a steel spring, so that the right forefinger rests one inch above the right eyebrow.

"Now . . ."

A bugle sounds. "I'm going to dismiss you for now," says Sergeant Nelson. "Just for fun, see if you can do me a right turn, like I showed you. On the command Dismiss, you turn smartly to your right, count three and then scram. Try it. Dis-*miss!*"

He doesn't call us back, or give us an "As you were." It is, after all, our first hour on the Square. We walk back to the hut to change for P.T. The novelty of the thing has made this first Drill Parade quite pleasant.

Bates catches up with the flying Sergeant Nelson, and says: "Please, Sergeant."

"What is it, son?"

"When you whistle to a dog, 'e pricks 'is ears oop."

"Are you here again with your dogs?"

"No, Sergeant. Yes, Sergeant. Oi mean, a dog is koind o' instinctive."

"There's a lunatic asylum next door to here," says Sergeant Nelson. "Either you'll go there pretty soon, or so help me, I will."

"Well, a cat, then," says Bates, earnestly. "If you go *pt-pt-pt*"—he calls an imaginary cat—"it cooms running up to yow, because it knows what yow mean. But a cat's got no sense. It's instinctive. It don't *know* what it does, or *why* it does it, but it *does* it, don't it?"

"Oh, definitely," says Sergeant Nelson.

He reaches the hut before we do. As we enter he cries: "*Hi-de-Hi!*"

"*Ho-de-Ho!*"

"Slippers, shorts, gym vests and sweaters, and a rolled towel under your arm. The muscle-factory, you weeds! The muscle-factory, you spineless gobs of calves' feet jelly, you. It made me what I am to-day, and I'm a one-man wave o' destruction! *Hi-de-Hi!*"

"*Ho-de-Ho!*"

"Trained Soldier Brand," says Sergeant Nelson.

"Sarnt?" says the Trained Soldier, leaping up.

"*I* don't want you," says the Sergeant. "I just said 'Trained Soldier Brand.' Just like that. 'Trained Soldier Brand.' Just as you might say: 'Blind O'Reilly' . . . Come on, *come* on, come ON! Ja want valets! Ja want ladies' maids? Ja want me to powder your little bottoms with talcum and put your little shorts on for you? Get out of it! Form up like I showed you just now, for P.T."

We march as best we can out to the hard green fields, where a Staff Sergeant waits for us—an Army Heavyweight Champion of practically everything, with the body of a boxer turned wrestler, the eye of a kind man embittered, and the face of an executioner who is kind to his children when off duty.

He bites off jagged spikes of verbiage and spits them out like fish-bones.

"Come close. Listen to me. First of all I want to have A few words. With you. Pay attention."

His grim grey eyes look us over; rest approvingly upon
the huge thews of Hodge and the long, quick boxing-
muscles of Bullock; appraise the wiriness of Johnson, the
sedentary slenderness of Old Silence, the stolid suet of
Shorrock, the ranginess of the Wire-Haired Boy from
Widnes, the neglected average torso of Dale. He rests a
great dark hand for an instant on Thurstan's shoulder.
Thurstan bobs up and back like a hammer in a piano,
tense and defensive. The Staff Sergeant glances at him
and yawns. Then he says:

"None of you are. Any good. Civilians. City-bred,
some of you. Doughy. Sloppy. Unfit. Most of you'd be
puffed after running. A mile. Hn. We'll alter all that."
He clears his throat, and then goes on, in the voice of a
lecturer, but with an undertone of weariness. (After all,
he has been saying the same thing over and over again,
day in and day out, for so very long.) He says:

"It is my duty to make you fit and strong in order that
you may serve your country to the full extent of your
capacity. Some of you went in for sports and physical
culture in peace-time. All the better for them that did.
You all ought to have done so. A man who neglects the
body God gave him is worse than a beast. And if you've
neglected yourselves and let yourselves get short-winded
and soft, well, you'll suffer for that in the first week or
two: it'll come hard, very hard. You get a lot of P.T. here.
You've got to be hammered into shape. I can't show you
any mercy, even if I wanted to . . . and I don't.

"I hope you enjoy the P.T. you get here. If you don't, it
makes no odds. So you'd better for your own sakes. It
isn't all arm-and-leg exercises. Now, we play a lot of
games and do a lot of nice running. Above all, we teach a
new kind of thing which we call Unarmed Combat.

"What is Unarmed Combat? Well, it's nothing more or less than dirty, rough-house fighting . . . self-defence other than Queensberry method. Call it All-In Wrestling . . . a bit of Catch-As-Catch-Can, Ju-Jitsu, Judo, anything you like. The idea is this: you're up against Jerry. Jerry is ruthless. Jerry won't lead with his left in hand-to-hand fighting: he'll more likely bite you in the face and kick. The principle is, that a break-hold, or a gouge, or a properly placed kick or twist, well applied, might save your life in an emergency. I teach you ruthless, unscrupulous, rough-house tactics, to be used if and when occasion demands. And furthermore, Unarmed Combat gives you confidence in yourselves, and helps you to a proper co-ordination of eye and hand and foot. For instance . . ."

The Staff Sergeant reaches out, casually, as one might reach for a cigarette; and almost as effortlessly picks up a great Sergeant Instructor in a blue-and-red striped sweater and a Sandow moustache.

"This kind of thing," says the Staff Sergeant, hurling the striped one to the earth and hauling his right hand back between his shoulder-blades, "is useful sometimes. But you have to be *quick*, not necessarily strong, but *quick* to do it, and speed is always useful, in every walk of life."

The striped Sergeant is black in the face and moaning. The Staff Sergeant releases him. "Sergeant Paul," he says, "rush me."

"*Must* I, Staff? You've demonstrated on me twice already to-day."

"Yes, you must."

The striped one walks twenty feet away, and then makes a desperate rush upon the Staff Sergeant. He hopes to bear the grim one down by sheer weight and vigour. A second or so later he is spinning through the air. "Watch him fall," says Staff. "If he didn't know how to fall he'd break his neck. Or maybe an arm." The striped Sergeant rolls over and over, and finally rises, covered with dry grass and somewhat angry.

The Staff Sergeant turns back to us. He has the calm, languid air of a man who has just thrown away an empty cigarette-packet. "You might go a bit easy on these demonstrations," says Sergeant Paul. "There was a stone where I fell."

"Well, the stone had no right to be there. All right. I just wanted to have a word with you. You can't be good soldiers unless you're fit. It's up to me to make you fit, and up to you to help me." And the Staff Sergeant repeats something we have heard before, and are destined to hear many times again:

"Work with me, and I'll be all right. Work against me, make things difficult, impede the progress of fitness and the war by any idleness, laziness, insubordination or funny business . . ." He grinds his teeth, leaving the rest unsaid but hideously implied.

Then he hands us over to the striped Sergeant, Paul, who lines us up and says:

"I'm the best fellow in the world if you treat me right. Work willingly and do your best, and I'm your pal. Play me up, and I don't mind telling you I'll make life a misery for you. I'll soon get that paleness off your faces and put some zing into those limbs. Now, let's see you run . . ."

An hour later we go back to the hut.

Sergeant Nelson grins at us.

"Well? Grown any hair on your horrible little chests? Get back into battle-dress. I, *I*, do you hear me, *I* am going to tell you about the Short Lee-Enfield Rifle. *Hi-de-Hi!*"

"*Ho-de-Ho!*"

Bates says: "Please Sergeant Oi think Oi've got a torn muscle."

"So what d'you want me to do? Darn it? Get going."

The little aches and pains of unaccustomed exercise affect different men in different ways. Some remember what their mothers told them about "over-straining" themselves, and fall into dismal panic. Others—heavy manual workers, and the like—consider them philosophically, without entirely ignoring them. Sedentary men, clerical fellows, black-coated workers like Dale, suffer considerably in the first weeks of Guards training, but suffer like heroes, saying nothing at all except an occasional "Owch," like the parrot that laid square eggs.

Months afterwards, Sergeant Nelson, speaking to the N.C.O. known as Corporal Bearsbreath, said:

"Bearsbreath, I definitely admit that the wartime Guardsman is not the same as the peace-time Guardsman. In peace time you can settle down to quiet training. You can chase your man into shape for months; and then again he's come into the Army because he wants to make it his job for a few years to come. Definitely. In wartime, you get all sorts and shapes and sizes of Guardsmen, within the height-limits. But you have to hand it to one or two of them, the way they take it.

"There was a guy called Spencer, some sort of a salesman of some kind of biscuits or some such tack, that had spent his life sitting in a little motor-car driving from boozer to boozer hawking this here stuff. He come in at fourteen-stone-seven, puffy as pastry, carrying maybe three stone of superfluous fat, and dead out of condition. Oh definitely. Built to weigh eleven stone; carrying three stone extra: thinnish in the leg, softish about the thigh, not too good in the feet. Well, Bearsbreath, you know as well as I do that the chief trouble with Guardsmen is their feet. There's practically a disease: 'Guardsman's Heels,' from excessive stamping. I thinks to myself: 'With all the good will in the world,' I thinks, 'this here Salesman wallah is going to turn out pretty poor . . . yes, I'm afraid he's going to be definitely steady.'

"And I watches him. Well, Bearsbreath, you know as well as I do that the first week or two cracks up quite a few rookies, for the time being . . . ammo-boots on their poor little feet, and stamp, stamp, stamp on the Square; and the Staff Sergeant in the muscle-factory; and the change of grub, and so on. This here Spencer drops weight like a Wop dumping his pack on the run. You can *see* stones and stones dripping off of him on the Square. Millions of stones that rook lost; billions. And sometimes, coming in at night to see if everything was hunky-doke, I'd see this here biscuit, or potato-crisp salesman, sitting on his bed with a pair of feet on him—I swear to God, Bearsbreath, they was like barrage-balloons painted red, only bigger. 'Sore tootsies?' I says, and he always says: 'It's all right, Sarnt.' Conscientious? I never see such a conscientious rook. And I see him shape, and I say to myself: 'This rook is a dead cert for the tapes, and pretty damn soon at that.' What I mean to say is, I run into him the other day, and he's a lance-jack. I would have sworn he couldn't have stood the racket, and I wouldn't have held it against him if he hadn't, because there's some fellers that aren't cut out for it.

"What I mean, Bearsbreath, is; for sheer sand in the belly, grit, spine, nerve, and guts, some o' these soft-looking civvies take some beating. He went through hell, that rook did. He was over thirty, too. Definitely, Bearsbreath, the war brings out the what-d'you-call-it in some blokes. There's big buck navvies would have laid down and had kittens at half what this here Spencer went through. Now my point is this: the Army helped to make a man of that geezer. He wouldn't have known how good he was if it hadn't been for the Army. But that's neither here nor there. My point is this: the kid of eighteen has soft bones, and he's young—he don't feel the strain much because it's helping him to grow. The working mug that's shoved barrows, or handled a pick and shovel, *he* doesn't notice it so much, because he's been using his muscles all his life, more or less. But the clurk, Bearsbreath, the clurk, the shopwalker, the pen-pusher, the bloke that's never used his muscles in his life—he's the bloke I'm sorry for and take my hat off to at the same time. He sort of feels that he's got to stand up to it as well as anybody else. And he does. And he won't go sick unless he's absolutely *got* to go sick. He's ashamed to. Toughish; definitely toughish."

Bearsbreath said: "We was all Civvies once, Nelson."

"Were we?" said Sergeant Nelson. "To tell you the honest truth, I hardly remember."

That evening, as we come back from tea, Trained Soldier Brand says:

"No talking, singing, or whistling. No smoking. No eating. Shining Parade. Remember, every morning the Officer comes round to inspect this hut. I noticed one or two greatcoats with buttons like old halfpennies this morning. I'm responsible for you. You land *me* in the muck if you don't watch out, and that is a serious offence. I want to see you fellers working till seven. Them gaiters have got to be blancoed every night. So's your belt, and et cetera. Remember, brush the surface of the webbing with water, first, then brush your blanco in thinly and evenly. Take your belts to bits and work on them brasses. A thin smear of polish, let it dry, and then rub, damn it, rub. Above all, work on them boots. I don't mind telling you, they're 'ot on boots 'ere. You'll be inspected soon. Say your boots is bad. What happens? The Company Commander hauls me in on Orders and says: 'Trained Soldier Brand, why is them men's daisy-roots in muck? Is this here the way you maintain the high standards of the Brigade of Guards? Are you a Coldstreamer? Or what the lousy hell are you? Why, you twillip,' he says. 'Take three drills just for a warning.' And if you think I'm going to rush round that Square with a pack just for you, you're wrong. So let me tell you something—any idle skiver I catch will find himself with such a load o' jankers he won't know where he is."

"What is jankers, Trained Soldier?" asked Johnson.

"It's a sort of general kind of word meaning punishment. You'll get to know the call: Defaulters—*You can be a Defaulter as long as you like, As long as you answer your name.* It might be *Show Boots Clean.* It might be *Extra Drill.* It might be C.B."

"What is C.B., Trained Soldier?"

"Confined to Barracks."

"But we're confined to barracks now."

"Yes, but only while you're Recruits. After you're done here, you're Guardsmen, and have the right to go out every night, duty permitting. You get a Permanent Pass, allowing you out of barracks from After Duty to Midnight. But if you get C.B., you can't go out. Defaulters sounds five minutes after Reveille. You've got to hustle to the

Square and answer your name double time. During the day, Defaulters blows about Dinner Time, and every hour after about five, till ten-thirty. You've got to answer your name every time. If you don't, you're for it. Then there's extra drills, in Fighting Order—small pack, with ground-sheet and mess-tins, pouches, braces, belt, rifle, bayonet, full water-bottle. And you've got to be spick-and-span, or you might get another few days. The drills, usually, are pretty tough, too. The game ain't worth the candle. For instance, you're very likely to get seven days or so for a dirty rifle. Well, a dust over and a pull-through 'll save you all that. Or being late for a parade: two minutes can land you seven days. Or over-staying your furlough, or being in possession of playing-cards, or answering back, or not answering back (answering back is Insubordination: not answering back is Dumb Insolence), or not being properly dressed, or forgetting to salute an officer, or having a dirty cap-star, or a dirty bayonet, or standing idle on parade, or being inattentive on parade, or speaking out of turn, or laughing, or crying, or using horrible—dirty words, or not walking properly, or not getting up at Reveille, or not putting out the lights at Lights Out, or skiving . . ."

"What is Skiving?"

"The same as Swinging It. Trying to get out of things; dodging a parade, wangling a fatigue, or otherwise chancing your arm. Slipping out for a tea 'n' a wad when on fatigue is, for instance, Skiving."

"What's a Wad?"

"Shiver-and-Shake. A Cake. (Get on with that shining!) There's no need to go round bobbing: just keep calm and do your dooty, and you'll keep out of trouble."

"What's Bobbing?"

"Oh . . . sort of bobbing; getting nerves, worrying. You, Dale, your boots are very steady."

"Thanks, Trained Soldier," says Dale, gratified; for to this good man "Steady" is the highest possible praise of a man or his job.

"Thanks? Thanks for what? In the Guards, son, 'Steady' means 'Absolutely lousy.' If you want to sort of spit in a man's eye, call him Steady. If, on the other hand, you want to give him a bit o' praise, then says he's Hot. 'Steady' means Awful, so get working. I know you're not used to it yet: don't get down'earted. Rub your polish well in, then spit nice clear spit, and rub it in with a circular motion. If you're using a bone, then bone your boots with a kind of smooth, stroking movement. . . . D'you hear that bugle-call? That's 'Yellow' . . . there's enemy planes about, so be on the alert. 'Red'—*There's a Jerry in the sky*"—he sings it—"means, go to the shelter with your tin hat and respirator. You also take your rifle and bayonet, to get you used to the feel of 'em. There's hundreds of calls: you've got to know them, from Reveille to Lights Out. There's little pomes to 'em. Frinstance: Picquet:

> *"Come an' do a Picquet, Boys,*
> *Come an' do a Guard,*
> *You think it's ruddy easy*
> *But you'll find it ruddy hard.*

"Or Officers' Mess:

> *"Officers' wives eat pudden and pies*
> *But soldiers' wives eat skilly.*

"Or Letters:

> "*Letters from Lousy Lou, Boys,*
> *Letters from Lousy Lou.*

"Or Commandant's Orders: After the Brigade Call:

> "*Justice will be done!*

"or

> "*Cri-ime does not Pay!*

"You'll learn, you'll learn in time. And what is Commandant's Orders, you ask? Well. If the Commandant wants to say something to you, he orders you to attend Orders, and you're marched in, first to Company Orders, and ordered to attend Commandant's Orders, and then you're marched into the Commandant's office, and get what's coming to you. Or say you've committed some crime, like being late, or absent. The Company Commander might not want to deal with the case himself. He might send you to the Adjutant for sentence, and the Adjutant might send you to the Commandant. So don't go and commit no crimes.

"Again, any man is entitled to interview the Company Commander, privately, about any matter. But he can't just walk in bolo and——"

"What's Bolo?"

"Cockeyed; anything not correct in the Coldstream Guards is Bolo. You don't just walk in and say 'Oi.' You see Sergeant in Waiting, and write out an Application for an Interview, and then, if the Captain is free to see you, which he always is, you're stood at ease outside the office, then, when your name's called you spring to attention and march in with your hands to your sides; mark time, halt; left turn, and, as your name's called again, take a smart pace forward and wait till you're spoken to. When the interview is over, you receive the order *Fall In*, and take a smart pace backward, left turn again, and out you go, fast, keeping your hands still. It's dead easy. A baby in arms could do it. If the officer says anything to you and you just want to say Yes, say 'Yes, sir'; not just 'sir.' The Billy Browns, or Grenadiers, say 'sir'; the Lilywhites say 'Yes, sir.'

"Another thing. Every week or two you'll have a Kit Inspection. That is to teach you to take proper care of the property entrusted to you. You have to show boots, battledress, both hats, one pair of socks clean, one shirt clean, sweater, gym vests, shorts, tin of black polish, tin of brown polish, tin of blanco, tin of metal polish, oil-bottle, pullthrough, mess-tins and cover, housewife complete with needles and et ceteras, knife, fork and spoon, steel helmet, respirator and respirator-haversack, slippers, button-stick, all your brushes sandpapered clean, and other odds and ends, all laid out in perfect order on a clean towel on your bed. Everything has to be marked with your number. They're 'ot on numbers, round here. And when the officer comes to your bed you stand smartly to attention, and say this: 2663141 (or whatever your number is) *Recruit Smith. Two Weeks Squadded* (or however long it is). *Kit Present, sir.* If anything is missing . . . it might be a pair of socks . . . you say *One Pair Socks Missing Otherwise Kit Present, sir.*

"I've got the numbering kit here, ink-pad, stamps, and doo-dahs. You've got to get yourselves a pennorth of tape each; stamp your number on a lot o' bits o' tape and sew 'em on everything you can lay your hands on. 'Cause things have a way of disappearing.

"Failure to comply with all this here is a very serious

offence, and I don't mind telling you that they're 'ot on serious offences in this mob."

"Hot means Good, doesn't it?" asks Dale.

"Yes. But not necessary. Frinstance, if I say 'Your boots is Hot,' I mean, they're good. But if I say 'The Drill Pig is Hot,' that means 'e's pretty savage."

"And what's a Drill Pig?"

"A Drill Pig is a Drill Sergeant. A Drill Sergeant is a sort of super-sergeant-major, an assistant to the Regimental Sergeant Major."

"But why *Pig?*" asks a lad from the Elephant and Castle.

"You'll soon find out," says Trained Soldier Brand.

The same lad asks: "And wot's a Regimental Sergeant Major do?"

"Well, 'e's a kind of link between the officers and the other ranks. 'E's a sort of an Archbishop."

"And the Commandant?"

" 'E's a sort of a Gawd."

The Wire-Haired Boy from Widnes, having stared for nearly fifteen minutes at a photograph of a peace-time Coldstreamer on a Buckingham Palace Guard, says to the Trained Soldier:

"I wanna sign on for twenty-one years."

As seven strikes we rise from our beds like men in a fairy tale released from a spell. "If you're going any-where at all, even to the Lat," says Brand, "you're supposed to take your respirators, tin hats, and gas-capes with you. This is to get you into the 'abit of carrying 'em wherever you go. And so you'd better. Say you're out one day on leave and the Gestapo sees you without your tin bowler and mask, you'll go in the moosh."

"Gestapo?"

"Another name for military police."

"Are they noice?" asks Bates.

Trained Soldier Brand says that while the Military Police are inoffensive to law-abiding soldiers, they can nevertheless be People Of Dubious Ancestry if they wish. "We got to 'ave 'em, I suppose," he says, "to keep law and order. If you pay rates and taxes you got to have law and order. Personally, I don't pay no rates and taxes, and I don't want no law and order. But there it is. There's military policemen in every town. They got the right to arrest anybody in uniform. They're the Army's C.I.D., kind o' style. They're coppers. They ain't popular, therefore. Nobody really loves a Gestapo man. It's unreasonable, but there it is. There ain't a soldier living that's never broken a rule—with the possible exception of Freddie Archer, R.S.M. of Scots Guards—the most regimental man in the British Army. Once, being two minutes late off leave, he put himself in the report and marched himself in to be punished. When talking to an officer on the telephone he salutes and stands stiffly to attention. But what was I saying? Gestapo. Personally I dislike 'em. That's a matter of opinion. The beauty of this here Democracy is, you can hate policemen and say so. But I ought to tell you that a Gestapo man is serving his country same as a sewer-man or a dustman. He's essential. And even if he wasn't, don't you go and get yourselves into no trouble, just for the sake of being properly dressed or anything.

"They sell beer in the Naffy. I, personally, have never met a man who could get drunk on it, though I have known many that tried. Wind pudden, that's what it is. All the same, it is alleged to be alcoholic, and if you bring any back with you you will have committed a terribly serious offence. They're 'ot on alcohol in barrack-rooms in this mob, I don't mind telling you. Red-'ot. Boiling-'ot. This is a military depot of the Brigade of Guards, so you don't go round bathing chorus-girls in champagne or knocking back bols of powl owl in the 'uts. Chocolate, yes. A nice packet o' wine-gums, yes. But beer? Beer is a serious offence."

We hurry to the Naffy.

In an immense room with an interminable counter, endless queues of Guards recruits, Lilywhites, Grenadiers, Jocks, Micks, and Taffies, writhe and mutter while a few frantic girls in blue cotton overalls dash out cups of tea, great jammy wads of cake, tins of boot-polish, bootlaces, vaseline, fruit-salts, pies, biscuits, pencils, chocolate, dusters, writing-pads, beans on toast, beer, cider, ink, cigarettes and sausages.

We wait in a queue. Everything is smoky and strange. A vociferous recruit with a brass leek on his cap is shouting: "That is unfair you are, look, to get a man in front to buy things for you, look! That is unjust it is!" And a dark recruit with a Cross of Saint Andrew worked into his Guards' Star says, in a fantastic combination of American and Glaswegian: "So hwhit?" A man on a remote platform singing a song about one Danny Boy is more unheard than a goldfish: he simply opens and closes his mouth. The uproar of the Naffy swallows his song, but he neither knows nor cares. There is some clapping. A sharp-starred Irish Guards' recruit near us says:

"There's a song that goes:

> "*You've lost an arm and you've lost a leg,*
> *You're an eyeless, noseless, spiritless egg,*
> *You'll have to be put in a bowl to beg—*
> *Johnny I hardly knew you.*

"I wish they'd sing that and cheer us up a bit."

But the singer, shoving his sharp tenor voice through a chink in the din, begins *Bless 'em all*.

> *Bless 'em all, Bless 'em all,*
> *The long and the short and the tall,*
> *There'll be no promotion, This side of the ocean,*
> *So cheer up me lads, Bless 'em all . . .*

Spencer the Salesman recognises a jar of the product he sells, and is cheered and saddened at the same time. Johnson, the fly Brummagem boy, says with sudden vehemence: "Oi bet Oi'll be a sergeant insoide six months." A dozen of our squad have arrived to swell the slow-moving queue. Old Silence comes out of his taciturnity and says: "Will you all have a beer?" We all say we will, if we can get it; for there seem enough men before us to drink all that was ever brewed. "Why are these places so short-staffed?" somebody asks; and somebody else replies: "They're short-staffed because they haven't got enough people working for 'em." "Oh, is that it?" asks the interrogator.

A querulous voice says: "So I says to the Sarnt In Waiting, 'I wanna go sick.' So I goes sick. So I sees the M.O. So the M.O. says: 'Now what's your trouble?' I says: 'Me foot, sir.' He says: 'Your foot isn't trouble. Say what you mean. What's wrong with your foot?' I says: 'It's swole.' 'Let's see,' he says. 'Ah,' he says, 'merely a blister.' 'Blister?' I says. 'Blister,' he says, and he sticks a ruddy great needle in that ruddy great blister and he got enough water out of that ruddy great blister—may I never get out of this here Naffy alive—enough water to fill a reservoy. And he sends me back to duty. Cruelty!"

"I wonder how we'll like it here?"

"Somebody told me it's horrible."

"The Training Battalion is worse."

"The Holding Battalion is worse still."

"The First is supposed to be worst of all."

"The Second is hell, somebody told me."

"Whether we like it or not we've got to stay here, so the thing to do is, get used to it quickly."

Suddenly a dreadful silence falls. *Jerry in the Sky!* cries the bugle. We run out. Thurstan pauses to curse and stamp his foot. Understandably: for, having waited twenty minutes, he found himself right against the counter. And then Red blew. Barker looks as if he has suddenly been smitten with all the miseries of Job, and has not been left with even a bit of pot to scrape his boils with.

From the back of the night comes the melancholy note of a siren. It gathers volume; shrieks, fades, and shrieks again. The distance is now full of something like muffled drums. "Lousy with stars," says Barker, referring to the sky, which is clear and beautiful. We hop down into our trench. The guns mutter loud now. We hear the queer, pulsating drone of raiders. Anti-aircraft guns bang. The night is full of steel.

Bates, in the middle of a story, will not be interrupted:

" . . . When Brummy Joe chucked this feller out o' that winder, 'e landed on 'is 'ead and split it open. 'E was proper frit o' Brummy after that, this feller was. Brummy could of showed yow some fight-ing. I see Brummy put 'is fist through a oak door. What? *'Urt* 'im? What, *Brummy?* A oak *door?* Don't be silly. Yow could a bashed Brummy wi' the door edgeways and not 'urt *'im*, not *Brummy!*

Well, another noice feller from Ull as we called Tyke——"

The ground seems to heave like a wrestler's back. The raider is weaving among the shell-splinters, dropping his bombs. The searchlights make strange patterns: shifting triangles, sprawling rhomboids, fabulous outlines that look like letters out of some half-formed alphabet. One great beam squirting up like a hose catches a silver speck and holds it. The batteries go mad. The sky twinkles with shell-bursts like a spangled skirt in a spotlight. "By God we got him!" somebody says.

" . . . So this feller asks Brummy for his two bob back. 'Yow want yow're two bob back?' says Brummy? 'Ah, Oi want moi two bob back.' 'Yow do, do yow?' 'Ah.' 'Oh?' 'Ah.' 'Roight yow are,' says Brummy, and picks up a eight-inch crowbar——"

The pulse of the raider has stopped. The searchlights wave uncannily. "*Look!*" There is something like a dust-mote in a moonbeam. It is a man, falling with a para-chute. There is something pitifully insignificant about this little thing, this bit of life drifting down out of the darkness suspended on threads from the edges of a bit of silk, caught in a net of light. He comes down slowly. The great beam circles, bumping against a little cluster of clouds. Through it, flashing electric lights, passes a Hurricane, roaring. Another siren sounds, miles away. Then our own siren, fifty feet from us, revolves and fills the world with a terrific whoop of triumph, so loud that you cannot hear it, but feel it in your bones.

We smile as we go back. It couldn't have worked out better if the Commandant had arranged it. In that little half-hour, we have begun to feel like soldiers.

" . . . Seventeen stitches over one of 'is eyes," Bates is saying. "Oi tell yow, seventeen stitches."

"Sleep and refresh your pretty little selves," says Sergeant Nelson. "Because to-morrow I'm really going to start in on you. Definitely, I'm going to chase you to-morrow. I got a liver. And when I got a liver I'd tear my own grandmother's tripes out and trample them underfoot. I'd definitely do all that and much more. Woho, am I going to chase you to-morrow! Any idle man here can make his last lousy little will and testament. Any chancer can go to the Ablutions and cut his scraggy little throat from ear to ear into a wash-basin. Sleep! It's an order! *Hi-de-Hi!*"

We roar at the top of our voices: "HO-DE-HO!"

We have suddenly become cheerful. We are getting the hang of things.

Quickly but smoothly, week after week, Sergeant Nelson drives his stuff into us; tireless, patient, with legs of steel and a throat of brass. Step by step he teaches us to march and drill. Slap by slap he instructs us in the handling of arms. Screw by screw he uncovers the mysteries of the Short Lee Enfield, Mark Three. Lunge by lunge he divulges the secrets of the bayonet, from High Port to Butt-Stroke and Kill. We pass our second, fourth, and sixth week inspections. The Company Commander says that we are doing tolerably well. Sergeant Nelson informs us that, in a long and varied life spent mostly among half-wits and the offscourings of the lunatic asylums of the earth, he has seen worse squads than us: which pleases us more than anything else. Like all Guards recruits, we have been working at concert pitch.

We have lived in a state of tense activity. We have become accustomed to the food. We grumble, as always. Once, when they gave us biscuits instead of bread for tea, and the officer came round to ask if there were any complaints, we all made barking noises; and the officer laughed, and we laughed to see him laugh, and even the Company Quartermaster Sergeant bared a terrible tooth in a bit of a smile. We have been lectured on gas, on regimental tradition, military law pertaining to the crimes of desertion, drunkenness, and neglect of duty. The Padre has had a few words with us. The Medical Officer has told us what every young Guardsman ought to know. The Staff Sergeant has been at us. The days in the beginning seem inexpressibly remote. We speak of recruits four weeks squadded, as Rookies. Eight haircuts have come and gone since the day we put off civilian clothes and looked at each other in brand-new khaki. Tactics are not altogether a sealed book to us. Our shoulders have experienced the pleasant kick of our rifles loaded with .303 ammunition. We walk very straight: it was a psychological rather than a muscular operation which brought this about. After three weeks we were allowed out for an afternoon: it felt good to walk in a street on our own, slamming down our great boots and swinging our arms.

And now we prepare for our last Inspection; the Commandant's Inspection.

If the Commandant approves of us, we will "pass out" to the Training Battalion, for another period of training. It doesn't occur to us, yet, that we have acquired merely the groundwork of Guardsmanship. We have yet to get down to the hard stuff, that makes Guardsmen into soldiers. The time is coming when we will know the fatigue of a thirty-two-mile route march, or of a midnight stunt in damp darkness among the bracken of a blasted common . . . the feel of a Bren Gun, like the stupendous gulping of wine out of a bottle . . . the smallness of a six-foot target at five hundred yards . . . the misery of half-dug trenches in a thin drizzle three miles from camp and an hour and a half from dinner . . . when there will be a C.O.'s parade every week, and other drill parades besides; and cross-country runs, and hardening exercises, and the tossing of live grenades, and the chance of seven days' leave, and the responsibilities of the ordinary trained soldier.

We dress with care. Debutantes flutter less than we do, as we put on our best battle-dress, with its cut-throat creases; and our best boots, glistening with quarts of spit and tins of polish; and our gaiters blancoed to a perfect pallor, and our brasses blindingly burnished. We help each other to dress. We pull each other's trousers over the web gaiters, and produce the proper blouse-effect in our coats. We touch things at their edges. One thumb-print may destroy everything. We pull down the great cheese-cutter peaks of our best hats. Trained Soldier Brand follows us to the Square, and, when we have formed up, inspects us, and runs about us flicking with a duster, like a harassed housewife expecting overwhelming company. Then the Sergeant, the terrific Nelson, inspects us. Then the Superintendent Sergeant looks us over, with an eye from which all hope has long departed. *He* comes, a sturdy figure with a resolute stride. "Sergeant Nelson's Squad, eight weeks squadded, and ready for your inspection, sir." We stand frozen, stiff as overwound clockwork. We don't see the Commandant. We are staring straight to our front. We feel him as he passes . . . a Presence, an Eye. Seven or eight years pass. His voice is heard saying that our turnout is, on the whole, quite good. Sergeant Nelson's lone eye seems to heave a little sigh all on its own. The buttons on his S.D. jacket rise several inches, and then sink luxuriously. Then comes his voice. We thought we had heard him shout. We never did. He is shouting now. He is using his best Parade voice—a voice of Stentor at a Stannoy Sound System. He roars like a lion at a water-hole. "*Squa-ha-haaaaaaaaaaaaAAAD . . . !*"

We stamp and wheel, right form and left form, salute to the left, the right, the front, and as improperly dressed. We take up arms, and slope, and order, and trail, and present them. We feel that we are doing all right. The Commandant questions us. We have swotted up everything he is likely to ask us, and, in fact, everything a Guardsman can possibly know. He asks us all that and a lot more. The autumn goes, winter comes and goes, more summers come and fade. Years pass. Our beards are long and grizzled. Our eyes are rheumy with advanced old age. He will dismiss us, and then we may lie down and die.

We are dismissed. It took about an hour and a half.

We drag ourselves away. "How were we, Sergeant?" And Sergeant Nelson says: "You were not like Guardsmen. You were like a lousy crowd of wild, undisciplined Soudanese bloody fuzzy-wuzzies trained by illegitimate Wog corporals in a stinking pot-house in Tel Aviv in 1890. You were awful. I can never look myself in the face again. But all the same, you have passed out."

We raise a wild cheer.

"I daresay you'll leave for the Training Battalion on Tuesday," he says.

Cookhouse sounds. We laugh, if only to relax our stomachs.

"*He saith among the trumpets, Ha, ha; and he smelleth the battle afar off,*" says Hodge, the Bible-reader. "Job, 39, 25."

"Who do?" asks Bates.

"The horse."

"I never heard a horse say 'Ha, ha,'" says Bates. "'Ave yow?"

Kitbag, big valise, little valise: Change of Quarters Order. We form in the road. Rather sadly, Sergeant Nelson cries *"Hi-de-Hi!"* We sadly reply: *"Ho-de-Ho!"* We are ready.

"Kill some Jerries," says Sergeant Nelson. "And *Hi-de-Hi!* for the last time, mugs."

"HO-DE-HO, Sergeant Nelson!"

"As for me," he says, "I got another squad coming to-day."

The order comes. Our left feet hit the dust.

We are on the march.

PART THREE

THE TEMPERING

SOMETHING stutters over on the Ranges. Five bangs on one string: that is the Bren Gun burst. A squad is firing at three hundred yards. There is always one man who fires before all the rest: *tu-tu-tu-tu-tut!* Then the rest open fire. The air rattles like a dice-box for sixty seconds or so. Then, *tu-tut!*—there is always one man who has a couple of rounds unfired. Hidden hands in the butts pull the targets down. A silence comes. Soon, somebody, somewhere, will make something go off bang. It might be a Mills bomb, or a mortar bomb; or in the distance the Artillery may fire a gun; or an N.C.O. may shoot fifty fat forty-five bullets out of a Tommy Gun; or a learner may squeeze six hoarse and hesitant explosions out of a revolver. Only night, or fog, quiets the Ranges. This, say some, is why it rains so often. A military policeman from Gloucester, who talks and talks in a voice like the monotonous scrape and squeak of a rusty pump, breathlessly assures all who will listen that the everlasting banging shakes the clouds. "D'you yurr it? Bang, bang, bang. It shakes all the water out o' them clouds, experts reckon."

For here, when it is not raining, it looks as if it is going to rain; except in the hottest part of the summer, when one fears that it will never rain again. There is a perversity about the climate. It will pour all day. But when a Night Stunt takes place, which rain might cancel, then the sky clears and a calm falls, the Dipper hangs empty in a lucid heaven, and a fat-faced moon sneers down at the men who wallow in the mire that the day's rain has left behind it. The feet of innumerable Guardsmen have kicked the ground to powder. The earth, when wet, is of the consistency of clotted cream. When dry it flies about. It is Passchendaele in the winter, and Oklahoma in the summer. One makes fantastic detours as the Quarter blows for C.O.'s Parade, to avoid puddles of unknown depth. But when the sun comes out, the very dandelions seem to blink in the dust. So say the old soldiers. From October to July, they groan, the place is like the countryside beyond the Malamute Saloon in "Dangerous Dan M'Grew" . . . it takes an Amundsen to get from the Post Office to the Y.M.C.A. From July to October, well, you might as well be in the Foreign Legion. And the flies, they say, are unnatural. The military policeman from Gloucester says that the flies are caused by the dust. "Dust creates flies, the experts reckon," he says, "just as earth creates wurrrums or shirts create fleas if you're not careful. It's a proof that thur's a God, the experts reckon . . ."

It is true that there are too many flies here in the warm weather; flies of exceptional intelligence, that might have come out of a Silly Symphony . . . flies that tickle and flies that drone; flies that bite, and flies that simply look threatening; dragon-flies, hover-flies, greenflies, even butterflies. On every side there stretches the decent, amiable Surrey countryside, full of gracious gardens behind trimmed green slabs of hedge. But the Camp itself is a shanty-town of huts. The adjacent villages are made up of skimpy little Edwardian villas, and look like little bits of Lewisham or Shepherd's Bush. The local barber complains that they know what you do in the village before you know it yourself: the other day his nose began to bleed; he hurried home, but his wife met him half-way with a wet towel—the news had preceded him, but only God knew how.

Some of the inhabitants complain of the soldiers: they dig trenches on the Common. . . . "Can't they make-believe to be at war without digging holes?" The villagers are familiar with the bugle-calls, which sound from dawn to dark and are audible for miles around: they hear *Lights Out* and adjust their clocks. All day long, manœuvring squads march out and back: Coldstreamers, singing *You'll Be Far Better Off in the Moosh,* or Scots Guards preceded by skirling bagpipes. They go out on Stunts, sometimes in the dead of night behind dim and sinister lamps; sometimes in column of route through spitting rain; sometimes armed with picks and shovels in the wake of a lorry-load of revetting hurdles and barbed wire. There is a coming and going of dispatch-riders, travelling like projectiles. All roads lead to the Camp. You get to it over a bridge that is all ready for blowing up. You pass a languid canal, brilliantly scummed with green algæ.

To the right of the road, going into Camp, lie the huts and the squares. To the left, the Messes of the gods and demigods; officers and sergeants. The road runs on, past the Y.M.C.A., past the Camp Theatre and the bright new huts that the Scots Guards live in . . . into a woodland of silver birch trees, and away to the unknown distance. To the right of the Guard-room, in the middle of a trampled desolation of clayey dirt, away from the jungles of gorse and bracken and bramble, lies a flat patch of beautiful turf. Day in and day out, in war or peace, a very ancient warrior strokes and caresses this turf, watering and anointing it, rolling it and smoothing it, clipping it and fertilising it, indignantly uprooting superfluous daisies with the forceful gentleness of a beautician depilating a lady's lip. This is the Cricket Field. Football is played at the back of the B. Lines Naffy, on rougher grass scattered with bits of metal—base-plugs, springs, and scraps of cast iron that have come yipping and whining over from the little No Man's Land where live grenades are thrown.

By night, the Camp is labyrinthine and mysterious, more baffling than Pimlico in the similarity of its buildings and company areas. He who steps aside from the road is lost in the maze of the Black Huts. The newcomer must develop something of the cat's sense of orientation: if he steps out of his hut after dark upon a harmless, hygienic mission, he is not unlikely to find himself wandering, groping in an enchanted midnight on the downtrodden grass at the back of the lavatories. Newcomers from the Depot sometimes fall into a state of despondency at the sight of the Black Huts. The huts at the Depot are brand new: the Black Huts have a sombre air of extreme age; the curses and grouses of innumerable Old Sweats have soaked into their wooden walls. Some of them are said to contain mice. On one occasion, at least, three huge Sergeants were seen, pursuing with drawn bayonets and slashing coal-shovels a miserable rodent no bigger than your thumbnail. The mouse got away, incidentally, but returned to forage that night, and caused Sergeant Hitchens of Wigan to shriek in his sleep by falling off a shelf on to his face. There is a rumour that two mice, bride and groom, consummated their union and brought up three families of baby mice in a suitcase in which a Guardsman known as Old Meanie used to hoard fruit-cake. Meanie (says the legend) was in the habit of waiting until his comrades were asleep before regaling himself on handfuls of cake and pie; but one night he put the father mouse into his furtive mouth, and thereafter was a changed man. The legend is particular about the sex of the mouse.

Here, where recruits become Guardsmen, one is permitted to exhibit over one's bed photographs of wives, relatives, fiancées, or close friends. Bed-heads break out in patchworks of snapshots. Men seize new arrivals by the arms, and, pointing to the blurred outlines of some nondescript form, say: "Isn't she a beauty?" or "Ain't she a smasher?" The correct reply to such questions is a sound which may be transcribed thus: "Mmmmmmmmm-mum!" One N.C.O., who keeps three cabinet photos of his pretty wife on his bit of wall, takes them down in the evening, for he considers it indecent that these pictures should look down on the spectacle of thirty men undressing. Regular Guardsmen always exhibit postcard snaps of themselves in scarlet tunics and bearskins. One man displays portraits of Loretta Young, Ann Sheridan, and Frances Day, on which he has written loving messages to himself in assumed hands. Another sometimes talks to a small snap of a big woman, saying: "If you're carrying on with anybody while I'm away . . ."

Soldiers, here, have responsibilities. They must "make themselves acquainted with the Detail." That is to say, nobody tells them what they are going to have to do. No Sergeant leads them from place to place. The blowing of the Quarter alone warns them that the hour of a Parade is drawing near. Baths and haircuts become, once again, the personal responsibility of the individual soldier. A hairy neck means trouble. "Dirty Flesh" is a serious offence. Men have got away with murder, but never with a rusty rifle. Beyond such matters as cleanliness, subordination, and punctuality, which are taken for granted, the Detail Boards are the Tablets of the Law. In the frames which hang on the walls outside the Company office, the Sergeant-Major pins the Roneoed will of the C.O., whose every word is an ultimatum. There one may read how it has come to the notice of the powers that Gambling is taking place, and the statement that this practice must cease forthwith; the game of Lotto, or Housie-Housie, being the only indoor game officially sanctioned in the huts. . . . And it was there that the N.C.O.s and men of the Guards learned that, in future, when rushing the enemy with bayonets, they must shout not "Hurray," but "Hurrah"; at which everybody danced round everybody else, making savage points with imaginary bayonets and mincing "Oh, HurrAH, Duckie, HurrAH, HurrAH!"

But the Detail is The Word. Your destiny is written, not on your forehead, but on the Detail. Man disposes: the Commanding Officer details him.

And in this place many things are learned.

The handling, cleaning, and use of rifles, Bren Guns, Tommy Guns, Mortars, and Hand Grenades, together with the firing, or throwing of same; tactics; marching; invisibility; trench-digging and revetting; cooking, if necessary and desirable; signalling; the manipulation of Bren Carriers; wiring; moving silently; moving at night; how to be a Corporal; how to avoid Gas; how to put out fires, together with the handling of fire-engines; map-reading; the Army Act; how to be a Military Policeman; speed; presence of mind; falling down; getting up; swimming; marching in formations; reading and writing if illiterate; foreign languages; how to be a C.Q.M.S.; the selection of position in action; observation as a fine art;

the laying of aims; the giving of fire-orders; how to lead a Section; how to mount guard; the whole mystery and art of the Sentry; the inner meaning and philosophic significance of Applied Discipline; how to drive Military Transport vehicles; how to crawl over enemy territory; how to attack; how to defend; how to fight, and when, and when not to fight; the timing of an attack, as it might be a punch to the jaw; how to harden the feet; what to do with bayonets, and when, and where to stick them; how to endure thirty-five miles on foot in rain or heat, with full fighting order; how to fire at aircraft; what to do when anything on earth happens, in any imaginable circumstances, in the teeth of any conceivable opposition . . . all these things are taught in official syllabuses. Above all, discipline; eternally and inevitably, discipline. Discipline is the screw, the nail, the cement, the glue, the nut, the bolt, the rivet that holds everything tight. Discipline is the wire, the connecting-rod, the chain, that co-ordinates. Discipline is the oil that makes the machine run fast, and the oil that makes the parts slide smooth, as well as the oil that makes the metal bright. They know things about discipline, here. They have seen the Prussians with it, and the Arabs without it. Somewhere between those poles lies the ideal. The principle of discipline here is divinely simple: you lay it on thick and fast, all the time; the Englishman takes it to heart and then adjusts it to the national character. The result is the type of Sergeant Nelson, disciplinarian of ferocity and patience and infinite humour, who, if he told you to go to Hell, would be perfectly willing to lead you there; who might run you into the spud-hole on Tuesday, but who would not fail to buy you a drink, and be damned to the regulations, if he met you outside on Saturday. Law and

Order make the world go round: the stars of infinite space couldn't move without the parade-ground discipline of the heavens; and without the severe regimentation of the organs, no heart would beat. But there's a time and a place for everything. So says Sergeant Nelson, type and pattern of the N.C.O. He, above all men, knows the inner mystery of discipline and the value of the unbroken line.

Nelson on Discipline:

"You seen an old lawn. Have you or have you not? Rolled flat, smooth as a billiard-table. Well, once upon a time, so a Yank tourist says to a gardener: 'Say, Buddy' —you know how Yanks talk—'how the gawdam hell do you gawdamwell get these 'ere gawdam lawns so gawdam smashing?' And the gardener says: 'You waters 'em and you rolls 'em, and then you rolls 'em and you waters 'em, and you goes on rolling and watering 'em for two or three 'undred years, and there you are.'

"It's the same thing with an Army. You work on it for hundreds and hundreds of years till you get a sort of foundation. That's Tradition. That's the stuff that's got to be sort of lived up to, kind of style. Discipline sort of comes out of that. Definitely, English discipline comes from English tradition. Have you got that? Before you make an English soldier, you got to make an English *man*. And then, when you lay the groundwork, you see how an English soldier will sort of discipline himself. That's *proper* discipline.

"You treat the Rookie a bit severe at first. But as soon as he gets the hang of things, you don't have to chase him. He takes everything in good part, and still stays a *man*. He fits into the machinery. On parade, he obeys an order like clockwork. Off parade, he'll argue the toss. That's what I like to see. But discipline, first of all, has got to be *taught*. You learn the ABC of it at the Depot. You pick up the Grammar at the Training Battalion. Get it?"

The idea is, that by the time you leave the Camp you will be capable of translating things on your own, if need be.

And where is this Camp?

A balloonist found himself in this place, early in the nineteenth century. An old lady, looking out of her bed-room window into a pale pink sunset, saw a great white bubble drifting down on to the Common. Hastily putting on her bonnet, she ran out. A hundred yards away a billowing mass of silk rippled among the gorse. As she watched, a man struggled out of a basket. He said:

"Where am I, my good woman?"

Falling on her knees and whispering in a voice com-pounded of joy and terror, the old lady replied:

"Pirbright, please you, God Almighty."

A century later, an Austrian refugee in Pirbright village, hearing a thunder of engines shaking the sky, ran into his landlady's sitting-room and cried: "Listen, please!"

Ancient and frail as rare porcelain, the landlady quavered:

"Why, don't you recognise them engines, sir? Don't upset yourself; they're only Hurricanes."

It is still the same old Pirbright. Only times have changed.

Here, N.C.O.s sleep in the same huts as the men. The beds are of iron: like Antæus, they are strong while they stand on their own feet; but lift them, and they disin-tegrate. The coir-fibre mattresses look exactly like what they are called, Biscuits. There are three Biscuits to a bed. At night, they are laid end-to-end upon the wire bed-frame, which, like the true-blue British institution that it is, has never bent or broken, or given way an inch under pressure. Hut No. 40, Z Company, contains thirty such beds, with their full complement of ninety biscuits; two six-foot benches of scrubbed deal; a galvanised iron coal-box, a tub, four galvanised iron basins, buckets zinc and buckets fire, a bass broom, two hair brooms, two scrubbing-brushes, one long scrubber, a slab of yellow soap as cold-looking and uninviting as imported Cheddar cheese, and a stove. No luxury here; none of your Depot pampering. When you rise in the morning, you grab yourself an iron basin and rush out to the wash-house with it. One man who keeps his own little enamel basin is greeted, every morning, with derisive yells: "Where's your water-jug, Darling? Where's your soap-dish and slop-pail? Ain't you forgot somethink? Where's your wardrobe and Jerry?" Sergeant Crowne fills a basin before he goes to sleep, so that he may shave in nice cold water the moment he gets up. He shaves with scrubbing-soap. "Cold water, good rough soap and a bluntish blade," he says, "and you *know* you've 'ad a shave." Sergeant Hands, however, goes in for brushless cream, and washes in a bucket, so that Crowne calls him Ramon Novarro.

Both Hands and Crowne wear the Palestine ribbon. We ask them if they ever met Nelson.

"One-Eye Nelson?" asks Sergeant Crowne, reflectively. "Once upon a time we used to call him Lipstick. Why Lipstick? Well, when he was a Guardsman, he used it, once. No, I don't mean on 'is mouf, silly. 'E got a stain on his best tunic—scarlet, you know—so 'e thought 'e'd cover it up with some lipstick. So 'e borrowed some lipstick from a nurse called Pinkie."

"No," says Sergeant Hands. "The nurse's name was Jenny. We used to call her The Vest-Pocket Drill Sergeant. Pinkie was engaged to Ding-Dong Bell."

"That's right. Jenny. 'E borrowed a lipstick from Jenny, and smeared it over the spot. That scarlet used to stain as easy as anything: rain 'd spot it. Well, Nelson smears this 'ere stuff over this spot, and it turns out to be tangerine-colour. So we called 'im Lipstick. Was old Nelson your squad-instructor? One of the best. 'E threw a plate of stew in my face once, in Egypt. Remember that, Hands? Best pal *I* ever 'ad. 'E didn't like to be called Lipstick."

Hands says: "You asked for that stew, Crowne. You would keep on calling him Gloria Swanson."

"Clara Bow. So 'e lets fly with this plate o' stew. 'Now am I Clara Bow?' 'e says."

"And what did you say, Sergeant?" asks Bates.

"I said: 'Of course you're Clara Bow.' After that we were best of pals."

Bates, who listens to everything with open mouth, says: "Oi bet it was noice in Palestoin, Sergeant."

Sergeant Hands replies: "A snare and a delusion. We was doing a kind o' police job. Oranges was cheap. We got them every dinner-time."

The giant, Hodge, with bated breath, asks if they saw Bethlehem.

"Certainly," says Crowne.

"What is it like?" asks Hodge.

"Little," says Crowne.

"Hot," says Hands.

"And Jerusalem?" asks Hodge.

"Pretty much the same," says Crowne.

"And what's all the trouble about?" asks Barker.

"Trouble?" says Crowne. "Well. The Yids make orchards and blocks of flats. And the Wogs want to cut 'n. So now and again a Wog shoves a knife into a Yid. Then a Yid goes and shoves a knife into a Wog. Then the Wogs get 'old of some live rounds and shoot a couple o' Yids. Then the Yids get 'old of some live rounds and shoot a couple o' Wogs. Then we come in and tell 'em to turn it in."

"And do they turn it in?"

"Yes and no," says Crowne.

"Who wins?" asks Bates.

"Order is kept," Crowne replies. "Order is kept."

John Johnson grins, and says: "Oi bet you 'ave a noice old toime with all them Arabian dancing-girls."

"No," says Crowne, "I can't say I ever did, not actually. They're fat. It's part of their religion to be fat. They ain't sort o' particular about soap. Their best friends are just the same, so *they* won't tell 'em. They ain't 'ygienic. Zmatter o' fact, I never saw a Arabian dancing-girl. Beer cost about a bob a boll. I don't believe Arabian girls *can* dance: I never caught one of 'em at it. I 'eard one sing, once. It sounded like somebody was twistin' 'er arm. I got a nice sun-tan, though. Yes, I did get that . . ."

"Ha!" says John Johnson.

"What d'you mean, Ha?" says Crowne. "You're from Brummagem, aren't you?"

"Yes, Sarnt."

"I thought as much. A fly boy. Okay, fly boy. Let me tell you one thing. Don't you get too fly with me. Got it?"

"Oi never said anythink, Sarnt!"

"You said Ha. It's the way you said it. I can smell a

chancer at five 'undred yards . . ." Sergeant Crowne looks around and his keen glance falls on Thurstan. "What's your name? ' he asks.

"Thurstan."

" 'Ow d'you like the Army, Thurstan?"

"I dunna lak it."

"Oh, you don't, eh?"

"Na."

"Why not?"

Thurstan struggles for words, finds none, and shrugs.

"Oh, it's like that, is it?" says Sergeant Crowne. "Look, Geordie. I'll tell you something for your own good. Don't get tough with the Army. People 'ave tried it. You can't do it, specially in wartime. I'm not saying you will, mind you. But fellers get browned off sometimes, and some of 'em try going absent. They always come back, most of 'em of their own accord. Make the best of it, Geordie. A man that goes absent is a mug: 'e can't get away with it. Besides, it's a sign of yellerness: a man that goes absent 'as no guts. Say you go absent. After three weeks you're posted as a deserter; and then the police of the 'ole country are on your tail. You can't get identity-cards, you can't do a thing, except perhaps lie low in somebody's 'ouse. And if you do that you lay them open to prosecution for 'arbouring you. You live like a rat in a 'ole. In the end, you come back. Then you go to the Glass 'Ouse, and you wish you 'adn't done it. Glass 'Ouse is tougher than a Civvy jail, Geordie."

Thurstan finds a few words. You can see them struggling to get out. Each broken phrase comes away from his white face like a limping, bedraggled, dazed chick from an egg.

"Civvy jell . . . Glass Oose . . . Ah'm no fred o't.

Ah . . . Army, too. Ah'm no fred of nowt; life a deeth . . ."

Then Thurstan does something shocking.

He rises out of his condemned-cell crouch, crosses the room in two or three springs, and strikes the iron stove a terrible backhand blow. His bare fingers make it ring like a cracked bell. We leap up. Thurstan strikes it again. Then he comes back and sits down on his bed. A trickle of blood crawls from under one of his bitten nails.

"Ah can't be hurt," says Thurstan. As Sergeant Crowne lays a restraining hand on his shoulder, he shakes it off and mutters: "Let me gang."

I hear Sergeant Hands murmur: "There's going to be trouble with that geezer."

We are all a little nervous. If the Depot filled us with the shyness of boys at a new school, the Training Battalion finds us exhilarated but diffident, like boys in their first job of work.

Saturday morning finds us trembling on the brink of our first C.O.'s Parade. It is Sergeant Crowne who reassures us:

"It's a bit of cush. It's a slice of pie. The purpose of a Commanding Officer's Parade is mainly to see that you keep yourselves up to scratch. They are raising a stink in some of the comic papers about 'ow silly it is to blanco your equipment. Well, we're still 'ot on cleanliness and tidiness 'ere, just the same. Say you blanco every bit of web you've got—big pack and straps, little pack, braces, pouches, belt, sling, and gaiters—'ow long does it take you? I say half an hour. You do it once a week. Praps you go over your gaiters twice. And you're neat and tidy. That's better than going about like Franco's Militia, ain't it? You feel better if you're neat and clean. In Civvy

Street, you wouldn't go about your business with a filthy face and a ten-days beard and fluff all over your coat, would do? No. Well, no more you do 'ere. All these grousers do is shout 'There's a war on.' Well, so there is. Certainly there's a war on. But that's no excuse for going about with your backside hanging out of your trousers and mud on your daisy-roots. War on! They're telling me there's a war on!

"Listen. War or no war, any man with dirty boots or dirty web or dirty flesh goes in the report. Now then. Grumble as much as you like, but wash! Moan your 'eads orf, but clean your boots! Grouse, but brush in that blanco! It takes a extra 'alf-hour. Alright. Let it. God strike me dead this minute—if I 'ad to walk out this very second to be shot against the wall, I'd prefer to die with clean 'ands and boots. It's our way. It's our style. Like it or lump it, by crackey you'll foller it. Do you get me?

"Look at young Sergeant Butts. You've seen 'im. 'E looks like a kid."

We have seen him. He does. He is very tall and lean, like the man in the O. Henry story who, if he carries any money with him has to carry it in one note folded length-ways . . . a man of six feet two, and no other dimensions worth mentioning. His face is round and innocent. He is all elbows and knees. When he walks fast he seems to have as many legs as a spider. There is such vigour in his skinny arms that he can draw a pair of new boots at five o'clock, and have a six-months' polish on them by a quarter to seven. Though fully twenty years old, he has not yet started to shave. Though merely twenty years old, he is already a Sergeant. His nickname is "Green-gage," nobody knows why. He is purer than a girl in a convent-school—he hasn't even any theoretical naughtiness. Sergeant Butts doesn't smoke. He says he enjoys a glass of beer, but nobody ever saw him drink one. All women, to him, are sisters. If he was born in sin, it doesn't show; or, like an unsuccessful inoculation, it never took. On the first blast of *Lights Out* he is asleep. One second before Reveille he is awake, ready to levitate rather than arise. He glows with soap and inner health. Upon his round pink head, with its Demerara-sugar-coloured hair, the cocky little S.D. Cap looks too ferocious. You feel that he needs a Scout hat and a pole. If a passing A.T.S. girl happens to say "Morning, Sergeant Butts," he blushes like a neon sign and grins like the negro on the Euthymol poster, and says "He-he!" He finds it difficult to frown at new recruits, for he has no eyebrows. He has one accomplishment of which he is proud—stroking an imaginary dog. Sometimes, for the amusement of tired soldiers in his hut, he pretends to be coaxing a dog across the floor; fighting with it, tugging at it—he can lean back at an angle of something like forty-five degrees without falling over—and finally falling, overwhelmed by the dog's caresses. Sergeant Butts is scrupulously neat in his dress. His S.D. tunic is tight as an umbrella-cover; it makes him look eight feet tall.

Young as he is, he has already had his baptism of fire and blood. He was in France when things cracked. The Corporal they calls "Bearsbreath" told us the story—that sour, hard-cased, gloomy Corporal who always sits, tough and self-contained as a Brazil nut.

Bearsbreath tells of the Retreat. "Roads choked. Civvies running. Bundles. Furniture. Everybody scramming; women, kids, and all. Once in a while some dirty Fifth Columnist yells 'Gas!' and starts a stampede. Kids trampled. I wish I could have got hold of one of those

Fifth Column boys. I'd of shot him in the belly and let him dig his own grave wriggling. You know that our mob was the last to go. Covering the withdrawal. Jerries dive-machine-gunning, women and all. I saw the body of a boy of about five shot through the face. His mother was still carrying him: couldn't put him down. That's the kind of people you're fighting. Nazis. They'd kill anything. Kill your kids, too, as soon as look at 'em. Well, Greengages was cut off; him and about six men.

"He had about twenty-thirty miles to go to the coast. So he started out. His boots was pretty well scuppered even then. He dumped 'em, and slogged it barefoot, still carrying his equipment, till he found another pair. He polished 'em up, even then, just out of habit, whenever they stopped to rest. Two of the blokes with him, taking him for an example, shaved, honest to God, with bits of broken mirror to look in. No soap. But they had the habit of living or dying clean. Got me?

"Going was rough. Jerry came down from time to time, machine-gunning. Our blokes tried to get one or two of 'em with rifle fire. Got one. Slogged on. Jerry got four of Greengage's men. The other two, dog-tired, had to dump their equipment. Feet conked out. Greengage hung on to his bundook and about fifty rounds. Every time a Jerry dived, Greengage had a go. Not a hope in hell. But he had a go. And every time it came to a rest, Greengage swabbed his boots and tried to clean up a bit. Another of his men copped it. Greengage went on with one bloke. Bloke's feet conked out. So did Greengage's. But he couldn't give up. He was a N.C.O.: it'd look bad. Besides, it wasn't in him to say 'die'. Helped the other bloke along. They come to a wounded feller from Birkenhead. Greengage and the Guardsman carry him. Birkenhead feller dies on the way, so they dump him. Slog on. Get to coast. Guardsman says to Greengage: 'Go on, Sarnt. I'm not coming. Can't swim.' 'I can,' says Greengage, and tows the feller out. Three miles. Gets him to boat. Climbs aboard. Salutes the officer and passes out. It wasn't the tiredness. He had two ounces of shrapnel in his back, and some more in his leg. So there you are. He's a good soldier, Greengage. All that way, under what they might call trying circumstances, he did his best to keep neat."

When Bearsbreath told us this, Dale asked whether Sergeant Butts got a medal.

"Medal? What for?"

"Heroism."

"Heroism? He did his duty. Jexpect him to stay and get caught? Jexpect him to leave his pal behind? Ja mean, heroism? Ja think they *chuck* medals away?"

"So there it is," says Sergeant Crowne. "Take it or leave it. The order for C.O.s Parade is, belt and pouches and side-arms, and rifle. You want to see them rifles are clean. Them barrels must gleam like Blind O'Reilly, and every nook and cranny must be dug out spotless. Mind your magazine-springs: one speck o' grit and Gord 'elp you. There's a rifle inspection right after C.O.s Parade; and to-day being Saturday, the rest of the day is yours to muck about in. Got me? Geordie, be a good lad and 'elp me on with this stuff."

Thurstan holds up Sergeant Crowne's webbing. The Sergeant could easily manage on his own, but he is trying to win Thurstan's confidence.

Watching, we experience something of the thrill of the circus ... The Tamer, with supreme confidence, kneels ...

the lion opens the red cavern of his mouth. . . . The brilliantined head rests, for a second, between the hungry-looking white tearing-teeth. . . . Then the Tamer rises, bowing, and pent-up admiration lets itself loose in applause.

"Thanks," says Sergeant Crowne, buttoning his epaulettes.

Thurstan, feeling every glance focussed upon him, shakes himself.

That man is dangerous.

A bugle sounds. "Quarter. Get outside to the Square," says Sergeant Crowne. Still unaccustomed to individual movement, we go down in a tight group.

Afternoon. It blows up cold. Yes, in from the North rides a muddy-piebald squadron of clouds, the spearhead of the advancing Winter. All of a sudden the air bites. Lance-Sergeant Dagwood, a languid-seeming, slow-talking, meditative, inexhaustible old soldier out of Birkenhead, breaks up some odds and ends of timber, using only his fingers and feet. He tears to pieces a piece of two-inch plank with quiet deliberation, as if it were a Japanese wooden puzzle to which he knows the key. He is a bony man with a plain, knobbly face: the best shot in the battalion, imperturbable as a carved image, with hands like wrenches, arms that have the lifting-power of cranes, and only one hot passion—the game and play of football. Placidly smoking an absurd little pipe, Dagwood shatters a twenty-pound lump of coal to bits with one calm and awful kick of his iron heel. "The times I've done this for my old woman," he says. A match rasps; the draught sighs, then bellows. The stove is going.

"Where's Bullock?" somebody asks.

Barker says: "Boxing. Officer says 'Do you box?' Ole Bullock says 'Yes'. 'Amatyer or Professional?' 'Pro,' says Ole Bullock. The long and the short of it is, 'e's gorn to the gym. Cord blimey, I'd 'ate to 'ave to take ole Bullock on. I can use me forks a bit, but nothing like ole Bullock."

"Can he go?" asks Dagwood.

"Go? One smack from that right 'and, and yer jaw's just the place where yer teef used to be. 'E's a pro, I tell yer. 'E met Nippy Oliver."

Dagwood asks: "Who's Nippy Oliver?"

"Nippy went ten rahnds wiv Young Kilham."

"And who's Young Kilham?"

"No kiddin', Sarnt? Don't yer know? Young Kilham drew with Hymie Gold. Hymie Gold went the distance with Fred M'Aharba. Ever 'eard of M'Aharba? It's a sort of an Irish name, but 'e's a sheeny: M'Aharba is Abraham spelt backwards. 'E could of been 'eavyweight champion. No jokes, ole Bullock can fight."

"Did he beat this Nippy Oliver?"

"Certainly 'e beat Nippy Oliver. On'y 'e was robbed o' the verdict. The referee was crooked. Everybody says ole Bullock won that fight. 'E's a wildcat, Sarnt, honest to Gawd."

"Well, that's all right," says Dagwood, easily. "He *looks* like a fighter."

"See that nose, Sarnt? See them ears? Oh," says Barker, hastily, "I know that sort o' thing don't count. But . . . well, talk o' noses. I knoo a feller that kept·a pub, and to look at this geezer you'd swear 'e'd fought bare-fist with everybody from the Pedlar Palmer to Joe bloody Louis. If ever there was any trouble in 'is pub, 'e'd simply lean over the bar and say: 'Anybody askin' for anyfink 'ere?' and people 'd shut up as if somebody's

shoved a sock down their froats. Well, one night 'e got
a bit you-know, soppy, and 'e told me abaht 'is face. It
'appened when 'e was a younkster—'e fell aht of a pear-
tree, and the branches 'ad sort of bopped 'im as 'e come
froo 'em. 'E'd never 'ad a scrap in 'is life. 'E couldn't 'it
'ard enough to shake a blamange. Didn't 'ave the nerve,
any'ow.

"But ole Bullock. I can size a bloke up. I've 'ad a
few scraps in my time. I——"

Bates snatches this opportunity of saying: "Did Oi ever
tell yow about Brummy Joe?"

"Shut up, you an' your Brummy Joe. I've 'ad a few
scraps, and I can tell who to scrap wiv and 'oo not. I
wouldn't start anyfink wiv ole Bullock."

"To me," says Dagwood, "he looks a bit slow."

"Maybe, maybe not," says Barker. "But 'e'd be a swine
to try and stop."

"Ah . . . that, yes," says Dagwood. "I don't say no
to that."

Bullock comes back. He has a black eye, and a general
air of calm satisfaction.

"Well?" asks Barker. " 'Ow dit go?"

"All right," says Bullock.

"Who d'you work out with?" asks Dagwood.

"Chap called Ackerman," says Bullock.

"What, a Corporal? A big feller? Jack Ackerman, of
Y Company?" asks Dagwood, with interest.

"That's it."

"Now Ackerman is good, son. How d'you do?"

"Oh, I did all right."

"He got you in the eye, I notice."

"Oh, that? That's nothing."

"Give him a pasting?"

"No, we didn't go on long enough. We just played about."

"Think you could give Ackerman a coating, son?"

"Oh yes, I could give Ackerman a coating, Sergeant," says the serious-minded Bullock. "I went a bit easy with him. He hit me a bit. I didn't hit him much. But if I had to meet Ackerman, why, I'd get him all right."

"You'll have to be pretty good to get Ackerman."

"I've never been knocked off my feet," says Bullock. "Except once. It was a foul punch. I think it was an accident. A Jamaica nigger called Rube did it, at the Pilfold Stadium. He swung and got me in the groin. I don't think it was the nigger's fault. His foot slipped, or something. Even then I was only down for five seconds. They wanted to give me the fight, but I went on with it."

"But you got that blackie!" says Barker.

"In the last round," says Bullock.

Between Barker and Bullock a firm friendship has come into being. I see Barker's eyes gleam with triumph. "There now," he says. "Ole Bullock could smash 'em all. Couldn't yer, eh?"

Bullock says: "I can't think of anybody I couldn't beat." He is not bragging. He really cannot think of anybody he couldn't beat. He contemplates his knuckles; screws up his face, and spits a little blood from a cut on the inside of his lip, his permanently-swollen upper lip "I think I could get most of 'em. I've seen Joe Louis on the pictures. Given time, I could get him, even."

Sergeant Crowne says: "What d'you mean, given time? You mean, if you could wait sixty or seventy years till 'e's nice and old, and slosh 'im when 'e's too blind to see yer?"

"Oh no," says Bullock, very earnest, "I mean, given

enough rounds. I'd wear him down and then I'd get him. Give me twenty rounds, and I'd get Louis."

We look at one another, not knowing what to say. The Boy from Widnes says: "Don't——" and then pauses; but he sees no aggression in the dour, battered face of the indomitable Bullock, and so goes on: "Don't be such a silly Git, Bullock!"

"Why am I a silly Git?"

"Joe Louis 'd knock you silly in one round."

"Oh no he wouldn't," says Bullock.

The Boy from Widnes protests: "I saw the picture of that thur Louis fighting Max Bur. He hit that thur Bur whurever he liked. And so he would you, Bullock."

"That's all right," says Bullock, amiably.

"Come 'n get a tea 'n' a wad," says Barker.

"All right," says Bullock, and they go out.

When the door has closed behind them, a stranger, a guardsman with a sagging, humorous face, not unlike Walt Disney's Pluto, laughs a peculiar quacking laugh.

"Joke?" says Sergeant Dagwood. "What's the joke, Hacket?"

The guardsman called Hacket says: "I've seen Bullock fight twice. I saw him fight that nigger, Rube, at the Pilfold Stadium. And I saw him fight a kid called Francis in Bedford."

"Well, what's funny?"

"Well, nothing. Only he's duff. He's terrible."

"In what way terrible? Did he win like he said?"

"Yes, he won all right, just like he said. That nigger Rube was pretty lousy too; he must of weighed seventeen stone, and he was as slow as a dray horse—but even then, he was about ten times quicker than Bullock. He hit Bullock with everything he had. It sounded like hammering nails into a packing-case. Biffity-biffity-biffity-bif! But poor old Bullock kept on coming back for more. Bullock kept swinging. He might as well have sent the nigger a postcard to tell him a punch was on the way. It was as easy as dodging a steam-roller, I tell you! And that foul punch: it made me sick to see it. I thought it would have killed old Bullock. But up he got, bent double, and insisted on carrying on with it. Game! Game as they make 'em. But my God, what a lousy boxer! In the end, the nigger got discouraged: there wasn't anything he could do about Bullock. He was tired of hitting him. Then Bullock sort of crowded him into a corner and let him have a sort of a right hook. It sounded like snooker-balls. The nigger just went flat. The same sort of thing happened with this kid called Francis, in Bedford. The crowd used to like poor old Bullock: they always got a laugh out of him. To see him sort of diving about after this kid . . . sort of doing the breast-stroke, and missing every punch. He's a swinger, old Bullock. He can't box any more than a windmill. He just kept rushing this kid Francis, and in the tenth round, again, he managed to get in just one swing. It was like a buck-navvy with a sledge-hammer—just about as slow, and just about as hard. Hit this kid Francis on the shoulder and pushed him over. The kid was too exhausted to get up. But the funny thing is, he thinks he's as good as Jack Dempsey. He'd fight anything. Poor old Bullock. He doesn't know what it means to be licked. He just can't see it. The expression on his face after he beat that nigger—you'd think he'd just won the Irish Sweep. Not that you could see much of his face. It's hard to understand why a man keeps on at a mug's game like that."

"A fighter, born and bred," says Dagwood, thoughtfully.

"Yes. But a man ought to have the sense to see he's no good at the game, when he pays more than he gets at it."

" 'E wins, don't 'e?" says Sergeant Crowne, stiffly.

"Yes, but——"

"There ain't no 'but' about it. A man 'as a fight. 'E wants to win. 'E wins. That's all there is to it."

"But he doesn't win in the end; not in the long run," says Hacket. "Bullock'll be punch-drunk in another two years."

"In the end, in the end!" snarls Sergeant Crowne. "In the long run! 'Oo cares about the Long Run? If you're 'aving a fight, go in and win, and to 'ell with the long run! Let Gawd worry about the Long Run! If it's boxing, shake 'ands and come aht fighting! 'It 'ard and often, and the end 'll take care of itself. In twenty million-billion years' time, the world 'll come to an end. But it ain't my business to worry over that."

"In how many years did you say?" asks Sergeant Hands.

"Twenty million-billion."

"What a fright you gave me," says Hands.

"How?"

"For the moment I thought you said only twenty thousand billion."

"I like a man that doesn't know when 'e's beaten," says Crowne.

"But it can be carried too far," says Hacket. "Moderation in all things, as Voltaire said."

"Who's Voltur?" asks the Boy from Widnes.

"Oh, some clergyman," says Sergeant Crowne. "What was you in Civvy Street, Hackett?"

"A book salesman."

"You know a bit about printing and paper and all that?"

"A bit."

"Then your swabbing-job will be tidying up the area round the hut. You'll find plenty of paper there."

The man we call The Schoolmaster rolls up the sock he has been darning, and says: "How do we know what happens in the long run? It's not for us to consider. Why, even if some very wise man manages to calculate where things will lead in just a little while, he's lucky and clever. Sergeant Crowne is right."

The Schoolmaster is a long, calm, fair man with receding hair, and a concentrated, studious expression which makes him look at least seven years older than thirty, which is his age. He wears glasses, and is a Bachelor of Arts; speaks in a slow, carefully-modulated voice, and even on a cookhouse fatigue manages to keep his large, thin-fingered hands in a condition of elegance. He has come into the ranks in order to get out of them—after his training here he will go to an O.C.T.U., from which he will emerge as a subaltern. Suspect, at first, on account of his accent, he won our hearts by plain good-nature and unconditional mucking-in. It was Barker who said, one day, when the Boy from Widnes muttered that the Schoolmaster made him sick: " 'E can't 'elp the way 'e talks. It's the way they're brought up, son; they can't 'elp it. Frinstance, you say 'Fur ur' instead of 'Fair 'air.' The ole Schoolmaster says 'Faiah haiah.' 'E's not smackin' it on. A certain class o' people talks like that. I know a Covent Garden flar-merchant that made a packet and sent 'is boy to be a doctor. Well, the ole man—we call 'im Gutsache, because 'e suffers wiv 'is inside when

'e goes on the wallop—'e talks the thickest cockney even I
ever 'eard: ole-fashioned slang, real market stuff that
nobody can make 'ead or tail of nowdays. Ole Gutsache'll
send a boy for 'is tea like this: 'e'll say: "Gemme a you
'n' a strike,' meaning a Cup of You-and-Me and a Slice of
Strike-Me-Dead, or bread 'n' butter. Well, some time ago
I run into ole Gutsache in the *Salisbury*, and there was ole
Gutsache, runnin' on sixteen to the dozen wivaht openin'
'is mouf, talkin' to a youngster dressed up like a toff. *Les
jum' in the jam 'n' gerra pig's 't Ella's*, 'e was sayin'. In plain
English: 'Let's jump in the jam-jar (car), and get a pig's-
ear (beer) at Ella's club.' And the youngster says: 'Whay,
certainleh, Fathah.' They'd taught Gutsache's kid to
speak Oxford. But the kid wasn't puttin' on no airs: 'e
just talked that way. Same wiv the Schoolmaster. Give
'im a fair chancet: 'e can't 'elp it, talkin' like that, any
more 'n' 'e could 'elp it if 'e stuttered."

The Schoolmaster goes on:

"We all hope to live through all this, don't we? Yet
every one of us is prepared to die if necessary."

We say that we suppose so.

"Yet," says the Schoolmaster, "I don't suppose that
many of us here care much whether there's an after-life."

Hodge says: "There is an after-life. I know it."

For fifteen minutes, twenty men talk all at the same
time, at the top of their voices. After-life: there is one,
there isn't one, the must be one, there can't be one, there
might be one, there is no proof of one, there are a thousand
proofs of one, it says so in the Bible. . . .

"No," says the Schoolmaster. "We don't know where
anything will lead to. We are all, so to speak, under
Sealed Orders. We all pretend to live merely for our own
ends, but it doesn't quite work out that way. If it did,

we'd run away from the first threat of danger. We should live and die like animals, like rabbits. Nobody would ever go away from the safety of his own little place. No new things would ever be discovered. No new ground would be broken. Men would still be living in caves. No, there is something in men that makes them go beyond themselves. That is what makes us men. Right back in the beginnings, men had a queer instinct to *leave* something, to make something that should stay when they were gone. Some time ago a cave was discovered in which men had lived tens of thousands of years ago. On the walls of this cave there were pictures, very carefully drawn, of animals. Now why do you think those dead-and-forgotten savages, struggling naked in the very dawn of things, wanted to leave pictures?"

"It is a fact," says Barker, "that if you give a feller a wall 'e'll 'ave to draw something on it, or write something. Step across the way and you'll see for yourself. You don't 'ave to go back no ten thousand years."

When the laughter subsides, the Schoolmaster says: "Men are always struggling against something. But the end must remain unknown."

"Mug's game," says John Johnson.

"I daresay that is what the Guards said in Nieppe Forest," says the Schoolmaster. "But in their hearts I don't think they believed it."

"What 'appened in Nieppe Forest?" asks Barker.

"Oh . . . last war," says Sergeant Crowne.

"I heard the story," says the Schoolmaster, "from a Captain of Engineers. . . . It was one of the things that made me join the Guards, as a matter of fact. I could never tell the story half as well as he did, because he was there, and saw it happen, and felt awfully deeply about it.

He was one of the first men to become an expert in chemical warfare, after the Germans started to go all out in 1918. He had been working at something for three days and three nights, and at last, he, a Corporal, and a runner paused to rest on the fringe of Nieppe Forest.

"It was a Summer night. The officer and the Corporal took their turn to sleep. The runner kept watch. The night passed . . ." The Schoolmaster becomes a little dreamy. . . . "I suppose it passed in a timeless flash. They lay there, between a deserted village and a dark forest. And so dawn broke.

"The Engineer says that he awoke, instinctively almost, just before dawn. So did the Corporal. They listened. There was silence. Birds began to sing—first of all one little bird perched on the wreckage of something a few yards away. They watched it. Then, they realised that the enormous German push was coming. They blinked themselves thoroughly awake. And then, in the distance, they heard a gentle *shup-shup, shup-shup, shup-shup*. Men marching. They looked at each other. The noise came nearer. The men were marching into the village. They heard a terrific voice shout: *March to Attention!* Only one sort of soldier will march to attention through a deserted village. The Corporal said, in a hushed whisper: 'The Guards!' And so it was. My friend watched them as they passed, dusty with a tremendous journey along those terrible roads; but marching as if it were a Saturday morning on the Square under the eye of the C.O. . . . left, right; left, right; left . . . left . . . left. . . . They marched into the forest, took up firing positions, and settled down, that mere handful of Guardsmen, to hold back the entire German advance.

"What they did in that forest has gone down in history.

But much later my friend had occasion to pass that way again. He found them still lying there. There hadn't been time to bury them. They had been wiped out to the last man. Even in death they still held their positions. Even their dead bones remained obedient to their will to stay unbroken."

A silence.

"Grouse about regimental bull-and-baloney," says Sergeant Crowne. "Go on, grouse!"

"All those lovely fellers," says Barker. "It sort of seems a kind of waste . . ."

"No," says the Schoolmaster. "An example of that sort has got to be lived up to. Look at Captain Scott, dying horribly, all alone in an awful desolation. He didn't achieve what he set out to do. And he died. He said: 'Had we lived, I should have had a tale to tell of the hardihood, endurance, and courage of my companions which would have stirred the heart of every Englishman. These rough notes and our dead bodies must tell the tale . . .' They did. I don't suppose anything could have been more eloquent. No man's gallantry is wasted. In the last War, for instance, hundreds of letters came to Scott's widow, saying that they could never have borne what they had had to bear without the strength that had come to them through Scott. Other examples can be futile. An example of pure courage never is. A true hero gives new power to all mankind. And if he comes of your own blood, it becomes impossible for you to let him down. And if he has worn your badge. . . . No. The traditions of the British Army may sometimes have given it a narrow mind, but they have never failed to make its heart very great."

"Did Oi ever tell you about Brummy Joe?" says Bates.

"Brummy Joe. Them Guards would a been frit o'
Brummy Joe. They wouldn't o' held no positions if
Brummy Joe'd been advancing again 'em. Eighteen
stun seven and six foot three in his stocking feet.
Mind yow, Joe's got a belly as stuck out like a basin.
They said: 'One punch in the belly and Joe's finished.'
Ah. But get there! I defy yow! Get near enough Brummy
Joe to 'it 'im there. Joe Louis couldn't, with a telegraph-
pole. When Brummy was on the beer the coppers went
about armed. Once, when they pinched old Brummy,
they broke seven cruncheons on 'is pore head. One night
when Brummy went into a nam-an-beef shop for a
samwidge, the man didn't give Brummy enough 'am.
Well, so old Brummy Joe picks up the 'am-knife and cuts a
slice off the man behind the counter. As true as I am
sitting on this form, a lovely thin slice. Once, Brummy
laid out nineteen Leicester boys in Chilliam's Dance
Palace with a guitar. .Talk about Captain Scott!

"Do yow know Chilliam's Dance Palace? Oi lived ten
minutes' walk away, in Parrot Close, when Oi was
married the first toime, properly married. Oi 'ad a noice
'ouse there. Moi wiofe was noice. She didn't loike me-ee.
She fell in loov wi' moi best friend. It was loike going to
the pictures. Moi friend came to me and said: 'Oi loov
Teena.' Oi says: 'Yow do, do yow? And does Teena
loov yow?' 'Yes,' 'e says. So Oi says: 'All roight, Jim.
Yow are my best friend, and so Oi give 'er to yow.' And
so Oi pommelled 'im till 'e was black and blue, and Oi
tells Jim straight: 'Oi don't loike to beat yow, Jim, but
Oi don't want the neighbours to talk.' And so moi wife
run off wi' moi best friend, just like the pictures. Ah. She
was a foine woman, but she didn't loike me. Oi loiked
'er, but Oi didn't loike 'er cooking, so Oi used to 'ave

my meals at my mum's 'ouse. And moi woife didn't loike that.

"So then Oi fell in loov wi' a loovly girl, and she 'ad a 'usband as 'ad deserted 'er, and Oi 'ad a woife as 'ad deserted me, so we couldn't get married, so Oi became 'er Unmarried 'Usband. It's all roight. The Army recognises it, and she gets moi money. It's respectable and proper.

"Oi gave moi married woife all moi furniture. We got another place, a cottage. But whenever moi unmarried woife went out shopping, moi married woife, as is jealous of 'er, used to wait for 'er and call 'er names in the street. And moi unmarried woife called moi married woife names back.

"Then moi married woife's mother, as thinks the world of 'er, used to wait outside where Oi was working and follow me 'ome, and call me names. Then my own mum and dad used to come and troy and make peace, but moi mum never got along wi' moi married woife's mum, and they used to foight in the street outsoide moi 'ouse. And moi unmarried woife's stepmother, as 'ates the soight of 'er, started wroiting anonymous letters to everybody about me. And moi married woife set Jim on me, and Jim used to wait for me to leave the 'ouse in the morning and pick on me, and Oi 'ad to pommel 'im. And then moi unmarried woife's 'usband turned oop, and 'e started waiting for me too, and Oi 'ad to pommel *'im*, only 'e was a rough 'andful and it took me some toime. So Oi 'ad to leave 'alf an hour earlier in the morning to attend to moi foights.

"One day moi unmarried woife made 'erself a new dress, and moi married woife waited for 'er and tore it off 'er back.

"The neighbours complained to the police about the disturbance. All the kids in the street enjoyed themselves and played Ring-o'-Roses round me whenever Oi went out. Moi mates started giving me nicknames, like The Mormon, and Ole King Solomon. Moi unmarried woife's stepmother scratched moi face in the street, and moi married woife came along and 'ad a foight wi' 'er; and moi unmarried woife came out an' joined in, an' all the kids started singing and dancing. That was on a Saturday noight. Moi unmarried woife ast me if loov was worth whoile, and 'ad 'ysterics and soom women came in an' soothed 'er down. Oi didn't get a wink o' sleep. Oi made up moi moind to join the Foreign Legion. Then, on the Sunday, war was declared. Oi was on the doorstep o' the Recruiting Office two hours before it opened. Oi loike War. War is noice: it gives yow a chance to 'ave a little peace."

"And what's all this got to do with Brummy Joe?" asks Sergeant Hands.

"Give me a chance to get a *word* in," says Bates. "Oi 'aven't started yet."

But *Cookhouse* sounds. We snatch up our knives and forks and go to tea.

In the course of this meal—mug of tea, slice-and-a-half of bread, two-thirds of an ounce of margarine, and a Cornish Pasty which Barker describes as "all pasty and no Cornish"—Dale, of all men on God's earth, does something silly.

He is at the foot of the table. He wants to attract the attention of Hodge, who is pouring tea out of a three-gallon bucket. He shouts. Hodge doesn't hear, for a couple of hundred men are eating at the tops of their voices. There is an odd crust of bread lying ready to hand. Dale takes careful aim and throws it at Hodge. The crust misses our gigantic friend and—it is one of those things that luck alone can achieve; a thing beyond human skill, like the falling on its edge of a tossed coin—drops very neatly into the hand of the Company Quartermaster-Sergeant, who happens to be passing at the moment.

The Quartermaster swells. His chin comes up; his eyebrows go down. "Who done that?" he asks.

Dale, white as paper, gulps and says: "I did, sir."

"Oh, *you* did. Do you realise that you're a traitor to your country? Do you realise that you're nothing better than a Nazi agent? Do you realise that if you took and blew up a power-station, that wouldn't be no worse than what you just now done? Do you realise that this is Bread? Do you realise that Bread is the Staff of Life? Do you realise that thousands and thousands of sailors and marines drown every second for this here piece of bread? Do you realise that this is sabotage? Do you realise that in wartime, there's a death penalty for sabotage? DO YOU REALISE THAT THERE IS A WAR ON, YOU HORRIBLE MAN, YOU?"

"No sir," says Dale, losing his head. "Yes sir."

"What d'you mean, No sir, Yes sir? Are you a Hitlerite?"

"No sir."

"Then what do you commit offences like this for?"

"I don't know, sir."

"Are you mad?"

"No sir."

"Then why do you do things and not know you're doing them, or why you're doing 'em? Do sane men do that?"

"No sir."

"Then you're crazy, aren't you?"

Dale twists his face into a sickly grin and shrugs his shoulders.

"Oh," says the C.Q.M.S. "Laughing. You think it's a joke, do you?"

"No sir."

"Then what are you laughing at?"

"Nothing sir."

"Laughing at nothing. Raving mad. You must be, or you wouldn't chuck lumps of nourishing food about in times like these. Don't let me catch you at it again. Carry on."

Dale moodily eats his Cornish pasty.

"You should have nudged him," says the School-master. "In a case like that, the shock weapon is to be preferred to the missile weapon."

"What's a shock weapon?" asks Dale.

As we walk back to the hut, the Schoolmaster explains. "A shock weapon is something with which you strike your enemy directly."

"Like a cosh," says Barker.

"Exactly. Or a bayonet. A missile weapon is something that throws things and strikes your enemy from a distance, like a rifle, or a crust of bread, or a bow-and-arrow. The development of armies depends upon the development of missile-weapons. Now we are highly advanced. An aeroplane armed with bombs and machine-guns may be described as a missile weapon. So may a tank. The missile-weapon is reaching its maximum efficiency. The rifle is being supplanted."

"Rifles have their uses," says Corporal Bearsbreath. "They're easy to clean, easy to use, and easy to carry. And when all's said 'n' done, a .303 bullet in your tripes is just as good as anything else. I bet old Wellington would have been glad of a few short Lee-Enfield magazine-rifles, Mark Three."

"I bet he would," says the Schoolmaster. "After all, any man trained to use a Lee-Enfield can be pretty certain of hitting his enemy at three, four, or five hundred yards. In Wellington's day, when we carried the old smooth-bore musket known as Brown Bess, the Guards musketry would have made you laugh. We practised at a hundred yards, with six-foot targets shaped like French Grenadiers. In the best possible conditions, the old brown musket misfired four times out of ten. You had to ram a handful of gunpowder down the spout, and put in a wad, and a ball, and then pour powder on the place where the flint struck a spark, and then pull your trigger and hope for the best. Training was at a high pitch at the beginning of the nineteenth century, when a Guardsman could load and fire about eight times in a minute. A musket, then, was like a cheap cigarette-lighter—a matter of flint and steel. The chief concern of the soldier, then, was to see that his musket misfired as seldom as possible. So the first shot, loaded into the musket at leisure, was the most valuable. You had to make the most of your first volley.

"Thus, at the battle of Fontenoy, the Coldstream Guards in the front line advanced for half a mile up a slope under a cross-fire of artillery against the French who were in trenches at the top. They received the French musket-fire without replying. Then, when they were right on top of the enemy, and one Coldstreamer in three had fallen, we let fly and swept them off the earth in an absolute hailstorm of bullets. If they had fired at longer range with their first careful loads, and then hastily reloaded, about fifty per cent. of the muskets would have misfired, and the attack would have lost half its effect.

"Now do you know what I think? Our Guards discipline, which is the best in the world, has its roots in the old-time need to conserve fire; to keep a line, stay unbroken, hold the trigger-finger back until the word of command, and then let loose one shattering volley. You see, the Coldstream Guards are the only survivors of the first highly-trained British Army. We have background. We have a start."

John Johnson says: "Oi wouldn't moind foighting in the Battle o' Waterloo. It was ea-*sy*. They didn't 'ave no shells and no bombs."

"They did. Major Shrapnel had already invented his shell."

"Ah, but nothing loike now. Them old cannon-balls just bounced."

"If you saw an eighteen-pound ball of iron ricocheting and flying over the ground towards you, what would you do?"

"Duck."

·"Do you realise that discipline was such that the British infantry were forbidden to step out of line, even in the face of round-shot: and didn't?"

The Boy from Widnes says: "I wouldn't like a bang on the head with an eighteen-pound ball of iron. As far as I'm concerned, it'd be just the same as a tank."

Hacket, whose rifle-sights, having a film of dust on them, were described as "being lousy with spiders and cobwebs and dirty filthy rust and verdigris," says: "For my part, you can keep the Short Lee-Enfield."

"You ought to have a matchlock," says the Schoolmaster. "The first Coldstreamers lugged a thing about four feet long, firing a bullet weighing an ounce and a quarter. He had to pour a charge of coarse powder down the muzzle, spit in a bullet which he carried in his mouth, pour some finer powder on the priming-pan, and set it all off with a match."

"Did they 'ave matches?" asks Barker.

"A kind of smouldering rope about three feet long. He took one end of the match between the thumb and second finger of his right hand, and then—bang! A fire order wasn't just 'Fire!' It was something like this: 'Take up your musket and staff. Join your musket and staff. Blow your pan. Prime your pan. Shut your pan. Cast off your loose powder. Cast about your musket and staff. Charge your musket. Recover your musket in your right hand. Shoulder your musket and carry the staff with it. Take out your match. Blow your match. Cock your match. Try your match. Guard your pan. Present blow your match upon your pan and give fire.' All that to get a bullet out."

"And now," says the Boy from Widnes, "a Bren gun, weighing, I bet, less than one o' them thur things, can fire a hundred and twenty bullets a minute. I bet it took them about five minutes to fire. In five minutes, you or I could kill six 'undred men with a Bren gun."

"Now that's what I call civilisation," says Hacket.

Alison, the glum blond man, suddenly says: "My old woman talks tripe. She says, why don't Hitler and Churchill 'ave a set-to all by themselves and settle the war that way?"

"That wouldn't be fur," says Widnes. " 'Itler's the younger man. Old Winnie's getting on in years."

"Oh, I dunno," says the Lad from the Elephant and

Castle. "Old Winnie's got plenty of go in 'im. It's the fighting spirit, see?"

"Winnie breathes 'eavy," says the glum blond man.

"Don't you believe it," says Widnes. " 'Itler breathes worse."

"You know what?" says Bates. "If it come to that we could make Brummy Joe Prime Minister just for the toime being. Brummy Joe's a terror——"

"Tommy Farr'd be better," says Alison.

" 'E could go over wiv 'is Foreign Minister," says the Lad. "We could make Len 'Arvey Foreign Minister."

"War Minister," says Widnes.

"Nah, it couldn't be done," says Alison.

"Why not?" asks Widnes.

"Who'd do politics?"

"They could make an arrangement," says Bates.

" 'Itler wouldn't fight," says the Lad.

" 'E'd 'ave to," says the Boy from Widnes. "It'd be a diplomatic arrangement."

" 'Itler'd fight dirty," says the Lad.

"So would Brummy Joe," insists Bates. " 'E carries a foot o' lead pipe covered wi' rubber bands orf beer bottles. Brummy'd feel naked without it."

"Would they charge an entrance fee?" asks Widnes.

"Bob a 'ead," says the Lad. "Make a packet."

"Oi bet yow there wouldn't half be some excitement," says Bates. "Wi' us and the Jerries in the audience."

"Proper rough-'ouse," says the Lad.

"We'd all 'ave a go," says Widnes.

"It'd be just like a war," says Alison.

"But we're 'aving a war now," says the Lad.

"Blimey, so we are," says Widnes.

"It wouldn't prove anything," says Sergeant Hands.

"Besides, all that kind o' thing is out of date. It'd make you laugh, Crowney, the way they used to fight in the olden times. You'd meet your enemies, and you'd bow, and you'd scrape, and you'd say: 'You fire first,' and they'd say: 'No, after you,' and then you'd fire at each other a bit, and so on."

"Don't be silly," says Sergeant Crowne. "War always was war, and when it come down to brass tacks, it was the same as it is now. You try and kill the other feller, and the other feller tries to kill you."

"It's true," says the Schoolmaster. "What Sergeant Hands says is true. Look at what happened when the Coldstream Guards fought the French at Fontenoy. They came face to face with the French Guards. They halted fifty yards away. Lord Charles Hay of the 1st Guards took off his hat, and drank the enemy's health. The Coldstream officers did likewise. The French Guards returned the salute. Then Lord Hay said: 'I hope, gentlemen, that you are going to wait for us to-day, and not swim the Scheldt as you swam the Main at Dettingen.'

"So Lord Hay turned to his own men, and said: 'Men of the King's Company, these are the French Guards, and I hope you are going to beat them to-day. Gentlemen ou the French Guards, fire!'

"The French Commander answered: 'We never fire first; fire yourselves.'

"The English Guards then cheered the French, and the French Guards cheered back. They were thirty yards away from each other. The French Guards raised their muskets. A Coldstreamer said: 'For what we are about to receive, Lord make us truly thankful.' Then the French Guards fired. About nineteen Guards' officers went down, and a large number of men. Then it was our turn. We

opened fire. Our musketry was known and feared all over
the world. The British officers were walking up and down,
tapping down the musket-barrels of the men to make
sure that they aimed low. We kept up a running fire,
wiped out the whole of the French front rank. And so we
cut through to the French camp."

"Well," says Crowne, "I'd see myself damned before
I'd invite any Jerry to fire at me first. ''It first. 'It 'ard
Keep on 'itting.' That's my motto."

"It depends, though," says Dale.

"Depends on what?"

"Who you're fighting, Sergeant."

"No it don't. If you fight, fight to win, and get it over.
If you got to fight, fight for keeps. If I *like* somebody, I
don't fight 'im, and so I don't take my 'at off to 'im or ask
'im to 'it me first. . . . It makes a nice story, Schoolmaster, and if it's in 'istory, then it must be true. But that
sort o' thing is a thing o' the past. If I 'ad to pick ten men
to lead in a bayonet-charge, I'd pick men that 'ated
Jerry's guts and wanted to see the colour of 'em. I
daresay there's two sides to any argument, but for my
part I don't care a twopenny damn. My side's the right
side, or I wouldn't be fighting on it."

"I agree with you," says Hands, "but you can't get
away from being English."

"Who says you can?"

"Nobody says you can. You can't get away from your
breeding, that's what I say. I've seen you myself, Crowne,
with my own two eyes, during that bit of a riot. You were
using your hands. In the heat of that fight, when there
was a Wog coming at you with a knife, you boxed,
Crowney, you *boxed*. If there'd been a referee watching
you you couldn't have kept more above that Wog's belt-

line. It's an instinct. It would have been all right for you to have used your feet. I used mine, I know. But it just didn't occur to you not to fight Queensberry. My brother talked just like you. But once, when he found himself wounded, in the same shell-hole with a wounded Jerry, last War, he shared his iodine and dressings with him. Though he would have killed him in a fight, any day, mind you. It's drummed into your head as a kid. You can't get away from it. But I don't mind admitting that what the Schoolmaster told us about letting the Frenchmen fire first is a bit too much of a good thing. Why, it's a wonder they didn't just come over and shake hands and call the war off, after that. *I* would of."

"It's good publicity," says Hacket. "I bet those Frenchmen said to themselves: 'What decent fellows these Englishmen are.' And it helped to undermine 'em."

Hands says: "English soldiers behave decent, instinctively; put Englishmen down anywhere and they'll be decent. Just as Guardsmen automatically form a straight line and keep their heads up. It's *in* them to do so. Isn't that what we're supposed to be fighting for?"

The Schoolmaster says: "A war can be an affair of honour just as a duel can be."

"You don't fight no duels with murderers," says Crowne.

"Hear hear," says Dale.

Hands looks at him. "What are *you* fighting for, Dale?"

"Well," says Dale. "The Nazis have got to be stopped or they'll be everywhere."

"You, Widnes?"

"Because there's a war on, Sarnt."

"Hodge?"

"Hitler is bad. If you give in to un, you give in to

wickedness. If you don't fight wickedness, you encourage wickedness. It'd be wicked not to fight Hitler, don't ee see?"

"Alison?"

"I don't know and I don't care, Sarnt. If the whole bloody country's fighting, what d'you expect *me* to do? Read a book or somethink?"

"Shorrock?"

"No Dictator tells *me* what to do."

"Crowney?"

"I like what I like. I'm not satisfied with England, not by a long chalk, but it's *my* country and I'm used to it. You can, at least, grouse round 'ere. Get me? I'd rather die grousing if I fancy grousing, then live bottled up. And there's something about those soppy goose-stepping mugs that I 'ate the sight of. I don't know what it is, but they set my teeth on edge. They get my goat. I wanna kill 'em."

"And you, Schoolmaster?—and you don't have to give us a song and dance about the Battle of Waterloo."

"I'm fighting for the same as everybody else . . . to preserve what there is that's decent and good in the world."

"Barker?"

"Sarnt, shell I tell yer the honest truth?" Barker imitates the portentous tone of a politician. "I am fightin' to make the sea free for the banana trade."

"Bearsbreath?"

"Turn it up," says Bearsbreath. "This sort of thing bores me."

"Me too," says Crowne. "Turn it up, Hands."

"I'm trying to find out our War Aims," says Hands.

"Let 'em keep their sights upright, 'old their bundooks

firm, and squeeze their triggers," says Crowne, "and they'll 'it whatever they're aimin' at."

"Yuh," says Dagwood, slicing his last, precious bit of twist with a jack-knife. In this knife you may find clues to the character of the good Birkenhead sergeant: he has guarded it for a dozen years, using it constantly. The big blade is worn narrow towards the point. He never uses the small blade: that is for emergency; but both blades are honed to razor-edges. If the need arose, he could mend his boots with that knife, or cut his way out of a place with it, or pick a lock, or perform a minor surgical operation, or carve a doll for a small girl or a boat for a boy, or cut a man's hair, or kill him. "Yuh. You've all got to learn to shoot. You do some revision on rifle and Bren. Then you fire your course, wearing fighting order. Like the School-master says, musketry is always useful."

John Johnson of Brummagem says: "Oi want to get moi 'ands on a Tommy-Gun." Quite unconsciously, he says this out of the corner of his mouth. One can see the filmic fantasy with which he is entertaining himself . . . gangsters . . . the roar of fast cars . . . *tupatupatup!*— and an enemy falls on his face.

"They're handy little things," says Dagwood, "at fifty yards or so, they're handy."

"Give me a Bren every time," says Hands.

"A Lewis, for rough work," says Crowne. "A Bren is too accurate, sometimes. You put too many rounds in the same place. You can't miss with a Bren. Any mug 'ere could score well with a Bren. But say you've got a mob rushing you, why, then it's just as well to spray 'em a bit, if you get what I mean."

"The prettiest thing I ever saw in my life," says Bearsbreath, "was a shot with an anti-tank rifle. In France. Did you ever come across Cocky Sinclair? He got a Jerry officer and seven Jerries with one shot. It was as pretty as a picture. And that was the only time I ever saw an anti-tank rifle fired from the shoulder. I didn't know it was possible. It ain't possible. But Cocky was as strong as a bullock. He's a stronger man than Ack-Ack Ackerman, even: stocky, a neck like a damned tree. He hoisted that anti-tank rifle up to his shoulder and let fly. And down went eight Jerries, plugged as clean as a whistle. The recoil knocked him down. While he was sitting on his backside, a Jerry plane came swooping down. He re-loaded, just like he was handling a short Lee-Enfield, and laid back, supporting the anti-tank on his foot, and fired at the plane. And so help me God he brought it down. I didn't learn till afterwards that the first shot broke Cocky's collarbone. The whole point was, he was annoyed."

"What 'appened to Cocky?" asks Crowne. "I put 'im inside, once, for insubordination."

"Oh, Cocky was always in and out of the moosh," says Bearsbreath. "He went absent once. The inside story of that was this: Cocky had a sister. See? She was all the relations he had. Cocky was sort of attached to this sister. Well, one day she got into trouble. Some bloke. This bloke treated her rough. She was a soppy sort of piece, and couldn't take care of herself. This bloke gave her a black eye one night when she asked him to sort of marry her. Cocky got to hear. He couldn't very well ask for a long week-end just to give a bloke a hiding. And Cocky never told a lie in his life. He couldn't. If he tried, he got tongue-tied and contradicted himself. So he just done a bunk, and went home. He borrowed the fare off of me.

That's how I knew. He got hold of this feller, and gave him the biggest coating you ever saw in your life. Then he came back, reported himself, and paid off fourteen days C.B. That was in peace-time. If he'd explained it to the C.O., I don't know, but I daresay the C.O. would have let him off light. He didn't like to. Said it made his sister out to be not respectable. The funny part is, this bloke married Cocky's sister, and has never raised a hand to her since."

"Where's 'e now?" asks Crowne.

"Oh . . . around, somewhere. I hear he pulled some bloke out from under a burning car outside Dunkirk: lifted the car up by the front axle and kicked the bloke away. I shouldn't be a bit surprised. He was a wild man in the Depot, but he got to be a good soldier afterwards."

"Some *are* wild," says Dagwood. "But as I see it, a wild man's all right, so long as he takes to a bit of discipline in the end. You've got to direct that wildness. Ever take the charge out of a .22 cartridge? It's little grey grains of stuff, sort of crystals. Put a match to it and it goes *phut*, a little puff of flame that couldn't hurt a fly. Pack it in proper, and that same pinch of stuff will send your bullet just where you want it, and pretty fast, too. Personally, I like a wild man. It's a sign of spirit. There are very few proper soldiers that haven't been inside once or twice. The officers understand that. They may talk all wrist-watch, but they're not mugs, most of 'em. You can be wild, but wild in the proper place."

Now in the hut there sleeps a Corporal who is an instructor of physical training. They call him Strangle-hold: he is an expert in Unarmed Combat. But his real name is John Ball. He came into the Army—it is an open secret—under false pretences, calmly perjuring himself.

Ball said he was thirty-one: he is thirty-seven, but of the type known as "Baby-Faced." He needs to shave only twice a week. There is a juvenile bloom upon his pink-and-white cheeks. An accidental-looking pinch of ash-blonde down on his upper lip represents the accumulated moustache of twenty years. His eyes are like the eyes of a baby, they are so full of quiet wonder and clear innocence: his teeth might be milk-teeth. The merest draught stirs his fine-drawn golden hair. He weighs thirteen stone, is constructed like a Greek hero, spent seven years in a Highland regiment, and at thirty-odd made a living as an all-in wrestler under the pseudonym of "The Child Wonder." His voice is high-pitched and peculiarly flat and metallic, with the carrying-power of a cowbell. When annoyed he can trumpet like a bull elephant. He spends most of his spare time writing interminable letters to a girl in Middlesbrough: she is a Baptist, and he is a Freethinker; his communications are oddly compounded of ardent love and passionate reasoning. He hates sentimental music. When he gets up in the morning he does handsprings, and sings at the top of his voice. Nobody has ever told him that he is tone-deaf.

Ball says:

"You talk about discipline and what not. Well, take a look at this." And he throws down a photograph. "Do you recognise me?"

We do and we don't. He is standing in a group. Seven or eight little men, dark little men, are leaning upon rifles. Ball towers over them, with his fair, shining face. He is carrying a rifle, also; but as the camera clicked he instinctively drew himself into a military attitude, and so stands, stiff as a poker, properly at ease. He is dressed in a kind of forage-cap, a shirt, and trousers. A blanket is rolled and slung about him. Fantastically, through his rags, there has burst the white fire of the good old British Regular Army. Everybody is covered with dust.

"Where's this?" asks Crowne.

"Spain," says Ball. "When the Civil War was on, I had a sort of crazy fancy to get into it. So I slipped into Spain and joined the Government Militia."

"Well I never!" says Dagwood.

"Bit of adventure, you know," says Ball. "I didn't care who won, so long as it wasn't Hitler and Musso. So I joined the Militia. I'd had seven years in the ———— Highlanders. I thought I might put it to some use, you know. And I had the chance of seeing good men with bad discipline. Nobody belly-ached about regimental nonsense more than I did before. But since then I'm dead regimental, as anybody'll tell you.

"Those dagoes had enthusiasm. They had nerve. They could stand the pace. But what bust them, apart from lack of equipment, you know, was their discipline. They'd got several different kinds of politics, too, you know, and that's always a bad thing for soldiers. They were *fighters*, you might say. But what was the use of it? Without discipline, they were a mob. The lousy Fascists were very little better, but they had better equipment, and what with one thing and another, they won. But it struck me that if my mob had got proper discipline, the Fascists could have been smashed up in Spain, you know; and then we'd have another ally at this present moment, instead of a Hitlerite in power in Spain. I did what I could, you know. But we were a rabble. With one battalion of Coldstream Guards, we could have taken Franco's shirt off his back."

"I bet you saw some sights," says Dale.

"I saw some sights. The Fascists had brought the Moors in. The Moors are used to torturing. Fascists like that kind of thing. I saw some of the things the Franco boys did, you know. We came into a sort of dusty, greyish-brown village. . . . Well," says Ball, "the other day I happened to look at somebody's bright red belt thrown down on a brown blanket. I happened to look at it while I was thinking of something else. And I didn't sleep that night, and when I did drop off about four o'clock I had dreams. You'd never believe what a woman can have done to her, and still live."

"But you gave them a taste of their own medicine when you copped 'em, I bet," says Barker.

"No," says Ball, "we didn't. You don't stop that kind of thing by doing it yourself. We strictly did not do anything of the kind. That's just where the Fascists are mugs, you know. They go in for tortures. That makes everybody hate them. They cut their own throats. I've seen the remains of people, all charred; soaked in petrol, you know, and lit. One of those dead bodies is a better argument against the Fascists than all the speeches in the world. And you don't think we were mugs enough to give them similar arguments against us? Besides, if you're fighting against a fellow because you don't want what he stands for, damn it all, you don't go and do just the very thing you're fighting to put a stop to. Do you? Even if you want to, you don't."

"I dunno," says Barker. "People must be mugs to stand for Nazis."

"People are mugs to stand for anything they don't want to stand for," says Shorrock.

"Don't be silly," says Old Silence. "Remember that Fascism and Nazism live by *compelling* people, in the first place. And so the Nazi becomes expert at making you do things you don't want to do, *making* you stand for things, *making* you betray people you love——"

"——" says Sergeant Crowne, using a rude term of disagreement. "I'd like to see anybody or anythink make me do what I thought was lousy!"

"Me, too," say several others.

Old Silence strokes his lank chin with a long, dark hand, and says:

"Assume something hard to swallow, Sergeant Crowne. Imagine—just for the sake of argument—that England was sold, and made a dishonourable peace with Hitler. *It can't happen*, but just *imagine* it."

"Well?" says Crowne.

"You're imagining that. Imagine that England did as Pétain did. All right. You're imagining that. The War is over. We are disarmed. We become a sort of vassal of Hitler. Are you imagining that? They still call us 'England,' but it's only a name, a label. The Nazis hold all Europe. The Army is disbanded. Time passes. Are you imagining it? Ten years pass. Ten years. And after ten years, you, Sergeant Crowne, meet Sergeant Hands in, let's say, Holborn. All right. If Hitler won this war, this is the kind of scene you'd find yourself in, Sergeant Crowne. You meet Sergeant Hands. And you talk. This is how it goes":

And Old Silence, making patterns in the air with his smoking cigarette, tells his impossible hypothetical story:

"Look," Hands might say, "how about a beer?"

And Crowne replies: "Whatever you say. I don't mind."

"Beer, then. Look, we're quite near the old 'Red Lion.' What about there?"

"Like old times," says Hands.

"Ah, those were the days, eh? Remember Bella?"

"Do *I* remember Bella? What about you? You always had a bit of a soft spot for Bella."

"Not me," says Crowne. "Well, maybe a bit. But she liked you best. She said you had nice eyes. Remember?"

"Ah, that was a long time ago," says Hands.

"Well, well, well. After all these years . . ." says Crowne.

"Yes. I've often thought about you. Time and time again I've said to my old woman: 'I wonder what's happened to old Crowne.' Ellen always liked you. She said you had personality. Over ten years, and you haven't changed a bit. Good old Crowney! I knew you as soon as you came round the corner. That walk. . . . God in Heaven, how it all comes back!'"

"They used to call us the Heavenly Twins."

"Didn't they, though?" says Hands. "Bella used to call us the Heavenly Twins."

"I'd have been jealous if we hadn't been pals," says Crowne. "But how is good old Ellen?"

"Best wife I ever had. Hardly a grey hair."

"And the kids?"

"All right, I suppose."

"What," says Crowne, "you only suppose?"

"No, no," says Hands, "they're fine. Only . . ."

"Only what?"

"Nothing. Nothing at all. But you know how it is. You sort of . . ." Hands pauses, and then says: "As an old pal. As one old soldier to another, and as man to man . . . you get sort of fed up."

"True enough," says Crowne.

Hands says: "I can see it in your face, too. Oh, well. In the old days we had our worries, but my God, Crowney, my God almighty, we were *men*, at least. Remember when they called you Grouser Crowne? Those were the days, eh? You had something to say, and you said it, straight from the shoulder, right out, bang, and done with it. Good old Crowney! Grouse now and see what it'll get you!"

Crowne wants to change the subject. He says: "It's a nice day." But Hands is full, you understand, and he talks a bit.

"Once upon a time we could talk, we could grumble. Things were different, then. You were a man. You still had your soul. Your thoughts were your own. As long as you've got a voice in things, as long as you can still say: 'I like this and I don't like that,' things aren't so bad! But now! Honest to God, Crowne, you can't trust anybody. They've got our kids. They've educated our kids to think their rotten way. But I'm talking too much . . ."

"I'm your pal," says Crowne.

"I know it," says Hands, "but things have got me down. Still . . . you'd never betray me. You never let me down. And sometimes I feel that if I don't talk, I'll burst. I'll go mad . . . and then . . ."

"Beer," says Crowne.

"It's such a price," says Hands. "Remember? We thought the beer back in 1941 was bad. Well, I'd give a lot for a pint of 1941 bitter and a packet of real tobacco fags. What *is* this stuff?"

"Chemicals."

"And the tobacco . . ."

"Muck."

"Do you remember, Crowney, when you used to be able to walk into a place and buy a steak? Underdone?"

"With proper chips," says Crowne.

"And peas? Why damn it, cheese! Remember Cheddar cheese?"

"They used to *give* it away! Well, practically. . . . A few pence a quarter of a pound."

"We live on German leavings," says Hands. "On rubbish. And we'll die on it."

"Us," says Crowne.

"Englishmen," says Hands.

"We should have died first," says Crowne.

Hands goes on: "After the steak we'd have a cup of tea, with real milk and sugar."

"Real tea," says Crowne.

"And change a ten-bob note and get some silver back."

"Look at me," says Crowne. "I got a rise last week. Know how much I get now? Seven hundred thousand pounds a month! Paper. My kids are getting thinner and thinner. Bread at two thousand five hundred pounds a small loaf . . ."

"And what bread? Acorns, sawdust, filth! By god, Crowney, sometimes I want to rush out into the street and shout—give 'em the old shout, the good old shout that made the rookies jump!—shout: 'Long live England! Long live Liberty! Long live Democracy! God blast the Nazis! Live free, or die fighting!' . . . and get shot down like a man, Crowney, like a *man*."

"And me, Hands," says Crowne.

"Honestly? Truly?"

"I saw my mother die of hunger," says Crowne. "Under my eyes she died. And my wife too. What do I keep going for? For my kids. They hate my guts. I'm not a proper

F.

kind of Fascist, or Nazi, or whatever it is. But they're my kids and I can't help loving them, Hands."

"I'm glad to hear you talk like that," says Hands. "Where are you living now?"

"Goering Boulevard. It used to be Victoria Road. Number 76. Always home by six. And you?"

"7, Hitler Avenue. Well, I've got to scram. You'll keep in touch?"

"You bet," says Crowne. "It's like a breath of fresh air seeing you again."

"Well . . . (look out, somebody's listening!) . . . Heil Hitler!"

"Heil Hitler!" says Crowne. And so they part.

Hands walks East. Soon he pauses: stands, biting his nails—just as he's biting them now—and then goes into a telephone booth. He dials a number and talks:

"Give me 55X," he says. "Here is CBH/888. Take this down. *Crowne.* Got it. 76, *Goering Boulevard.* Got it? Yes. Seditious talk. Subversive activities. Spreading discontent. Treasonable propaganda. An enemy of the Reich. Go get him. He will be home at six."

A pause. A horrified silence. "What?" says Hands. "What? Do you mean to tell me that I'd do that? Me? Me, Hands? Why, you. . . . What, me? Turn nark? Turn informer? Rat? Me? On my pal? On my pal Crowne? Or on any man, let alone Crowne? You . . ."

Old Silence replies: "Listen a moment, Sergeant Hands. We were imagining a case. Still imagine that the Nazis came to power here."

"Well?"

"You've got a daughter."

"Two."

"And a son?"

"Two."

"In ten years' time, your daughters will be young women, and your sons young men. You love them, Sergeant?"

"Better 'n anything."

"And if a Nazi official threatened to send your girls to a House, for the entertainment of German soldiers, or workers? And to do some terrible things to your sons? You'd do anything on earth to stop that, wouldn't you? You'd consider your daughters and sons more important than your old pal, wouldn't you?"

With a strange touch of tenderness, the savage Sergeant Crowne says: "Hands. I wouldn't bear you any grudge if you turned me in to save your kids. I'd see your point, and we'd still be pals."

"By Christ," says Hands, quietly, "I wouldn't be alive to see that day, Old Silence. Not while I had even a tooth left to fight with."

"That is how Dictatorships are kept going, though," says the Schoolmaster.

"Over my dead body," says Hands.

"And mine," says Crowne.

Sunday. We rise thirty minutes later. This being a day of rest, we only have to scrub the hut. The Catholics go out early, for Communion. There is a United Board service; a spiritual coalition of Baptists and Congregationalists, held in the place called the U.B., in which there is a tea-bar . . . a good tea-bar, at which there presides an old soldier with one finger missing, and an Alsatian dog with a nonconformist air. Almost everybody else is marched off to Church Parade. The Camp is silent.

F*

In our hut only four or five men remain—three Catholics, a Jew called Shaw, and Old Silence, who is down as an Agnostic.

Shaw is the four letters in the middle of *Warshawsky*. The name was sawn down to fit English tongues, when Guardsman Shaw's father came West from Czestochowa, where the Black Virgin is, in South West Poland. There had been rumour of a pogrom. In Kishinev, unborn children of Jews had been delivered prematurely and posthumously with bayonets. Warshawsky got out. Guardsman Shaw was born on British soil; but only just. He is a tallish, slender, pensive man, to whom are attributed strange rites and outlandish ceremonies. During eight days every year, he eats no bread, because the bread of the ancient Israelites, delivered from the Land of Egypt and the House of Bondage, had not time to rise before they packed it. There is a period of twenty-four hours in which no food and drink passes his lips, and he keeps the Great White Fast in a synagogue, to the accompaniment of ardent prayers and strange, nostalgic songs. Here, he eats what he gets; but at home nobody would dream of cooking meat which did not come from a beast that chewed the cud and also had cloven hoofs, and had not been killed according to a certain ritual. His father has never shaved, in obedience to Mosaic law, and would die sooner than eat a milk pudding after a dash of meat, and wouldn't eat at all if he couldn't wash his hands first. Shaw has never tasted pork, oysters, lobsters, eels, rabbits, or anything that creeps or crawls, or any fish that has not both fins and scales. He gives away his breakfast bacon, and will not smoke after sunset on Friday until after sunset Saturday, on account of the law which forbids the kindling of a flame on the Sabbath. There is money in

his family: his father made a good deal out of gowns.
Guardsman Shaw, in civilian life, is an accountant. He
went to a good school. A studious and on the whole
unworldly person, he abandoned his office and volunteered
for the Guards because he felt that in this manner he
stood a good chance of getting at some Nazis hand-to-
hand. Beneath his bookish exterior, something simmers.
He is the type of the fighting student that held the walls of
Jerusalem against Titus, and argued over the split hairs of
the Law as the catapults quivered and the javelins hissed
past. He smokes interminably, never drinks, and possesses
a kipper-coloured violin upon which he plays melancholy
music. He needs to be watched: otherwise, he will switch
the radio on to a quartette in Something Minor or a
Concerto in D before you know where you are.

A young Catholic named Dooley says, rather severely:

"You know what, Shaw? I bet they wouldn't let you do
things like this in Germany. Believing what you like, and
all that."

Shaw, who tends to sententiousness in argument, says:
"They couldn't stop me believing. They could stop my
expressing my beliefs," and he picks a phrase of Bach's
Toccata and Fugue in D, pizzicato, out of the violin on his
knee.

"You ought to think yourself lucky," says Dooley.

"I do," says Shaw; and tries to get the viola parts
of Beethoven's Quartet in C Moll, but fails. "I am
lucky. This is the best place in the world to live in.
My father came from Poland, when Poland was part
of the Russian Empire. He was astonished when he
found that the English police were polite to him, and
that they didn't expect bribes. He couldn't believe that I,
his son, would have equal rights with any other British-

born man. Jews had no rights worth mentioning where he came from.

"He came here just before I was born, with my mother and a sister of mine, two years old. Well, it happened that he did fairly well after a good deal of hard work, and after a year or so was actually able to afford a holiday at the seaside for us all. I was a very little baby. My sister could walk: she was a beautiful child. One morning, my father took my sister and me for a walk along the front. He was pushing me in a pram, very slowly, while my sister toddled along by his side, holding on to him. I believe he was just about to cross the road, when a great big man—my father must have told me this story a hundred times—a great big man in a check suit, with a beard and a fine swaggering air, stopped and looked at me, and gently pinched my cheek; and looked at my little sister, and patted her on the head, and said: 'Fine children.' 'Thank God,' said my father. The gentleman in the check suit then asked him how old we were, and my father told him: 'The boy is eleven months old, and the girl is four, bless them, Mister.' Then the gentleman put a hand in his waistcoat, and took out a golden sovereign, and gave it to my sister; said: 'Good morning to you,' and walked on. My father, looking after him, saw men who were passing raising their hats to him. He asked somebody who it was. It was King Edward the Seventh.

"My father was overwhelmed. There was a country for you! A King, an Emperor! And he walked along without a bodyguard, and stopped a poor Jewish tradesman, and was civil to him and kind to his children, in the open street! And my poor old father, who had some very bad times still fresh in his memory, burst into tears. My sister cried too. I, catching the infection, howled at the top of

my voice. After that my father walked with his head held
high. He felt he was part of a wonderful country, and he
would have died for England after that. So would I.
Sometimes I feel that even the English don't realise what
they've got, in England. That wireless. . . . The other
night somebody got Hamburg, and we listened to Lord
Haw-Haw: listened, and laughed, and of our own accord
cut him off. Does it occur to you how marvellous it is that
we can do that? Fascists and Nazis are sent to prison for
listening to English broadcasts. And in the library, there's
a copy of *Mein Kampf*, though nobody bothers to read it.
Think myself lucky? I am lucky. So are you."

"And you, Silence," says Dooley. "I bet you wouldn't
be allowed not to believe in anything anywhere else."

"And you, Dooley," says Old Silence. "The Catholics
have been persecuted in their time, too. But who says I
believe in nothing?"

"You've got no religion," says Dooley.

"Well?"

"Then what can you believe in?"

The man called Old Silence sits still and looks out at
the bright morning, while Shaw, caressing the strings of
his violin with the white bow, produces a gentle melody.

"The other night," says Old Silence, almost to himself,
"I couldn't sleep. I was thinking. I was thinking of gods,
and men, and prayers; and there came into my mind
something . . ."

"What?" asks Dooley, for Old Silence has paused.

" . . . something that might be a prayer."

"To *who*? To *what*?" asks Dooley.

"*For* what?" asks Shaw.

"It went something like this," says Old Silence.
Half-closing his eyes, and looking at a beam of sunlight

in which the tiny dust-motes dance, he gravely declaims:

"*I can't believe in the God of my Fathers. If there is one Mind which understands all things, it will comprehend me in my unbelief.*

"*I don't know whose hand hung Hesperus in the sky, and fixed the Dog Star, and scattered the shining dust of Heaven, and fired the sun, and froze the darkness between the lonely worlds that spin in space.*

"*The world flies through the night towards the morning.*

"*Oh Universe, so far beyond human understanding! I know that a thousand worlds may grow cold and die between two of your unending heart-beats. I know that all the sciences and philosophies of man—all his findings and seekings—all his discoveries and inspirations—are like flashes of a mighty, misty panorama seen through a chink in a rushing train.*

"*I know that man, in his little space of time, may catch only a glimpse of Truth, like the last deseprate glance at heaven of a lost wayfarer falling into an abyss.*

"*I know that suns wane and earths perish. But I also know that I can see the light of dead and forgotten stars.*

"*I am lost in awe at your beauty, immeasurable Universe! Yet I am not afraid of you, and so I know that between the handful of grey slime in my head, with which I think and plan, and the threads of my nerves which miraculously tie my thoughts to my eyes and lips and fingers, there is something more. It is something that is Man's. It is a Soul.*

"*About this I cannot reason. I do not know. I believe that the soul of Man cannot die. I do not know what it is, or why it is, or how it comes, or where it may go. It made the beast-shaped dawn-man conquer his instinctive terror of the elements. It looks out of me with calm love for the greatness of things, with joy in its power to praise noble things and wonder at eternal things, and with hope in its yearning to cleanse from life the squalor of unclean things.*

"Oh Life! Light! Universe! Let me have strength to struggle always and keep unsoiled my pride in the presence of Fear! Give me the power to bear with a straight back all the burdens that Life can heap upon me! Give me the will to find new horizons and build new things! I am a poor creature; a shadow. But since I stand on a mountain of dead men and breathe the dust of a million years of man's broken endeavours, let me be no less than the first speechless man who with fine faith and blind courage crossed the first river! Give me strength to live and work, knowing that every movement of the finger of the clock beckons me towards a hole in the ground!

"I know that this life, and the death that goes with it, are only phases. Let me keep out of my heart the ancient, terrified ape that clutches, howling, at the breaking branch! Give valour to this dust and dignity to this clay! Give me kindness, patience, understanding and endurance, so that I, who love poor lonely Man, may help him to find some happiness on his way upwards to his unknown end!"

"Dust of a million years," says Barker, who has come in meanwhile. "Let's get this swabbing over 'n' done with."

Beds crash back. Buckets clank down. Brooms clatter. Corporal Bearsbreath begins to shout: "C'mon! Thirty of you! This hut ought to be dug out and finished in thirty minutes! Get a rift on! Get a jazz on those scrubbers! Johnson, don't let me catch you skiving!"

The Lad from the Elephant, in mad enthusiasm, hurls down a bucket of water and runs amok with a long scrubber.

In forty-five minutes, the hut is damply clean. Later it will rain. To-morrow the hut will be dirty again. For the next seven days we will conduct a sort of Lucknow against the detritus of the earth which the rain will turn to mud, and the warmth of the hut will turn back to dust . . . against the dust and ashes which always lie in wait.

"In the East," says Sergeant Hands, "there's whole cities buried under yards and yards of muck. That's what comes of not getting the place properly dug out. So be warned! Dirt buries you alive if you let it. Furthermore, as senior N.C.O. in this hut, I get the blame if the place is in tripe. And that," Sergeant Hands mutters, "is worst of all."

Barker says: "My mum's been digging aht our 'ouse for forty-two years and a quarter. It's still as dirty as it was when she started . . ."

"You'll find," says Crowne, "that even this little bit o' dampness will get into your rifle-barrels. Watch out for your barrels. They're sensitive as a young girl's cheeks. And you're going to fire your course. So nurse them barrels."

And so the course is fired. Those of us who flinched a little at first (when, on the thirty-yard range at the Depot, the noise of a .303 rifle-shot seemed to smash and reverberate like a cannon) find a strange exhilaration in the clear, crisp bang of rifles in the open air. A nice sound, accompanied by a pleasant nudge which hints of huge power, and a clean, keen antiseptic smell of burnt explosive. Those good, noisy, bleak-looking ranges, muttering with echoes! We fire gravely, and with concentration. We lie down with bucko sergeants and fire our Bren-gun course, and see the sand splashing brown on the butts, and the black or white discs hovering, oscillating and coming to rest where our bursts have punctured the targets.

We are becoming soldiers. The first strange excitement wears off; and so does the first uneasiness. The Depot seems very far away. We swore we'd never forget Sergeant Nelson, and yet we have already begun to forget him. He, at this moment, is hammering the crude stuff of brand new recruits . . . working, as on us, with frenzy and patience; pleading, roaring, urging, damning, dropping rare hints of praise; manufacturing more of us. But we, seeing new squads coming into the Training Battalion, stand, in our baggy canvas suits, and comment upon the manner of their marching. "Not bad," we say; and "Likely-looking rookies"; and "They're not getting too bad a mob of kids at Caterham these days."

A C.O.'s Parade has no terrors for us. In the ancient days, seven or eight weeks ago, we dressed for our last inspection with the tremulous, dewy-eyed anxiety of brides on the last dawn of virginity. Now, rushing back five minutes late from P.T., and having fifteen minutes in which to change before the Quarter blows, we curse hideously but are not in the least dismayed, and turn out smarter than we ever turned out at the Depot, to march with something resembling the proper swing, the subtle swagger . . . "As if you owned this ground you march on! And if you owned the ea-hearth!" the R.S.M. roars, in his voice which shakes a little from its decades of thunder.

We are acquiring experience in field training. We begin to get the diagnostic intuition of the soldier looking for cover. We can keep an Arrowhead Formation without looking. Night and the open heath have restled to our crawling, when we started to pick up the secrets of prowling on patrol. Any one of us can clean a Mills Grenade, and put the fuse in it, and screw it tight, and throw it so that it bursts in a mean spray of jagged iron at thirty or forty yards. They have given us Bren until we are slightly sick of Bren; but we can handle that invaluable light machine-gun with the slightly bored accuracy of mechanics with familiar tools. Night, dark midnight, has seen us marching away to the shadow-lands behind the golf-course, where, in black invisibility, we have dug weapon-pits. And we know all about trenches, because we have dug them: buck navvies in uniform have sighed with a strange joy at the feel of picks and shovels; and sedentary men among us, puffing and grunting, have learned the technique of making holes and paid for their learning with little coin-shaped bits of skin.

Some of us, who would have shrunk like tickled oysters at a hint of punishment, have committed crimes and paid them off with carefree laughter. Yes, the serious Dale, the good clerk whom a rough word depressed, got three days C.B. for missing a parade. He said he didn't know: the Company Commander said he ought to have known, and so Dale had to answer Defaulters three days running, and did some drill that would have reduced him to a gibbering heap six months before. And he said: "What the hell, anyway"; to which Sergeant Dagwood said: "That's the spirit."

There is no getting away from the fact that we are changing. Shorrock is down to eleven stone ten, and there is, so to speak, meat-juice in the dumpling of his face. What is more, he argues less frequently, and lays down less law. He is the same Shorrock. But he has seen something of the world; of the wide and varied world that is England. He'd never spoken to a Devon man before, for example. To him, Rockbottom still represents all that is brightest and best in England, but his contempt for the rest of the world is tempered a little. He has had to listen to people telling him things, for the first time since he left Rock Bottom Wesleyan School. He has mixed with new men. He despises the Cockney, but concedes to him certain virtues; which he didn't before the war. He has acquired patience. He has lost flesh and gained outlook; narrowed physically, and broadened mentally. "There is no Rockbottom but Rockbottom, and Shorrock is its Prophet." This will hold good until the Pennine Chain is down to its last link; but the dogma has softened, admitting the Moderation of inter-county tolerance. Shorrock, meanwhile, having decided that he has a genius for driving, and being attracted by the sturdy little caterpillar-wheeled Bren Carrier (which somehow resembles himself) has gone into a Carrier Platoon.

Hodge, the giant, the man impregnable; Hodge, of huge thews and rock-founded faith, never changed. There was never anything in Hodge that needed to change. Hodge is an elemental force. If ever Hodge struck down an enemy, he would be striking not a man but a wickedness: not that the man, as representative of wickedness, could hope to be spared! He has gone into a Suicide Squad. A man in a Suicide Squad does not want to commit suicide: his career in it is a denial of the possibility of death. The Suicide Squad man is a man with a mission. He, personally, discounts Death as a possibility while his mission is unfulfilled. In the Canal, Hodge swam like a fish and dived like a seal. On land, he was indefatigable. He was immense, but proportionate; could run like a hare, perform unheard-of leaps, and hurl things to uncalculated distances. To Unarmed Combat he applied a certain grave, sober concentration. Imagine a statue of the Farnese Hercules endowed with a will. Even Corporal

Ball was clay in his stupendous clutch. Yet Hodge is gentle. His fingers, large as a baby's arms, have a strange delicacy of touch. The Lad from the Elephant and Castle will tell you how Hodge took a splinter out of his finger, which no tweezers could reach. Hodge yearned to come to handgrips with the Devil. It was natural that he should go into a training-place for parachute troops. By now, his training completed and his vast arm embellished with a pale blue winged parachute badge, he will have been called back to get in the harvest; and that being done with, he will return to fight the good fight with all his terrible might—the old, elemental Anglo-Saxon.

Dale, as I indicated, has toughened. He always had everything in him that a man needs, but it took the rough society of soldiers to peel from his essential self the pale sheath of the city. A certain primness has dropped from him like a cloak, and there has come into his face a look of confidence. His shoulders seem to have set, as a boy's shoulders do when he loses puppy-fat. It happens—I tell you, it happens! Dale was a man (pardon the expression) seated on his bottom. He has learned to use his hands and feet—and behold, the riddle of Samson is reversed! Out of the meat comes forth the eater, and out of sweetness comes forth strength. The Schoolmaster has gone to his Officer Cadet Training Unit. But that gentle soul has got himself a certain physical resolution which nothing in his life before could ever have given him. Nothing could ever make that man less than a gentleman: but he has got something more than a theory of manual labour, and something deeper than a bookish sympathy with the thing he calls The People. He has come across the units that go to make up the strange, docile, cantankerous, trusting, suspicious, colourful English Masses. He will be a better officer for that, and a wiser man.

Certain people, of course, don't change, and never will. Barker is the same. So is Bullock, his bosom friend. They remain the same for different reasons. Barker, the eternal Cockney, is supple. He is bamboo. He is many-jointed, but straight and tough. He will bend with every wind that blows, because that is how he is constructed for the stern business of survival. He has only one real shape and attitude, and springs back to it. The hurricane thinks it has levelled Barker to the ground; but the wind grows tired, and Barker stands upright. Bullock is unchangeable because nothing but death will ever move him. He stands stiff, and will break before he bends. Dour, solemn, narrow-minded, cautiously good-hearted, his great flame of indomitability always burns hot and strong. He is intransigent; a gnarled tree. He met that smashing fighter, Ack-Ack Ackerman, and they fought a draw. A poor boxer, but a dreadful man to fight: that is Bullock. If he changed, there would be the end of him. We ought to thank God that such men do not change.

Widnes, the boy who used to have wire hair, has taken to the Army. You have seen, perhaps, a new-hatched waterhen slipping into a pond and instantly swimming? Widnes, as soon as he felt his way among the back-alleys of army procedure, found himself in his element. He has put on weight, and will put on more. He took a Corporal's Class, and, having triumphantly come through the hell that the Drill Sergeants hand out to prospective N.C.O.s in the Coldstream Guards, went On Orders and was told that he had been awarded the rank of Acting Unpaid Lance-Corporal. He is making the Army his career. Soon, he will be a Corporal, then a Lance-Sergeant, then a Full Sergeant, then Company Quartermaster Sergeant, then Company Sergeant-Major, then Drill Sergeant, then Regimental Sergeant-Major; and then an aged man, erect as a telegraph-pole, with a voice like a football fan's rattle and an impermeable respectability—a man like the great Charlie Yardley of the Training Battalion, or Britton, whose voice still paralyses men at eight hundred and fifty yards. Wars may come and go. Widnes will perform his duty, and take world calamity in his stride. It is feared, in certain quarters, that he may turn out to be heartless; but Sergeant Dagwood says that this kind of thing passes, like the gloom of adolescence; severity in a Young Corporal, he says, like wildness in a Recruit, is not necessarily a bad sign.

But John Johnson changed. He, fundamentally, is the Brummagem Fly Boy. But the Army has dealt with Fly Boys, since time immemorial. When dogs bring forth cats, then Fly Boys will get away with things in the Guards. There was one incident which, I think, undermined Johnson's confidence in the fly technique. There is a shambling, big-boned man from the wildest moors of Yorkshire, a sort of peasant who falls down rather than sits, and has to get words up out of himself with a conscious effort. This man is called Old Jeddup, because Sergeants are always saying to him: "Hold yer head up. C'mon! Old Jeddup!" He weighs sixteen stone. A young subaltern, on a night stunt, tried to teach him how to move silently. Old Jeddup melted into the heather like a weasel and came back with a buck rabbit: he used to be a poacher. We have thousands of such healthily law-breaking sons of the soil in this army. Old Jeddup, bar by bar, bought five shillingsworth of chocolate to send to his little son. He packed it in a small box. He fumbled and tangled himself with the string in the presence of the

Fly Boy, and ultimately got the box tied up and tucked away in his tin of personal effects. Then he took it out again, and looked at it. John Johnson winked at us all and asked him how much he wanted for it. Old Jeddup said: "What's it worth?" Johnson, being as fly as they come, said: "Quick! Half a dollar!" Old Jeddup said "Cash?" "Cash," said Johnson; and Jeddup said "Done." He handed over the box, and took the half-crown. But the box he handed over was empty; he had prepared a duplicate in advance. Then he told Johnson how this was the oldest of all confidence tricks, and gave him back one shilling. It undermined John Johnson, who, thinking thereafter before he demonstrated, automatically became more wise and less fly.

Johnson, with all his false ideals, makes a good soldier, if only out of vanity; for he would die a thousand deaths rather than look silly. Bates, that simple man, has the profoundest admiration for him. But Bates is basically the simpleton. He has nothing in his nature more complex than a punch in the mouth. He is beloved. Bates is affectionate. He has a childish ingenuity. If somebody sends him for a left-handed monkey-wrench he assumes that such a thing must be procurable, and won't go away until he gets it. He believes what he is told, and the more firmly a thing is said, the deeper his belief in it. Then if a mob-orator shrieked Fascism at Bates, would he swallow that, too? He might repeat as gospel what he had heard, but he is the last man on earth who could live in the state of affairs that would come out of it, because he sets a vast value upon his personal liberties. A bit of a fool, Bates: but never, if you value your profile, never push him around; unless you happen to be his wife. And even then, not beyond a certain point.

But what happened to Thurstan?

The Hut. Evening. Sergeant Crowne sits, setting up a new S.D. cap. In order to achieve the rigid rectilinear front beloved of the Guards, men evolve arrangements of adhesive plaster and bachelor buttons that might have been worked out, in fun, by Heath Robinson. So Sergeant Crowne struggles, muttering.

I shall not forget that night. It was the death-night of my beloved friend Old Silence. The occasion fixed itself in my memory. It is possible that I may forget my name. But that time, that place, and that atmosphere I can never forget. I did not learn about Old Silence until later. He had got seven days' leave, to be married. He had been a lonely man, like Larra in the legend, living like a shadow on a horizon beyond the ordinary cares of humanity. Just before he had been called into the Army, Old Silence had fallen in love with a woman, who fell in love with him. Life, thereafter, had a new and fine significance for him. He discovered new things, deep and high. And so he had left us for seven days, singing in the cracked, uncertain voice of a man unaccustomed to singing, after we had slapped his back, and yelled encouragement, and helped him to put on his webbing, which John Johnson, of all men, had helped him to blanco. Everybody loved Old Silence. The Lad from the Elephant stole a horse-shoe and made ready to hang it over the vacant bed.

He was due back that night. He did not come. A week later, when conjecture had exhausted itself after every man had rejected the possibility of desertion, a letter came. Old Silence had been married. There was a breakfast. The letter stated it nakedly . . . a small breakfast for four guests. He was a man who loved everybody, and therefore loved nobody in particular. He had few friends, for he had a habit of silence, as his nickname implies. A raider dropped a bomb, and the remains of Old Silence were found with those of his bride. He had arched his back over her, trying to protect her. They were both dead in their first and last embrace. He died with his song unsung. There are few of us who would not have interposed ourselves between a bomb and him. Peace to Old Silence in the immensity! This is not the time to tell of the kindliness, the magnanimity, and the strength of that man. He was my friend. He died that night.

The radio was on. Because, at that moment, there was nothing available that was more to everybody's taste, we tolerated a record of Caruso singing some *Ave Maria*. The Sergeant In Waiting, who, that week, happened to be Sergeant Hands, pushed his head into the hut and said: "Well . . . Humphrey Bogart's gone absent."

Thurstan was called by the name of that distinguished actor of criminal roles, because of a certain hangdog trick of the head and his brusque manner of speech. Besides, Humphrey Bogart can look every inch a killer; and although there was no actual resemblance, Thurstan resembled him in his manner.

"Gone absent," said Crowne. "That settles it."

"Pore——" said Barker.

"Why pore——?" asked Sergeant Crowne.

" 'E's crazy," said Barker. " 'E's not right. There's somethink wrong with 'im. 'E ought not to be in the army at all."

"Mug," said Hands. "Where'll it get him? But I've been expecting this all along. He was working up towards it. I could see it. He's been in trouble since he's been here.

Remember when he socked Tucker for touching his boots? He's never been out of trouble from the first week. You could smell this coming. I despise a man that goes absent just like that. It's a proof he's got no guts. Even if he don't like it, he ought to stand the racket. *I* didn't like it. Nobody does, at first. No. Well . . ."

Sergeant Hands went away on his bicycle, about the complex and endless business of the Orderly Sergeant.

It was the Schoolmaster who said: "You ought to understand Thurstan. I could see this coming, too. I'm about the only person who ever talked with him.

"Thurstan is a wild animal. But I assure you that he's all right. He's had a rotten life. Don't condemn him too quickly. He's a decent fellow and a proper man. Don't laugh at me when I say that. You don't understand what the trouble is with Thurstan. Shall I tell you what? He can't talk."

"How d'you mean, can't talk?" said Crowne. " 'E's got a tongue."

"Sergeant Crowne! You've got a tongue. But tell me— can you explain exactly what you mean by the first pressure on a trigger?"

"Well, no, not if you want me to put it altogether in words. No, I can't."

"Can you explain what you mean by a corkscrew?"

"In actual words? No."

"Can you describe what you see when you see a puff of cigarette-smoke?"

"No."

"But you've got a tongue. And a tongue isn't always enough. It's like saying: 'You've got a pen. Write a book.' I'm about the only person who has talked to Thurstan, and I'm telling you that the thing that has made that man ferocious is, that he's never been able to say what he's wanted to say. That sounds crazy. But I've had his story from him.

"His father was an animal. He used to beat his mother. She was a silent woman. Thurstan never really learned to talk. Nobody talked to him. He came from a village in the wilds of the North. He hardly went to school at all. Do you remember how he'd always ask somebody to tell him what was on the detail: usually me? He couldn't read or write. He's ashamed of it. He was ill-treated by everybody except his mother, and she never talked to him, and he was unable to express his sympathy for her. As soon as he was old enough—and he was a strong kid—he went into a mine. I can't get a clear idea of what he did, because I don't know the circumstances. But he was in charge of pit-ponies, or something of that sort. And it seems that he had reason to be scared of one of them."

A Northern collier says: "Ah. They can be orkard."

"It seems there was a black pit-pony. It went mad and chased him. He saved himself by pushing a lamp into its mouth. But he hadn't the nerve to go back. He was ashamed of that, too. When he went home his father beat him. He couldn't explain himself. He got a terrible thrashing. He ran away from home. After that he lived as best he could. He never learned to say what it was necessary for him to say. You know how necessary it is for a man to talk a bit. Thurstan never did, never could. He married. His wife was afraid of him. She found somebody else. He couldn't do anything except fight it out, and went to gaol for three months. When he came out, he fell in with a mob of dock-rats. He went in for robbery. He was let down by his associates, and caught. He didn't talk: he wouldn't, and anyway, he couldn't. He did another six months. He went to Liverpool, and fell in love with a girl there. But he couldn't get around to talking to her. He not only had nothing to say, but he couldn't even begin to say the things that he felt he *had* to say. He didn't have confidence. He'd start a word, and end by grunting. You've heard him.

"Now everybody knows what it is to feel that he'd like to have a chat, and yet have nobody to talk to. Imagine poor Thurstan, poor old Thurstan. He comes of a race that loves to talk and tell stories. He felt he had a lot to say. But it was choked back in him. So he became silent. The most dangerous thing in the world is, for a man to become silent. That's what happened to Thurstan. There was only one way in which he could express himself; by using his hands. He knew only one argument: physical violence. He felt inferior to things, except when he could hit them. He has had terrible fights. He's a fighter. But he's always run away. To Thurstan, there has never been any use in explanation: there was nothing he could explain. It was all in his head, but he could never get it out. When things became too much for him, he simply left them. It wasn't cowardice: it was that he didn't know any other way of dealing with things. He ran away from the pit to somewhere else. From there, elsewhere. He's horribly alone. Life was too much for him, and he welcomed the war. He ran away from life, as he knew it, into the Army. And then—poor fellow—the Army was too much. He felt he didn't fit. And so he's run away. And I am willing to bet on something."

"What?" said Crowne.

"He'll be back in two days," said the Schoolmaster. "He's never spoken, but he's listened. He'll go away from here, right into the teeth of everything he ever wanted to get away from. Here, he has men fighting with him, instead of against him. Here, people are willing to teach him things for nothing, even to read and write. Thurstan is silent, but only because he *can't* talk. He's no fool. He'll think it out. I'll bet a hundred cigarettes to twenty that he'll be back in two days. Two days from to-night. A hundred cigarettes to twenty. Who takes me?"

Pause.

"Well?" said the Schoolmaster.

"Taken," said Hacket.

It happened quite dramatically. At that moment, Sergeant Hands came back. "He's in," he said. "Reported himself to Sarnt on Guard. Talking! Says: 'Take me back. Here I am. Shove me inside. I'll pay it off. I'm willing to be a soldier.' And then he says it's on account of Captain Scott. Nuts, I tell you, nuts, crazy, crackers!"

With a radiant face, the Schoolmaster said: "Give me that twenty cigarettes! I'm telling you that Thurstan is a good fellow."

"Or the value thereof," said Hacket, and laid down one shilling and one penny; the price of twenty Woodbines. "Fags are scarce."

Fourteen weeks have eaten themselves up. Our Company Sergeant-Major, the Iron Duke, wily old soldier, case-hardened roughneck veteran, has warned us. The Detail confirms it. We are for the Holding Battalion. This is a sieve through which all Guardsmen must pass; a clearing-house; a pack from which one is dealt. Companies go there, stay a while to mount guards in London, and so depart to rougher and dirtier work. This parting, now, fills us with no such sense of amputation as we experienced when we left the Depot. We have almost lost—though we never could quite lose—our tendency to thrust out roots wherever we rest. We have forgotten what it means to have any but portable property. All that we need to eat with, march with, sleep with, and defend ourselves with, is contained within the ninety pounds or so of our equipment. We have the habit of mobility. We have become soldiers.

As we hammer down the stuff in our big packs—(with what hopping anxiety did we assemble our first Change Of Quarters Order in the prehistoric period before we came here!)—Sergeant Dagwood looks at us and smiles. He has an ugly, lumpy face, every wrinkle and pore of which is a secondary masculine sexual characteristic, like hair on the chest; this powerful, gentle Sergeant. It breaks into a smile of remarkable charm. Years of command have hardened it: you cannot shout an order and look pleasant at the same time. But when he smiles, friendliness shines through his countenance like sunlight through a bomb-battered wall.

"You're off," he says.

"Yes," says Bates, "we are, yow know, Sergeant!"

"Yump," says Dagwood. "It's a long time since I was at the Holding Battalion. I'll never forget my first Buckingham Palace Guard. As soon as we were took off, I was run into the cooler. I'd lowered my butt an inch in turning. *I* didn't know. What was it I got? I forget. I think it was seven days. I can't remember. It's nice to be going to the Holding Battalion for the first time. It's nice to be young. Look: do your best on guard at Buck or Jimmy. It's not nice to let the mob down. So do the best you can.'

"You can be good to look at, and a good soldier at the

same time. No, honest to God: the better you are, the better you look. It's true. It's a fact. There's no argument. Do your best: be good pals and do your best, eh? All the old regulars, all the old sweats, tough guys, were particular about putting on a good show when they just had to be show-soldiers. Harry Wyatt of the Third Battalion—Number 5854—he did a good guard, and he got the V.C. That goes for the Lance-Jack, Bill Dobson, too. And Brooks, and Tom Whitman, and Norman Jackson: V.C.s too, all Last War. It's not all bull and boloney. *I* tell you it's not.

"Last War. People used to say: 'We can sleep to-night: the Guards are in front of us.' Well, keep that up. As a personal favour to me, keep that up. The Last War was only a war, a sort of ordinary war, compared to this one. It starts slow, but it doesn't finish, you know, till one or other of us goes down. There's going to be rough stuff. There's going to be hell. Well, that's all right. You know me. I'm a Sergeant. It's been my duty to tell you what to do. You know that if I've opened my mouth and bit your heads off on parade I was always one of you, and your pal, off parade. Man to man—keep it up, for Christ's sake keep it up. After all these hundreds of years . . . no, it'd look bad, *bad!*

"Anybody got a light? . . .

"The proper fighting hasn't come yet. It's coming. Now, in Civvy Street, old geezers of eighty are heroes. You can't do less than them. You won't. It's not possible. This isn't a lecture. I'm not demonstrating something out of the book. Just talking to you. You're Guardsmen now. You know the whole story. Well, fight good! Keep it up! It might be that any one of you finds himself alone, right in a ditch. Still keep it up! And keep it up in proper order. Go to heaven or go to hell, but wherever you go, go clean!

"But what am I talking about? *You're* all right. Good luck to you. The best of luck. In this mob your best pal never writes to you. It doesn't matter. He's still your pal: you know him and he knows you. I'll never hear of any of you again, unless you get a V.C., or something. That's all right, quite all right. Only: keep it up! Do you get me? *Keep it up!*"

At this point there comes into the hut a razor-lipped man with immense shoulders and the icy eyes of a killer, no less a person than Ack-Ack Ackerman. He looks down his beaked nose at Bullock, and says:

"Fair is fair. Wanna tell you. The worst smack I ever had in my life was that right you landed on me. My head rung like a bell. I could never wish for a better fight."

"Nor me, neither," says Bullock. "And thank you very much."

"Thank *you*," says Ack-Ack Ackerman. "Well . . . good hunting. And watch that left. Adieu, but not good-bye. . . ."

And so we march away.

PART FOUR

THE FINISHED PRODUCT

EVERY midday the old sweats foregather at the Naffy. There is a Company clerk, a crumpled man, who has seen more years in service than he cares to remember. He is the leader of the little group of elderly soldiers. They meet at twelve and drink a species of watered bitter. He always buys the first round. He says one word, "four", and the barman puts out four pints of mild ale. Then, the crumpled Company clerk hands out the beer. An ancient warrior, medal-ribboned in all the colours of the rainbow, the withered man who waters the cricket pitch, snatches the first pint. This man is called Geordie, because he comes from somewhere far north. He snatches his drink says "uh" then sips it; puts it down, and then invariably explores his right ear with a matchstick. He is a very old soldier; a sombre man of twenty years' service; but he was old when he joined. There is another man, also from the far north: they call him Jimmy, and it is said that in thirty-five years of Army life he has never quite escaped trouble. Jimmy has an outrageous, an uproarious cheerfulness. No press in any civilised land could reprint his language. His imprecations are horrible. His blasphemies are unbelievable. He invokes impossible diseases, strange gods, and non-existent physical organs of unmentionable saints. Thirty years ago he was a corporal. Now, in the twilight of his life he is a Guardsman; a wicked, old Guardsman, still huge, still terrible and still riotous. It is odd to hear the somehow youthful flamboyance of his language tumbling out of that ancient, sunken mouth. And there he sits, invariably to the left of Geordie; both drinking acidulous weak beer. With them, always, sits a little tubby tailor. Rumour has it that this tailor owns thirty houses, and is a man of landed property. Everybody applies to this tailor on questions of real estate. Tradition has grown up about him. If he died with nothing in the bank, the Guards would feel that they had been cheated.

He has a greyhound.

He calls it a greyhound. It is a long dog. He calls it Bartholomew. Between Bartholomew and the enigmatic little man there is a dark understanding. The tailor, though a warrior, I mean an old soldier, is a man of peace: yet one kind of talk with him is fighting talk—talk against the dog Bartholomew. If you cast any aspersion upon the heredity of that dog you have Tubby, the tailor, to contend with. It is a greyhound, a greyhound of greyhounds, compared with which Mick the Miller is as stationary as a bedstead and a mere thing on four legs.

If you give him half a chance he will not fail to tell you the legend of the dog Bartholomew.

"Listen," he says, "look. Just look. Look at that back. Look at that chest. That dog is all lungs. So help me God, if he took a deep breath he'd raise up into the air, so help me God, like a balloon. So help me God. And this dog, this here mortal dog, Bartholomew, you may believe me or you may believe me not, was the fastest thing that ever walked. The fastest thing, so help me God. And he was owned by a toff. Are you listening? Do you hear me talk? By a gentleman, so help me God, a gentleman. But this gentleman—it can happen to any of us—so he was down on his luck. And you know how, good God, there can be all of a sudden a sort of a stroke of sort of luck? Well, this here gentleman, so it seems he has a sister who has a dog (excuse me) a bitch, a greyhound bitch. It's all right! A bitch, for a dog, isn't swearing. Well, this sister of this gentleman, so she goes so help me God, to Southdown and this here bitch sort of goes out and then she sort of comes back and then she sort of has pups. Five. Five pups. Well, this gentleman's sister is a judge of dogs.

"These five pups.

"Two, so help me God, she drowns. Three she gives away, but one she keeps.

"Did I say five? I said six.

"Now, this gentleman's sister, so the pup she keeps is this here pup. And no sooner can this here pup walk than—so help me God it runs. Listen, I am telling you something. I suppose you know that every living thing when the sun shines upon it casts a shadow. There is a law about it. Look. This here dog, this lovely dog Bartholomew, if he took off—and so help me God he did take off pretty frequent—you could see, just for a second, a sort of black patch on the ground. Not for more than a second, mind you, he left his bloody shadow behind him. But of course, only for a second.

"Well, the gentleman, this here gentleman, he was down on his luck. So he says to his sister: 'Irene, lend me a monkey.'

" 'Monkey,' she says, 'I ain't got no monkey. But I'll tell you what I'll do. I'll give you this here dog Bartholomew.'

" 'What do you mean you will give me this here dog Bartholomew,' this gentleman says. But they take him out on the Sussex Downs, and they say 'Run!' and so help me God this here dog runs so that this gentleman who is a judge of dogs swears that he has never seen anything like it in all his life.

"So this gentleman says 'Thank you very much,' and takes the dog to Brighton, and trains it up and down the Palace Pier. And so help me God it is a fact that nothing that ever ran was one millionth as fast as this here dog Bartholomew.

"And so, this here gentleman he goes here, and he goes there, and he borrows a fiver from this one, and from that one, and he raises two hundred and fifty nicker, and he enters this dog, this dog Bartholomew, for a race, and he shoves this here two hundred and fifty nicker on this here dog Bartholomew.

"O.K. O.K.? All right, O.K. Comes one day before the race. All this here gentleman has to do is to take this lovely dog to the White City for the race he has entered in. But this takes train fare. And this gentleman—mind you, a proper toff—has not got the price of the fare. He asks his sister. No go. He has sort of tapped his sister sort of heavyish in the past, and she will not stand for any more of it, no, not even for tosheroons. Well, so this gentleman finds some mug, and this mug has a motor-bike, and what does this gentleman do?

"No, no, that's all right, not a drop. Well, half a pint. All right, a pint.

"This gentleman borrows the motor-bike and a couple of leather straps. He straps this here dog Bartholomew on to the back of the motor-bike and, so help me God, he burns up the distance between Brighton and London, and then when he comes to unstrap this dog Bartholomew, the wha'd-you-call-it—dumpity-dump—vibration—of this motor-bike has imparted itself, as they call it, to this dog Bartholomew. And he trembles, poor thing, like a leaf. He bobs like a recruit. I am telling you that this here dog Bartholomew has a nervous breakdown on account of the vibration of the motor-bike, and when he is let out of the trap at the beginning of the race, instead of running after the rabbit, he runs the wrong way. He bites three stewards, he does a sort of a death-howl, but nevertheless he does something like half a mile in something like fifteen seconds. But, so help me God, in the wrong direction. And so, the gentleman sells him to me for a dollar to get his fare back to Brighton where he hopes to tap this here sister of his.

"And even to this day this here dog Bartholomew, whenever he hears a motor-bike, has hysterics. Otherwise this dog would make Mick the Miller look like something that crawls on a whatsaname. You may laugh."

And the dog Bartholomew crouches at his feet. It may be a greyhound, but a purist would call it simply a long dog, with too much chest and too much ears and too much tail and not enough legs. But the tailor's faith in that dog is something beautiful and profound, and nothing in the world could shake it.

To this group there also attaches himself a military policeman, a member of the dreaded Gestapo. He is the weather expert whom I have had the honour of mentioning once before: a man with a mild face and a West of England burr—a man whom, at one glance, anybody might recognise as the father of a family. He upholds the law, but with apologies. He joined the military police because he felt that this, somehow, would keep him closer to his wife and five sons. They call him Himmler. He resents this. He is a mine of misinformation upon every subject under the sun. If you wish to know the opposite of the truth about anything, ask Himmler. It is Himmler who knows that to have your ears pierced is good for the eyes. He knows that a cancer is either male or female, and, when removed by a surgeon, cries out of its own accord. If you want to know all that the moon can do, ask Himmler; for it is he who can tell you that the moon, and nothing but the moon, turns hair white, breeds fleas and is responsible for dust.

The group sits. Between the library and the main body of the restaurant, there is a kind of a closet containing a bar scarcely more than three feet long. This dog-end of space belongs to the group. The old sweats. They sit here from precisely noon until the stroke of two, after which they go about their unknown business.

The Old Sweats sit, full of small beer and big talk, puffing pungent Woodbine-smoke. They are mostly Camp Staff. This was a Summer Camp before the War: they used practically to hibernate in that canteen throughout long Winters, spinning endless tales of which nine-tenths were lies. Sometimes they are joined by a dried-out old Scots Guardsman and a fifty-year-old Grenadier nearly seven feet tall.

The Grenadier, whose origins are in Cumberland, has a gift of dramatic diction. He can make a story out of anything—nearly always a tragedy, an epic of martyrdom and injustice.

"Ah!" he says. "I knew Harry Nicholls."

"And who's Harry Nicholls?" asks Geordie, scornfully.

"What? You don't know Harry Nicholls? Why, he got the first V.C. in this war!"

"It's a dirty lie," says Geordie. "A dirty, filthy, rotten,

stinking lie. The very first V.C. in this war was won by one of our kids, a Coalie, d'ye hear?"

"I know this for a fact," says the Grenadier, with a tremendous gesture. "The first V.C. since 1935. Number 2614910, Lance-Jack Harry Nicholls. He boxed for the Battalion. Heavy Weight Imperial Service Champion. May 1940, he was wounded in the arm by shrapnel. But he led his section on. Over the ridge they go, the whole company. Do you hear this? And then, biffity-bif! The Jerries open up with heavy machine-guns, at pea-shooter range. So what does old Harry do? He gets hold of a buckshee Bren, he does, and he rushes forward firing from the hip. From the hip he fires. He gives one machine-gun a burst, and he wipes it out. Then he gives another one a burst, and silences it. They filled Harry full of lead. But he went up to a higher bit of ground so he could get a good look at practically the whole of the Nazi infantry. And he shoves in another magazine, and lets the Jerries have it. He killed about a hundred of 'em. But he didn't stop firing till he had no more rounds left. It is the truth, as sure as there's a God in heaven, kids—my ole pal Harry Nicholls held back the whole German army single-handed, and got his company safe across the River Scheldt, though he was filled so full of bullets that there wasn't room in him for any more and he was walking in a great splashing pool of red blood. What happened to him then? He was dead. He must have been dead for half an hour. But the soul of that man was such that he couldn't stop firing until he hadn't a round left to fire with. So the company gets over the Scheldt, by crackey, and poor old Harry was left behind. Dead, says you. Dead, says they. Dead says all of us, and the King gives his widder a V.C. on his behalf. And then what news comes through? Why, Harry

Nicholls wasn't dead at all. You can't kill a Grenadier. I'm telling you, you can't. Nicholls is alive, in a German hospital, getting over all them wounds. And God help Jerry when Harry Nicholls gets better again! He'll come smashing out, he will, he'll come crashing out of that heap like a fire-engine out of a shed, and he'll be back. My old pal Harry."

"Your old pal nothing!" says Geordie. "You never met him."

"Say that again!" cries the Grenadier.

"You 'eard," says Geordie. "How *could* you of met him?"

"Never you mind how I could or could not have met my old pal Nicholls," says the Grenadier. "My old pal Harry was the first V.C. of this war, and that's all there is to be said about it."

Geordie says a naughty word, laughs heartily, and says: "A Coldstreamer was the first V.C. of all. A chap called Strong. Crimea. Shell comes over and drops in among a mob of our boys. All right, laugh. A shell, I tell you. A sort of holler iron ball, crammed with gunpowder, and fizzling with a fuse. Like a firework. Only dangerous. This thing comes plonk at their feet. It's due to go off in a split second. It's too big to run away from, and too heavy to lob back over the parapet. So Strong, a Coldstreamer, picks up this shell, and hugs it to him, and runs and runs and runs, gets to the parapet and tosses the shell over, just as it bursts."

"He wasn't the first V.C.," says the Scot, and the argument that follows may be heard a hundred yards away through all the noises of the Camp.

Then somebody says: "What d'you mean, 'first V.C. since 1935?' There wasn't a war on in 1935."

"Get out of it," says the long Grenadier. "There's always a war on. There's always something, anyway. Up on the Indian frontier, there's raids, and there's all manner of skirmishes all the time. Nobody hears anything about 'em. But there are. And I tell you that medals get won every day, war or no war."

"You're a liar," says Geordie. "I don't believe a word you say. You and your Harry Nicholls. Don't make me laugh."

"I tell you it's true."

"Was you there?"

"No, I admit that I wasn't exactly there."

"Then how d'you know?"

"Why, you ignorant ——, you, it's history! Do you think they give V.C.s away for nothing?"

"I don't know! Why, you lousy Billy Brown, I've earned the V.C. a thousand times."

Roars of laughter.

Geordie shouts: "I have! Thousands of times. And what did I ever get? Damn all is what I got. I don't believe anything about anything. If you ain't seen it with your own eyes, you don't know it's true."

"Dinnot talk rubbish," says the Scot, sourly; and says no more.

"Ever see a conjuring trick?" asks the Grenadier. "I once saw a man cutting a woman in half. All right. I saw it. So was it real? Was that man really sawing that woman in two?"

"Well, not properly, not thoroughly," says Geordie, evasively.

"Then how can you believe what you see?"

"I don't believe nothing!" cries Geordie.

"Look," says the Grenadier. "You can be mistaken.

But if a thing *actually happens* to a lot of people at once, it's *true*."

Geordie replies: "A lot of people all at once see that man sawing a woman in half."

"That didn't actually happen. They was made to think it was happening."

"Same thing," says Geordie.

"Why, you obstinate swine, you swining obstinate pig! Don't you dare to fly in the face of History. You drunken slob! Didn't you once tell me with your own two lips, you dirty liar, that you'd seen a ghost outside the Y.M.C.A. one night?"

"And so I damnwell did," says Geordie.

"You're a one to talk, then, about not believing in anything. That's what *you* are: I fluff you, all right. Truth. scientific fact like a V.C., honest scientific fact like my old pal Harry, you don't believe. But ghosts, oh yes! You fairy!"

"That was no joke," says Geordie. "It was sober truth as true as I sit in this chair. God strike me down dead this minute if I didn't see it. Outside the Y.M.C.A., I tell you. And it wasn't night-time, but broad staring damnation daylight. I was going along that road, and coming the other way there was a bloke covered wi' dust from head to foot, and walking as if he had sore feet. I takes a look at him, and I see he's got a funny sort of a uniform on. Red coat, knee breeches, and a long sort of cardboard hat. So I thought he was one of these so-called Czechs, but he comes up to me and says: 'Comrade, have you heard the news?' So I thinks he's one of these Communists, and I says: 'No, Comrade, I ain't. What news?' And he says: 'Napoleon is back,' he says, 'and I've got to rejoin my regiment.' And I says: 'Are you trying to take the mike out of me? Or are you just potty? Or what are you?' Then he looks at me, and shakes his head slowly, and with my own eyes I saw him sort of get thinner, thin-drawn-out, kind of smoky. And then he wasn't there any more."

"It could have been a dream," says the Barman. Geordie glares at him, and growls: "It was no more of a dream than you are, you squirt! Why ain't you in uniform, anyway, you . . ."

The Grenadier, who has been smiling on one side of his face, says:

"You and your dreams. To you, Geordie, dreams are real. Well, look. Look at this and tell me if I lie about Nicholls. Look." And from a deep pocket of his S.D. Jacket, the tall man takes a bit of newsprint, creased almost to nothingness, but religiously preserved between two bits of cardboard. It is a copy of the London *Gazette*, dated Tuesday, 30th July, 1940.

"Look," he says. "No. 2614910 Lance-Corporal Harry Nicholls, Grenadier Guards. And there's the story. Dead true."

"Then why didn't you pull out that bit o' paper in the first place?" asks Geordie.

"Because you ought to take my word for it."

"Anyway," says Geordie, "I knew it was true, because I see it in the papers at the time; and I believe I saw this kid Nicholls box, once."

"Well then, what did you say you didn't believe me for, then?" asks the Grenadier, angrily.

"Just for the sake of a argument," says Geordie. "What's a V.C., anyway?"

"A honour," says the tailor.

"Point is," says Geordie, "there comes a point where you got to go forrard or get kilt. You take a last chance, and fight mad. If it comes off, you're a hero. If it don't, you're a corpse."

"That depends," says the Grenadier. "I've seen plenty men surrender, Jerries, in the last bust-up. I've seen plenty of 'em raise their hands and shout for mercy. They're like that when cornered, though they're cocky enough when things are going their way. But I never saw one of our mob doing any surrendering. Did you, Geordie?"

"No, never."

"It's a matter of temperament," says the Grenadier. "Some people are made one way, others another way. Englishmen hate to look silly. So they go and die rather than make a laughing-stock of themselves. Anything for the sake of proper order! I've seen a man crawl out over, good God, a bit of No Man's Land that was a death trap where a man stood no more chance than a fly in a gear-box—go out under machine-gun fire, and shrapnel, good God Almighty, with the Jerries limbering up a flammen-werfer, a flame-thrower. He crawled out when the odds must have been say two or three hundred to one against him getting back at all, and thousands to one against him getting back unhurt. He went to pick up a bloke with a busted hip lying out in the open. Now as things were just then, it was about a million to one against any of us getting out alive, because there was only nine or ten of us, and Jerry was advancing under a curtain of heavy stuff, and we was cut off and hopeless to look at. But this bloke goes out to get this wounded man, who wasn't even a china, not even a pal in particular. He couldn't help it. It was in him to do it. Once an Englishman, always an English-man. Medals don't make any difference. You don't go and get a V.C. because you think it'd look nice pinned on your coat, or because there's some twopenny-halfpenny little pension attached to it. You aren't a hero on account of a medal."

"A medal encourages you," says Geordie.

"Don't you believe it," says the Grenadier. "A medal is a bit of tin. A *medal* don't encourage you. I've seen Italian colonels covered from head to foot with crosses, and stars, and bits, and pieces, and medals of every possible variety and shape and size. And they ran like rabbits. No. It's the *act* that is the encouragement. A bloke like my old pal Harry Nicholls, now. What's a bit of a bronze cross to him? Or to anybody? But when kids get to hear about him, when they read stories about old Nicholls, they say to themselves: 'It'd look silly if after all that we went and let Nicholls down.'

"And again, look at my old pal, Lance-Sergeant Rhodes. He had a Lewis gun section. Well, so Rhodes sees the Jerries leave a pill-box. Our own barrage was coming over thick and strong. It was the good old death trap again. But Rhodes, after picking off Jerry after Jerry with the Lewis and with his good old bundook, went out single-handed, with machine-gun fire right on him, and the shells bursting right in his face; and God only knows how he done it, but he took that pill-box, single-handed, he did, and brought back nine Jerry prisoners. All alone he did it. They give him a V.C. for that."

A dark and excitable old soldier with a brass leek in his cap says:

"And what about my friend, look, Bob Bye, a Glamorgan boy, look! Did he not do all that and more? With these eyes I saw him do it. He took two German blockhouses, *two*, that is! First of all, look, he rushes one blockhouse and kills the whole lot of the garrison, all alone.

Then he takes the second one with his company. Then a party was detailed to clear up a line of blockhouses which had been passed, see. Bob Bye volunteers to take charge. He cleans them all up. He takes a third objective. That is a man, he was! A Glamorgan boy, from Penrhiwceiber. Like me."

The Scot says, with a grim air of acrimony:

"Did you hear of Freddie McNess, in 'sixteen? He was wounded so that his neck and jaw were pretty well blown away, while organising a counter-attack. But he went through a bomb-barrage alone, to bring us fresh supplies of bombs; wounded and alone. He kept us going, shouting and swearing and cursing and laughing, throwing bomb after bomb like a mad machine. And then he fell down with hardly a drop of blood left within him. Hum. V.C."

"Tom Witham did pretty much the same," says Geordie. "A Burnley boy. Coldstream Guards, 1917. V.C."

"And Johnnie Moyney?" says a giant Mick, an Irish Guardsman with a stiff leg, and a shrapnel-pocked cheek. "Old Johnnie Moyney. Didn't he hold the post with us for ninety-six solid hours without water and with no food? And on the fifth day didn't he take us out and give Jerry hell with the Lewis and Mills bombs; and cut a way back for us; and cover our retirement, and bring every last damned one of us safely back? There was a V.C. for you, a real V.C.! I wonder what happened to Johnnie Moyney . . ."

"I daresay the same as what happened to Olly Brooks of the Third Battalion," says Geordie. "Blown to hell and back at Loos in 'fifteen; recaptured two hundred yards o' trench: feared nothing. I daresay he's one of two things. Alive, or else dead. V.C.s. Oh, *phut!* Some are noticed,

others aren't. Some get V.C.s. Others get headaches.
It's all the same in the end. Have another beer. Hi, you,
you twit! Pour these out agen. To hell with the bits o' tin
and brass! Medals! I saved an officer's life once, and
ought to have got a V.C. for it. Near Loos. I lifted up a
burning car that he was pinned under with these two mitts,
I did. I was as strong as a bullock then, and still am, too!
I lifted up that car by the front axles, and it was blazing
like a busted lamp, flaring like crackey. I turned that car
over. Sandow couldn't have done it. I felt sort of strong,
with all the shells bursting round me and the little bits o'
red-hot shrapnel yipping and wheeing in my ears. Yes.
I saved that officer's life. But he was dead. So nobody
knew about it, and I didn't get no medal. Waste o'
time."

"Did you know he was dead?" asks the Grenadier.

"How could I have known, you stupid? Would I have
gone to all that trouble and burnt the skin off of myself
for a corpse? I kind of suspected that he might be dead,
mind you, but I thought I'd give him the benefit of the
doubt. And much good it done him or me."

"Ah," says the Grenadier. "If I could have my time
over again!"

"What'd you do?"

The Grenadier has not the faintest idea. He covers his
confusion by picking on a young recruit who has edged
into the alcove and is lighting a cigarette. "You," he
says, "what do you mean by coming here and eavesdropping on our conversation?"

"I wasn't eavesdropping, I was just listening."

"Oh, you were. What's your name?"

"Dobbin."

"How old are you?"

"Nineteen."

"Where are you from?"

"Luton."

"What work you do in Luton?"

"Nothing."

"Do all right at it?"

"How d'you mean?"

"Didn't you have a trade?"

"No."

"Like the Army?"

"No."

"It's the greatest life in the world, son."

"Yes?" says Dobbin, with a grin. "It don't seem to have got *you* anywhere."

"Shall I scoff this little nit?" asks Geordie.

"Let him alone," says the Grenadier. "It's not for you to say, Dobbin, where anything has got us. It's not any man's place to say. Do you hear? We've been in the Guards all our lives, and we might grouse and grumble day and night, but we're proud of it. You see us now, son, getting on a bit in years. As the Dagoes put it, our roads are nearing the sea. But there's more to a thing than you see in one second, at one time. You bear that in mind, Dobbin. You might see an empty brass cartridge-case lying on the ground, and you might kick it aside without a word. Yet that cartridge-case might be the one thing that won the War. Yes. You might see an old rusty nail lying around, and throw it away. But there was a time when that nail was bright and sharp, and for all you know to the contrary, that nail might have been the thing that held the very roof up over your head, in its time. If you saw us rolling about in Rolls Royce cars, I daresay you'd think we really had got somewhere, wouldn't you? When you've knocked around as long as we have, you'll know that everybody goes the same way to the same place in the end. A shilling blanket or an oak box with brass handles: there's only one way for any man to go, Dobbin. What a man has got, doesn't matter. *What a man has done, and what he's stood or fallen for, that's what matters.* That's where he's got. There was a City man that made millions out of swindling. On the Tuesday, you would have said he'd got to the top of the world. But on the Wednesday he blew his head off and the whole town knew him for an empty crook. Where had he got? Really and truly? Nowhere. *Never* anywhere. Us, we've got nothing. We've got our pay and our grub, and not too much of either. But we were keeping you and your mum safe in your beds when you were too little to walk, and keeping this country all clear for you to grow up and do nothing in. Where have we got? Into the Guards, and into a bit of history. That's something, if there was nothing else, Dobbin. We held our lines, by Jesus, and we came out fighting and we managed to get through. We've been hurt. Nothing can hurt us much any more. No, the rain can't wet us, the cold can't freeze us, the wind can't shake us, and the sun can't burn us. There's no man, or beast, or nightmare, or bluff that can throw a scare into us. There's no force that can put us off a thing once we go towards that thing. Not even a lump of iron through the head can stop us, because we are the ones that hand on the stuff that makes us go. Put us in a desert, and we can make ourselves at home. Put us in a hole full of mud, and we'll still keep calm and play the man. We've got no homes. A plank is comfort to us. A bit of meat is luxury. If we ever had any folks, we just lost 'em. The hut is our house. Our feet feel funny out of ammunition boots. We've known what it feels like to come face to face with a day or a night that must be the last . . . only somehow we came through, and saw the dark, or the daylight, and laughed it off whatever we felt. We've had our share of troubles. We can take an injustice and swallow it. We grouse, but never whine. We yell before we're hurt; but never because we're hurt. We'd lie for a pal, but not for ourselves. We break all the laws except the important ones. We can lie doggo under destiny like Arabs, but we never give way to it or anything else. We don't believe in anything except that we've *got* to be on parade when the bugle blows, whatever the parade is, and wherever it is. And we like to keep ourselves clean, and don't do too many dirty tricks. Where has it got us? Son—didn't anybody ever tell you? Manhood! That is what it's got us. We may be a bit dilapidated, but we're men! Isn't that something?"

A heavy old voice says: "Well said, my boy."

It is Old Charlie.

Although he is neatly dressed in a blue tunic and trousers; although his boots have upon them a dye, or shine, such as only years can impart; and although he has an air of smartness, a dapper alertness, a prim elegance such as only Guardsmen acquire—turned out, though he is, with a calculated neatness, he somehow looks as ragged as a battle-tattered banner. There is that about him which suggests that he is deathless. He looks as if he might be some trophy over which nations have fought. Perhaps he is. He is one of the oldest of all the Coldstream Guards.

His forehead is something against which Time has sharpened its scythe: it is scored and creased and wrinkled beyond the aspect of flesh. Some strange fatality has saved him, throughout incalculable years, for some unknown destiny. He was born in 1860. Charles Dickens was a man-about-town when he was a boy. Once upon a time he was a child, and then he was devoted body and soul to an elder brother whose name—what a pig this Time is, that snuffles up everything!—he has almost forgotten. This brother, with the Foot Guards, went to a place called Russia on some fool's errand and came back with one leg and a thousand tales. Where is this brother? The worms know. But it was out of hero-worship for him that this old man joined the Guards, the Coldstream Guards. There was, in his mind, some bluish picture of smoke—some strange blurred scene—a haze, in the midst of which men in red struggled hand-to-hand with men in grey: some adolescent fantasy of Inkerman, where the Guards fought tooth and nail and, turning their muskets round, banged down the soldiers of the Czar with the butt of Brown Bess. He should be dead. He belongs to another day and age. His father remembered Waterloo. He can tell awful stories. Geordie has seen him looking at a short Lee Enfield rifle and shaking his head—it seemed to him such a small thing, with such a small hole in it. How could so petty a weapon stop a man? In spite of everything, years or no years, he stands erect. Nothing but putrefaction will bend that back. He is rigid with the uprightness of sixty years of service. The last time a sergeant told him to hold his head up was in 1881. He was an old soldier before the Boer War. His age had reached two figures—about ten years—when his mother, with a look of vexation, said: "This Napoleon." She was referring to Napoleon the Third.

They call him Old Charlie. It is impossible for him to appear without some outbreak of badinage. Even

Geordie says: "Where's your bow and arrow?" There is a legend that he was put In The Book for having a dirty powder-horn at the Hougoumont Farmhouse. Apart from the fact of his long service, his antecedents are wrapped in darkness. He never had a home. If he ever had a wife or children, nobody ever heard about them. He is a legendary figure, like the old horse that still survives in the depot at Caterham—the slow, stately regimental horse, which represents nothing but a half-forgotten sentiment. He says little. The oldest have borne most. He knows it. He carries the weight of years and memory. None of us will ever live so long. Age has worn his cheeks into little pits and nodules: he is a monolith. Geordie is an old soldier, but Old Charlie might have had a son older than Geordie. "You may be young," he seems to say, "but you never saw 1860. Live as long as you like, you never will have seen 1860."

Sometimes he comes into the little bar; says nothing, drinks nothing, does nothing—simply looks about him with an expression curiously compounded of bewilderment and ineffable dignity. It is then that the nonsense starts; not that there's any man in the place who would not defend Old Charlie with his life.

There is only one person to whom he talks. This is a little girl whom men call Star. She is the daughter of some old sergeant who lives beyond the camp. They call her Star because her mother, drenched in regimental matters, has embroidered the eight-pointed star of the Brigade upon the grubby yellow jersey which she invariably wears. She is a naughty little girl, sullen and intractable. Her face is fixed in a forbidding scowl. She got that from her father, a savage old N.C.O. She is not like other little girls. She is not interested in childish things; nor has she any of that budding womanliness which is common and proper to little girls. I believe that her real name is Jess, or Tess—anyway, it ends in "ess". She likes soldiers, but in no flippant or flirtatious way. She likes to contemplate them. When the long brown lines go out in column of route, she may always be seen standing still as a graven image by the roadside; not cheering, giving no sign of recognition—merely gravely watching. Her lower lip protrudes; her upper lip is compressed. Her brow is corrugated; there is a ferocious look in her small dark eyes. This is a peculiar little girl. Nothing can melt her. If you offer her coins or sweets she takes them gloomily and thanklessly. She seems to be full of trouble. She plays only one game, and that seems to have no meaning. She walks up and down dragging after her a peeled branch of silver birch—saying nothing, and never smiling; simply dragging the branch. Her mother says that she is eight years old, and will grow out of it. It is alleged that she takes after her father—a man whom nobody loved, nobody understood, and nobody wanted to understand.

She has one boy-friend. This is Old Charlie.

They have assignations. They meet, by a kind of instinctive arrangement. At about a quarter past one every afternoon the little girl Tess, or Jess, walks gravely past the Guardroom and walks, as it were accidentally, up and down the road outside the Sergeants' Mess. She is self-possessed, preoccupied and rather sombre. She never ceases to frown—in fact the habit of this facial contortion has already cut two tiny lines between her eyes. She walks swinging her arms, her small fists clenched. At other times she might drag her branch; but never at one-fifteen. She walks up and down. In due course, out of the Officers'

Mess where he is employed in some not too laborious capacity, Old Charlie comes striding, dressed all in blue. The mystery of it is, that in all those years—all those years—awful, monotonous years of military service—he has never managed to acquire even two stripes. Lance-Corporals of the Coldstream Guards always wear two stripes: (it looks, somehow, better) old as the hills, he is less than a Lance-Jack. Was he stupid? It seems hardly likely. Was he a bad man? A bad soldier? One would say not. The fact remains that he is ending as he began, having got nothing in the service but age, which any man can get anywhere if he lives long enough. He walks solemnly and pauses just by the Catholic Church—a cold old man with moustachios like icicles, disciplined and aged beyond ordinary humanity. The little girl walks to within four or five paces of him, and then she stops, boring the toe of her right shoe into the gravel. She has all the appearance of one upon whose shoulders rests the weight of the universe. She looks almost as old and almost as responsible as Old Charlie. She pretends not to have seen him. He pretends not to have seen her. His huge right hand, which resembles a bunch of red West Indian bananas, slowly opens: he always carries his pipe in his hand, for fear that the bulk of it may spoil the outline of his skin-tight blue mess suit. From a trousers pocket he produces a match; strikes it, lights the pipe, spits once and lets a big blue cloud crawl up to heaven while he contemplates, with God knows what strange sad thoughts, the bare and hideous Guardroom, the White Huts, and the hidden distance which ends in the trees beyond the cricket field. This never varies. His forefinger, indestructible as asbestos, tamps down the glowing ash in his pipe. Holding this pipe in his right hand, while his left arm hangs straight down;

slightly inclining his head in deep thought, he walks up to the Guardroom and stands still.

The little girl watches him out of the corners of her eyes. Then she follows him, walking exactly as he walks—in long, stiff strides. They pass each other three or four times. The ancient one pauses and his tangled white eyebrows come down in a savage and forbidding scowl. His poor old washed-out eyes, which might be blue or grey or green, fix themselves upon the little girl in a glare which is meant to be terrifying, but which, alas, is nearly vacant. She in her turn, glares back at him and in her glance there is something oddly lonely. They confront each other: the child, dark with the clouds of sorrows which nobody will ever understand; and the old man, inarticulate and encumbered with an awful weight of half-remembered things.

He clamps the teeth the Army gave him down upon the yellowish stem of his burned-out pipe and holds it unsteadily between his wavering jaws. Then he shoots out his right fist clenched tight, and slowly peels away from it one finger—the fourth. The little girl looks at it, frowning, and then grabs this extended finger in her left hand. No word is spoken. They walk off together. It is believed that neither of them has another friend in the world. Old Charlie has outlived everything and everybody; and Jess (?) or Tess (?) seems to feel that she is going to have much to live through.

A meeting of the currents of Life and Time. They walk away, past the Officers' Mess, past the Pioneers Yard, to the Y.M.C.A., and then back.

And it happens that only I have heard what they say to each other.

Near the nice new huts of the Scots Guards, between the road and the canal, lies a strip of woodland, mostly silver birch. From here they cut twigs to make revetting hurdles. Men go in with slash hooks, and come out with great armfuls of slender and elegant budding branches; yet, the woodland remains dense and almost primæval. We come here sometimes in field training: there are dents and gashes in this strip of earth which present all the varying features of potential cover. From the road it looks like . . . merely trees, but if you go in among these trees, you lose sight of the road . . . the dark grey dreary road . . . and find yourself under a pattern of foliage which waves gently and mysteriously, and among slim, straight, speckled silver trees which stand between you and the world. Men come here sometimes on Sundays or on Saturday afternoons, when they want to be alone. There is a time when every man wants to be alone, for a little while, among trees.

It was Saturday afternoon. I was lying there and looking up. In the distance rubber tyres purred over tarmac; and some bird, some high-flying bird with a voice of ineffable sweetness sang a song in four notes. The branches moved. In that moment I forgot all the grandeur and misery of the war and the world, and almost fell asleep. I heard them coming, but the sound of their feet seemed to come from far away and hardly penetrated the gentle coma into which I had fallen. I saw them—the very old man and the very young child, both scowling, she clasping the little finger of his right hand in a determined left fist. This must have been a place to which they often came. They walked straight to it and sat down upon a patch of grass between two banks of bracken. I could not see the little girl: she was too small, and the fronds hid her.

But the stiff blue back of that impenetrable old soldier stood up sturdily, conspicuous against its background of green. He took off his cap. I don't know why I was surprised to see that he had no hair.

He spoke:

"Woman. Look. Trees. Do you like trees, woman?"

No doubt the child nodded; she said nothing.

"Listen."

The bird still sang.

"Do you like birds?"

Silence. She must have nodded again, for he went on:

"I like birds too. Birds are nice things. Wherever you go you find birds. Anywhere you like, there is always birds. Go to Africa—right out into the desert, where there is nothing at all; and there are still birds. Out on the veldt: you look, and you see nothing. But fall down, just you fall down. And what will you see then? Why, woman, right up, right up in the sky, as it might be a speck, a tiny little speck, you'll see something coming down. What is it, what is it coming down out of that empty sky right down on to that empty land?"

The little girl said "God."

The old man said: "Vultures. A kind of a bird. They wait, hanging up in the sky so high that you can't see them, but all the time they're watching you, watching you all the time. And when they see you fall, or if they see you die, they drop. They don't fly down. They wrap themselves up in their wings and fall like stones, and then, two or three hundred yards off the ground they spread their wings out all of a sudden as it might be, great big flowers opening, and you hear them go slap! Yes, slap! And they slide down, and they stand round you, wrapped up in them wings of theirs, like cloaks, and they wait."

"What for?" she asked.

"They wait for you to die."

"Why?"

"So as to eat you."

"Not till you're dead?"

"No."

"Ah."

Silence again. Then the little girl said: "What are they for?"

The old man replied: "To clean up. You can't have things lying around all over the place. They clean things up. They are . . ." he paused and then said "on fatigue. They get a wilderness dug out. If it wasn't for them horrible birds the desert would stink. Because everything is dying all the time. Yes, in them hot places it is easy to live. If you put your walking stick into the ground, roses would come out of it. And if it is easy for one thing to live, it is easy for another thing to live; and it is easy for you to get along, and also for your enemy likewise. Yes, woman, the easier it is to live, the easier it is to die. But woman, you look at me. I'm ten times older than you are, and I'm alive. I'm eighty."

"Eighty's not much," she said.

He went on rather dreamily: "I see every day fellas fretting—fretting like prisoners behind bars—at being in this Army. But woman, do I say to them: 'Young fella, I have been in this Army over sixty year'? No I don't. I don't say nothing. Woman, I don't talk to 'em. I ain't got nothing to say, woman. Why? Because talking makes no difference. Talking makes no difference. Talking never helped anybody nor never will. There is nothing to be said woman, nothing. Sometimes I think that in the Army the first thirty years is the worst but woman, when I think again I don't know. Everything is rotten while you're going through it, and everything is lovely when you look back on it. I don't know woman, and I don't care. I'm old. But I will see 'em damned before I die. I ain't going to die."

He said this almost to himself. Then he seemed to remember something, and his tone changed. He said: "You like me, don't you? And I like you. I think you're a nice little girl. You like holding on to my finger don't you?"

She made a non-committal noise: "Mm."

"If I had anything to give you, I'd give it to you. But I ain't got anything. No, after all these years I got nothing to show. But does that matter? You take it from me woman, having something to show don't matter. Show yourself to yourself, at the end of everything, and if you can pat yourself on the back and shake hands with yourself and like yourself—like yourself like you might like a stranger—well, that's alright. I've seen rough times. I've had field punishment. I've seen wars. Yes, woman, I've drunk my medicine. When they lay me out, there'll be some marks for them to see. But that don't matter. I was saying, if I had anything to give, I'd give it to you, or to your mum to hold for you. I had a matter of a hundred and eighty-two pounds that I saved up. But I ain't got it any more. I give it away. Tell me, woman, am I crazy?"

Her voice said very firmly: "Yes."

"Yes, says you, yes says everybody. So I don't talk. A certain party comes to me and says: 'Charlie, I've got to find a five-pound note.' So I thinks. 'A five-pound note,' I says. 'Alright,' I says, 'I will give you a five-pound note.' So I draws out a five-pound note to give him. And then I says: 'What do you want with the dirty money? What have you saved it for?' And I draws it all out, and I gives it away. I gives it to charity. Never mind what. It makes no difference, I give it away, woman, and I felt the better for being without it. I'm a soldier, see? And I travels light.

"There's a young fella they calls Bearsbreath. A sort of a lance-corporal. A kid, a little kid, a kid of no more than thirty-six or seven. And yet, woman, I see that kid Bearsbreath, with these two eyes I see him give away everything he ever had. And do you know what it was? A belt. Do you understand?"

"Course I understand."

"Course you understand. You're a woman of the world and I'm a man of the world, and I'm talking to yer, because you got savvy. Me, I joined the Army—do you know why? Because I idolised my brother. He was in this mob. He was at Inkerman. That was in the Crimean War. Why," said Old Charlie, with a kind of hushed amazement in his voice, "if he had lived Edward would be ninety-five. But he's dead. Everybody's dead. That was a battle, Inkerman, woman. The Coldstream Guards come over, and when their guns was empty they picked up stones off the field and beat the Russian' 'eads in with 'em. Yes, we took that position with sticks and stones, that's what we did. And we'd do it again, woman, we'd do it again, sticks, stones, boots, or just bare fists.

"But this kid Bearsbreath. What was I saying? Oh yes, his belt. Young Bearsbreath has been in this mob all his life, practically. He was a Barnado's Boy. Do you understand what that is, woman? He didn't 'ave nobody. He didn't 'ave no mum, he didn't 'ave nothing. I believe they found him in a basket outside a door. Soon as he was old enough he went into the Army. Guards. Coalies. Got 'im nowhere. Regular old sweat like me. Never had nothing and never will have nothing. Except what? Don't laugh, a belt. Dirty old leather belt. You understand woman? Course you understand. An old soldier has a belt. Wherever he goes and makes a friend he gets a badge. He swaps badges, cap badges, with whatever pal he might make in another regiment. And he fixed this here badge on to his belt. Time comes when his belt is covered with badges, and that is a very nice pretty thing. This here young fool of a Bearsbreath, he had a belt.

"Hah! Well, so there was a kid in the drums. Ginger kid. I don't know his name but they called him Ginger. One day, so there's a rehearsal for a pantomime or a concert, or something. Somebody or other says: 'What's the dateth to-day?' and somebody else says: 'The dateth to-day is the nineteenth.' This kid Ginger—you wouldn't cry, would you, woman?—this kid Ginger busts out crying. Well, young Bearsbreath says to young Ginger: 'What's the trouble?' and young Ginger says: 'Nuffink.' This kid Ginger was a good drummer. It was a pleasure to hear him blow Defaulters. This kid Ginger says: 'Nuffink' and this kid Bearsbreath says to 'im: 'Somebody been bullying you, Ginger?' and Ginger says: 'No.' Then Bearsbreath says: 'Why did you bust out crying when they told you the dateth?' and this kid Ginger says: 'I wasn't crying.' 'I should bloody well think not,' says Bearsbreath. 'A big boy like you. 'Ow old are you?' And this kid Ginger says: 'Sixteen.' 'Oh,' says Bearsbreath, 'you're a big boy for your size, and when was yer sixteen?' This kid Ginger says: 'I'm sixteen to-day.' 'Why,' says Bearsbreath, 'what's that to cry about. You ought to be laughing. You should be thankful you're alive, or something. Gord blimey,' says Bearsbreath, 'whether you're thankful or sorry, God damn and blast it all, you should be ashamed of yourself for crying. Are you a man or are you a woman?' 'I'm a man,' says Ginger. 'No you're not,' says Bearsbreath, 'you're not a man, crying like that! Why,' he says, 'what's the matter with you. Did you want your mummy to come and wish you many happy returns or something?' This kid Ginger says: 'I ain't got no mum.' 'Oh,' says Bearsbreath, 'you ain't got no mum. And I suppose next thing you'll tell me is that you ain't got no dad.' 'Well, what if I ain't,' says Ginger. 'Ain't you,' says Bearsbreath, and Ginger says: 'Well, no, I ain't.' 'Brothers, sisters, uncles, aunts?' says Bearsbreath. 'No,' says Ginger. 'Oh,' says Bearsbreath. 'A sort of orphan.' Then Ginger says: 'Sort of.' 'Well,' says Bearsbreath, 'then you ought to be ashamed of yourself,' and he walks out. Well, about five minutes later he comes back into the hut with four tuppeny bars of chocolate, and he gives them to this kid Ginger and he says: 'Oh well, many 'appy returns,' and hands these bars of chocolate to young Ginger, and Ginger says: 'Thanks.'

"Nut-milk chocolate?"

"Yuh—that's right, nut-milk chocolate. And then Bearsbreath sort of stands on his two legs wide apart, and he says: 'I'm surprised at you. You and your birthdays. Blimey,' he says, 'what's the younger generation coming to. Personally,' he says: 'I never had a birthday in me life,' he says. 'Only cissies have birthdays. Only effiminate young women have birthdays. Why,' he says, 'personally, I'd be ashamed to own to having a birthday,' he said. 'So,' he says, 'you ain't got no mum and no dad and you ain't got nobody, and you go around 'aving birthdays, do you? Alright, young fella,' he says, and this kid Bearsbreath shoves his hands under this here rubbish, this sloppy stuff they call battle-dress, and takes off his belt. Bearsbreath was proud of this belt. It was a good bit of cowhide with a big brass buckle, and this kid Bearsbreath had stuck on to it eleven or twelve regimental badges of all sorts, and in particular a silver stag's head of the Seaforth Highlanders, and a Scots Guards warrant officer's starred cross in some sort of silver metal. He was proud of that belt, because in a way, apart from a sort of a stiffness in the back and a sort of way of walking, this belt was all that young Bearsbreath had to show for about twenty years in the Guards, woman, twenty lousy years. Bearsbreath takes off this belt, and I thought for the moment that he was going to give Ginger a lamming with it. (In case you want to know, a belt of that sort is very handy if it comes to a rough house.) Bearsbreath drops this belt into this kid Ginger's lap and says: 'Here you are, you little crybaby. Here's a birthday present for you,' and walks out. Young Ginger sat there sort of staring, and a couple of other drummers who had been pulling his leg about him piping his eye stood around and sort of went green with envy, and somebody says: 'Gord blimey, I wonder what come over old Bearsbreath,' because, you understand, woman, that that belt was much more than money to a man like Bearsbreath. Dammit, woman, that was his Army life. That was bits and pieces. That was all he had to show. That was all he'd ever have to show. A Lance-Jack, good for nothing but the lousy Army . . . but that belt, well, that belt was something.

"Me, I only gave away a bit of money. That was nothing. Money's nothing."

"Have you got a belt?"

"Yes, I've got a belt."

"Can I see it?"

"Yes, but you mustn't touch it."

"I won't touch it."

"Honour bright?"

"Honour bright."

I heard the snick of a buckle, and a little scream of admiration.

"Isn't it lovely."

"Yuh, isn't it? There's badges on that belt that you'll never see the like of again. Do you see that one there? That dates back to 1855, and that's pretty nigh a hundred years ago. There's twenty-two badges on that belt, woman, and every one of them badges belonged to a good comrade of mine, a good friend. And every one of them men is dead and that's all there is to show, so what do you think of that, woman?"

A silence.

Beyond the frail branches of the silver birch trees, the bird still sang. The ancient soldier had risen to his feet and was putting on his cap. I could see the little girl now, for she had risen too. Her forehead was smooth. Her eyes were clear and wide open and the frown was gone from over them. For a moment they looked at each other.

"Your belt," she said.

The old man said: "Keep it."

He stuck out his little finger and she clutched it, and then they walked away.

EPILOGUE

NELSON ON DEATH

PIRBRIGHT VILLAGE: the pub called "Fat Fan's." Once upon a time "The White Hart" was owned by a plump lady. The wife of the present landlord is slender; but in the Army, tradition dies hard. Go to the Brigade Naffy in Pirbright Camp any day at noon, and you will see a little knot of old, old soldiers in the wet canteen, drinking a species of ale so weak that it falls flat as soon as it is poured out. The most ancient of these warriors is a Coldstreamer of about thirty-five years' service—a veteran of every military vicissitude, old as the hills and as indestructible; wise as Gideon, in battle, though not so wise out of it; huge, uproarious, heavy-jawed and voracious; a drain through which half the beer in England has passed; a graveyard of Naffy pies; a dictionary of strange language; a mine of information about the Other Ranks. He has been in Pirbright since time immemorial, but has never heard of the "White Hart." But "Fat Fan's"——oh, *he* knows "Fat Fan's." Let outsiders call the place the "White Hart." Coldstreamers and Scots Guards in every square of Mercator's Projection know the place as "Fat Fan's"; and "Fat Fan's" it will be for ever.

I say: Pirbright Village; the pub called "Fat Fan's."

The carriage trade gets there now. Captain Hobdey, who took the place, dug down through strata of wall-paper and found, like a gem in a Christmas cracker, an ancient inn. Bits of the "White Hart" thus discovered,

213

strike old soldiers as new-fangled. The seventeenth century is all very well, but it is nothing like the good old days. Nevertheless, they drink there, because it is "Fat Fan's." If a cataclysm washed the place out, the naked site would still bear the name . . . Fan's, Good Old Fan's, Old Fat Fan's. There is nothing to be done about it.

Sergeant Nelson is down on a visit. He was entitled to seven days' leave. He had nine pounds in credit, and has drawn the money. Beyond the Army, that one-eyed hero would be lonely. It is true that he has a relation here and there; but nothing that you might describe as a family. To him, Sergeant Crowne's handclasp is the touch of a vanished hand, and the faded echoes of the Pirbright bugles the sound of a voice that is still. The Black Huts are home sweet home. The ranges are the lost horizons of sweet youth. "Fat Fan's" is a tender memory of the springtime of things. Time is a swine that snuffles up everything; but some things Time can never swallow.

You can imagine with what grimly-suppressed eagerness he made the roundabout journey. But he comes into "Fat Fan's" with perfect nonchalance. It might be his own mess. His heart bounds like a rabbit in a bag as he sees Crowne, Hands, and Dagwood, at the bar. But his face remains rigid. Only his eye celebrates. He says:

"Ah-ha, Crowney. Ah-ha, Hands. Yah, Dag. Drink?"

"Ole Lipstick," says Sergeant Crowne.

"Whattaya mean, Lipstick?" says Nelson. "Tcha gonna drink?"

"Mild," says Dagwood.

"Bitter," says Crowne.

"Brown," says Hands.

"Place changed hands? Lady! Two bitters, a mild and a brown. Big 'uns. Well?"

"Well?" says Crowne.

"Long time since we met," says Nelson.

"1937," says Hands.

"8," says Dagwood.

"7," says Hands.

"9," says Crowne.

"7," says Hands. "What d'you mean, 9, you Burke?"

"What year did War break out?" asks Crowne, patiently.

"I can tell you," says Hands. "It was the year Big Arthur threatened the Drill Sergeant with a bayonet."

"That was 8," says Dagwood.

"1938?" says Crowne. "You sure? Well, all right: 1938. Big Arthur threatened the Drill Pig in 8. The year the War broke out was the year I got a Severe for sort of 'itting a feller that 'it me first. I know, I got this Severe, and then the War broke out. Yeamp, I got it: the War must of broke out round about September, 1939. Ye-amp, it sort of broke out then."

"Definitely," says Nelson.

"So what's been happening since then?" asks Hands.

"Oh, nothing, nothing," says Nelson. "You?"

"Nothing," says Crowne. "Sort of squads you gettin'?"

"Oh, just squads," says Nelson. "I teach 'em: you skive with 'em."

"I unlearn 'em all you learn 'em, and then I learn 'em proper," says Crowne.

"*Phut!*" says Nelson.

Hands introduces a newcomer, a burly Sergeant with a blue scar on his nose: "Know Clark? Nobby, this is Nelson."

"Stameetcha," says Nelson.

"He was in the Foreign Legion," says Hands.

"Well, have a drink. Have a short one. So you were one of these Foreign Legionaries, were you? Was it like on the pictures?"

"The uniform was," says Sergeant Clark.

"There long?"

"Five years."

"How d'you come to join that mob?"

"I was a kid. I saw *Beau Geste* and got tight afterwards. When I come to, I'd joined the Foreign Legion."

"That's how I joined the Guards," says Nelson. "Well, was it all right?"

"All right."

"Tough?"

"I done tougher marches with our mob in Egypt."

"Well, well, so we meet again," says Sergeant Nelson.

"Um," says Crowne. "Well? Drink? Same again please miss. So what's goin' on, Nelson?"

"Browned off," says Nelson.

" 'Angin' on to you," says Crowne. "Need instructors. Won't let you go. Yah?"

"Definitely hanging bloody on to me," says Nelson. "I'm browned off."

"Me too," says Hands.

"I'm thinking," says Dagwood, "of getting myself bust. Then I might get abroad."

"Me too," says Crowne.

"And me," says Nelson.

They have been talking like this for about seventeen years.

Nine-thirty.

Private lives have been discussed and disposed of in five

minutes. Grievances have filled two hours. Reminiscence has scuttled in and out of everything; ubiquitous, ir-repressible and unreliable as a pup. It all comes back to shop; soldiering. All roads lead to that.

"They'll do all right," says Nelson.

"Mmm-yeah, maybe," says Crowne. "Some of 'em are steady. But on the whole, they'll do. I 'ad some of your kids."

"What kids were they?" asks Nelson.

"They came in the Autumn. Sort of October, round about."

"Oh yes. I remember. It was . . . no it wasn't. Was there a kid from a place called Brighton that worked his ticket on account of asthma?"

"No. There was a bloke called Thurstan that kept on getting into trouble."

"Glass House?" asks Nelson.

"No," says Crowne. "Went absent once. Came back. Went straight. Bit mental, but 'e come to 'is senses."

"Some people definitely do, and others definitely don't," says Nelson. "I remember the wallah you mean. I could see there was going to be trouble with that geezer. Definitely. So, he turned out all right, eh?"

"A nice kid," says Dagwood. "Well, anyway, not so bad."

"Wasn't there a po-tential officer they used to call The Schoolmaster?"

"Yes," says Dagwood. "A bookworm."

"Kay?"

"Yes," says Crowne. "Okay."

"When he left," says Dagwood, "he wrote a bit of poetry."

"What, made it up?" askes Nelson.

"Oh, I shouldn't be surprised." Dagwood rummages in a breast pocket and gets out a greasy little autograph-album. "Look."

Looking over his shoulder, Nelson reads:

Here dead we lie because we did not choose
To live and shame the land from which we sprung.
Life, to be sure, is nothing much to lose,
But young men think it is, and we were young.

"Now there you are," says Nelson. "Dead we lie, and all that sort of bull and boloney. Life to be sure is nothing much to lose. Now where do they get that stuff? God blimey, where do they think that kind of tripe is going to get 'em? Education. There's a man of education, and look at what he makes up. Before they do anything, they've got to write something on their own gravestones. They've got to make a song and a dance about it. Definitely, they've got to make a fuss. We were young! He *is* young! What's the big idea, Dagwood? What's the big idea? Crying over their own dead bodies before they're killed! Here dead we lie. So what if here dead we lie? Eh, Crowney? A pack o' tripe. I'd like to see anybody sort of encouraging a squad of rooks with that sort of slop. Me, I give 'em the old Hi-de-Hi! And I make 'em give me the old Ho-de-Ho! Dead we lie. Why, we been dead dozens of times. Haven't we, Crowney? Or pretty near dead. As good as dead. But what did we say? We said: 'Let's give 'em rough stuff and bust through.' Didn't we, Handsey? We did, Dag, didn't we? Definitely we did. Where do they get that stuff? God blimey, I nearly did a Dead We Lie on the way along: I nearly went smacko on the line. I tripped over a sort of trunk on the platform.

Why, Dagwood, old cock, we lie dead, more or less, every five minutes from the time the nurse smacks our backside, to the time they chuck dirt in our face. But do I write poetry about Dead We Lie? Did you ever catch me at it, Dagwood? Definitely not. Did he, Crowney? Well then. Tear that page out and——"

"Order your last drinks, please," says the landlord.

"Last drinks? *Last* drinks? What d'you mean, last drinks?" asks Sergeant Nelson, ordering one more round. "Well, mud in your eye, old skivers! This time next week payday on the Field! It'll be nice, ha? The dear old Active Service! Death? I spit in his eye! *Last* drinks. Not by a definitely very long chalk, my cocko! Here's looking at you!"

"Time, gentlemen, please," says the landlord.

"Yes, Time—that's all we need—Time!" says Nelson.

THE END